It happened
in **BOSTON?**

It happened
in BOSTON?

❧ RUSSELL H. GREENAN ❧

Random House / New York

for my
Mother and Father

1 ૐ

LATELY I have come to feel that the pigeons are spying on me. What other explanation can there be?

The Public Garden across the way attracts them, which is natural enough since there are trees there and grass and water in the lagoon and, of course, a few fools who insist on scattering birdseed about. But it is hardly natural for them to flock to my window ledge early each morning and to remain there all day long. And it is certainly unnatural for them to peer into the room and scrutinize my newspaper clippings, my books and my private actions.

Yesterday, as I sat in the Garden, I examined this apartment house. There are forty-six windows facing Beacon Street but only one—mine—was graced with those evil-looking birds. Forty-five without, one with. Significant.

To be sure, I chase them, but they soon return. What draws them there? Why my window?

This morning I put some poisoned bread outside the dining-room window. If nothing else, it should lure them away from my ledge, and if the stuff exhibits its customary efficacy, some will perish. I can't hope to destroy every pigeon in the city, of course, but if I am lucky enough to get some of the ringleaders, it might serve to discourage the rank and file.

EACH MAN lives his life in a manner peculiar to himself alone. Even the most well-oiled, precisely machined cog in the complex gear-train of modern society—and I am not one of these, much as I crave order—has within himself a unique core that distinguishes him from those about him. This inner being exists only for itself and is forever at war with the inner beings of others.

Except for Sundays and holidays my daily schedule rarely varies. I rise early, wash, have a hard-boiled egg and coffee and then go out to sit in the Garden. There I reverie. Yesterday morning I was in Venice on that day in 1380 when the news of the great victory of Chioggia reached the city. I was Guido Pochi, a saddle-maker. All the neighbors had gathered in my shop. We sang and laughed and I entertained them by twirling about on the end of a strip of cowhide that I held with my teeth alone. We drank many bowls of red wine—even my wife, Angie.

An explanation is needed here. For the past year or so I have been developing a curious faculty—a kind of mind translation. This strange gift, which I suspect I share with few if any others in this world, permits me to visit different places in space and time and there assume an appropriate alien identity. It all began quite without warning one night as I was lying on my bed reading the life of Cagliostro. Suddenly I was aboard a ship on a sunny sea. The entire experience lasted no more than a couple of seconds but there was no question about its validity. The next day, while sitting in the Garden, I was abruptly carried off to the steppes of Asia, and thereafter these journeys took place with astonishing frequency. I found that I need only sit quietly for a while—preferably in the open—and I would soon be in another setting. Of course, my mind must be clear and calm. If it's cluttered up with thoughts or if I am agitated for any reason, nothing will happen no matter how long I sit.

With time, these excursions grew in length. A moment in Siberia expanded into a minute or two in Cyrene, then an hour in Baeda's England or Tierra del Fuego and, at last, as much as half a day in Babylon or Bangalore. One of my earliest transportations was to another planet, somewhere out in the blue. I spent about fifteen minutes walking about a mountain of what looked like gold and vermilion glass. Above it the sky was olive and speckled with crimson clouds. A sun, barely half the size of our own and colored the dark red of drying blood, hovered above a perfectly level horizon that seemed unbelievably distant.

My bench in the Public Garden has become a magic carpet. It whisks me about the universe without regard to charts or calendars. There I sit, with my eyes wide open and people strolling by within a yard of my nose, with the sounds of automobiles, children and birds all about me, with the sun of Boston warming my back and a Boston breeze caressing my cheek —yet I am not really there. I am eating oysters with Massena at Nice. I am beating my wife on Panay. I am wielding a spear at the Battle of Pydna, or talking with Zurbaran, or baking bread in Neopolis, or playing bezique in Djibouti, or swatting flies in Djambi, or fleeing the Medes in Thessaly, or hunting golden lizards in the blue desert of another world, or kissing a woman in Peru, or arguing with Numa, or fishing in the Gulf of Bothnia, or praying in Kathmandu, or going up the Kennebec with Arnold.

And yet, as authentic as these psychic transferences are, a small part of my consciousness remains forever with my body there on the bench. Should someone speak to me, I am not at all startled. I respond at once, easily and lucidly. The thread is then broken, however, and I cannot return to the scene of the reverie.

I am most careful to maintain an expressionless face, regardless of the nature of the events transpiring on the further side of my brain, and though in the beginning my lips sometimes moved in response to words spoken elsewhere, I soon learned to repress this waywardness. Were anyone to look at me, he would see only a pensive young man—neither tall nor short, dark nor fair, fat nor thin—languidly sunning himself in the park.

As a rule I have one reverie in the morning and another after lunch. If I am frequently interrupted, as sometimes happens, I might travel to four or five different places in the course of an hour, however. What baffles me most is my ability to speak so many strange languages in my different roles—to speak and to understand them as exactly as I do English. But as swiftly as I return to Boston, all these strange and lovely words are swifter still in fleeing from my head. Though I remember everything else, all recollection of alien speech vanishes.

All this, no doubt, sounds peculiar—maybe even unbelievable—but I swear that it is true. I am not the sort of man who tells lies, whatever other shortcomings I might have.

> Guard grimly your veracity,
> With desp'rate pertinacity.

So urges the clever Le Sur, and I couldn't agree with the man more.

Following my morning reverie I go to the cafeteria on Charles Street and there have a cup of coffee and a hard-boiled egg. If possible I sit at one of the windows, for I am very fond of this old street and can never observe it enough. The brick buildings with their gray slate roofs, their bright green shutters and their delightful window boxes never fail to delight my eye. I like the fine, solid form of the venerable church and the greenery of the florists and the hoary treasures of the numerous antique shops. The people, too, have a charm and quaintness that is most engaging. They are generally courteous, knowledgeable and independent in matters of dress. They have a freshness that captivates me. Only this morning I observed a very ancient lady carrying a Queen Anne mirror from one of the basement boutiques, and though it was obviously heavy, never once did she falter beneath its weight. Her eyes sparkled like those of a maid of sixteen in the throes of a first ardor as she made her way across the street. Into a doorway she went, casting a single, almost furtive, look over her shoulder, as though fearful that the dealer—having realized his mistake in selling such a gem—would suddenly appear, money in hand, and renounce the transaction. On the other hand, of course, she may have been a particularly daring shoplifter.

When I leave the restaurant I meander down the east side of the street and return on the west side, glancing cursorily in all the shop windows. It was in one of these places that I got the Bourg Angel. My crystal ball was sold to me by an old gentleman with a white beard and a back so bent that he had to teeter on his heels to look up at me. This sparkling sphere sits in a teakwood cradle. I have stared into its glittering depths for hours, and though I have yet to see anything, it affords me much satisfaction and is marvelously soothing. One day, at some critical time in my life perhaps, it will reveal something of significance.

From Charles Street, I walk to the library at Copley Square. If the weather is mild I sit in the courtyard and watch the play of the fountain or simply study the square of sky overhead. Sometimes I try to hear the sunlight or to imagine colors not derived from the primaries or to visualize the universe with all the space removed. If the day be cold or rainy I ascend the stone staircase to the reading room. There I might read a few pages of a book chosen at random or I might simply sit for a while, staring sightlessly at the words.

I have lunch at Brant's—liver and bacon or spaghetti or Salisbury steak with mashed potatoes or frankfurts and beans or, in the hot weather, tuna, sardine or salmon salad with slices of tomato and hard-boiled egg and maybe a hemisphere of sherbet alongside. Brant's is an excellent place. My criminal activities have acquainted me with many cafeterias—some quite pretentious—but none to match Brant's for the quality of the food, the efficiency of the staff and the near-perfect tidiness of both the dining room and the kitchen.

The afternoon finds me back at my bench, where I remain until the shadows begin to form. I might stop at Salvucci's for some provisions, otherwise I go directly home. After chasing the pigeons away, I usually lie under my bed for a half hour or so before having my dinner. After that I read a little of my Casimir book or listen to my records or study my newspaper clippings. Last night I made another list of restaurants. Unfortunately, the miserable telephone book abbreviates street names to the point of total unintelligibility. That will be revised, too.

I go to bed at ten-thirty or eleven. Just before that, however, I have a cup of coffee and a hard-boiled egg. Lately I have been sleeping pretty well.

3 ಶ

"GOOD MORNING," said Randolph.

"Good morning," I replied, returning from Cuzco to Boston with the speed of light. "Where's your frog?" Randolph is a seven- or perhaps eight-year-old boy who plays in the Garden almost every day. His father is a surgeon at Massachusetts General. Randolph attends a private school in the afternoon during the winter, spring and fall, but in the summer he scampers, tumbles, rolls and dances here on the broad islands of green grass. His best friend is a hand puppet in the form of a frog. It is the color of the cloth shamrocks worn on Saint Patrick's day and is named Sebastian.

"Still sleeping," he answered.

"He is, is he? Do you know the difference between a cat and a frog?"

"A cat has nine lives but a frog croaks every night. You told me that one three weeks ago. It was on a Saturday."

"Of course. Just giving your phenomenal memory a little test, my boy," I replied evenly. "Does he usually sleep this late on Wednesdays?"

"Today is Friday. He hardly ever sleeps late. This is the first time. He has a toothache," he said, sitting beside me.

"Do frogs have teeth?"

"Sebastian has—not too many, though. Want a jujube?" His small hand emerged from the depths of his shirt pocket and opened like a somewhat grimy flower to reveal a small gummy object covered with fuzz.

"No, thanks," I answered hastily. The candy disappeared into his mouth in one quick and perfectly efficient gesture. We fell silent. Thirty yards away a speckled brown duck who had wandered too far from the lagoon was now hurrying back as best he could while a French poodle, leashed to a stout young lady, urged it along with a series of shrill staccato barks. We watched with mild interest. The duck's awkward gait at last brought it to the water's edge. It fell in and sailed away.

"What's your name?" Randolph asked.

"Alfred," I said.

"Alfred what?"

"Alfred Omega."

"That's an Irish name, isn't it?"

"Oh yes."

"Last Tuesday you said you were Spanish," he declared, but without a hint of indignation in his accusation.

"I did, yes."

"And Saturday afternoon you said you were Chinese."

"Ah yes. I know it sounds strange, but on Saturday afternoon I was Chinese."

"Yes," said the boy severely.

"Yes what?"

"Yes, it does sound strange," he said, shifting the gumdrop in his mouth.

"Of course. Have you ever heard of the two Chinese gentlemen who met on a cobbled thoroughfare in old Tsingtao? The first said, 'Hi, Lo!' and the second replied, 'Lo, Hi!' "

"Yes. My father told it to me and it happened in Chinatown, not where you said. I told it to you Saturday afternoon when you said you were Chinese. Don't you remember?" He was quite exasperated. "Don't you have any new ones?"

"You're probably right, Randolph. I seem to remember it now." I was annoyed but I lost none of my poise. I even smiled. "What kind of a joke would you like to hear? I have tens of hundreds—thousands, as a matter of fact."

Randolph probed his ear with his little finger, then scratched a scab on his knee. "Another Chinese joke," he said emphatically.

"Oh, good! Splendid! Another Chinese joke, eh?" I said as I searched the dusty recesses of my mind for some old jest that could be orientalized. "I've got one right on the tip of my tongue. Can you wait awhile?"

"How long?" he demanded.

"That's it!" I announced triumphantly. "How Long is a Chinaman! Get it?"

He granted me a short, charitable laugh. "I get it. That was too short. Another one."

"This time an Italian joke, all right, my boy?"

"No, another Chinese joke but a long one."

"Variety is the condiment of existence, Randolph, but you have placed me on a very bland diet." I was not a little aggrieved by his persistence. At that moment, however, the speckled duck returned to the bank, where it flapped its wings and began to saunter about the grass, and its happy appearance jogged my memory.

"There once was an Englishman who visited the court of the emperor of China. Unfortunately, the poor fellow neither spoke nor understood Chinese, and none of the Chinese knew any English."

Randolph smiled in anticipation and looked intently into my face.

"You see, it's funny already, isn't it?" I said. "Now, the emperor, wishing to impress this foreigner with his liberality, arranged a sumptuous banquet in the most magnificent hall of his most magnificent palace and favored him with a place of honor at his own royal table. The Englishman was delighted. The food proved to be elegant and savory, and being unable to join in the conversation, he was free to give it his full attention. One dish, a kind of meat pie, was so incredibly delicious that he helped himself to second and even third portions, scorching his mouth in his eagerness to satisfy his palate. Anxious to learn the name of this tasty meat, he turned to his neighbour, one of the emperor's venerable ministers, and pointing to his plate, said interrogatively, 'Quack, quack?' The minister looked at him for a moment, then smiled graciously, shook his head and retorted, 'Bow-wow.'"

For a while Randolph said nothing. Then he leaped from the bench and exclaimed, "Bow-wow! I like that. He was eating a dog but he thought he was eating a duck. Bow-wow! That's a good one. He was eating a cooked dog."

"That's correct," I said, gratified with my success. "I never told you that one before, did I?"

"No. Quack, quack!"

"I don't always repeat myself, do I?"

"Bow-wow!" he answered and galloped away in the direction of the lagoon, where the speckled duck, as if sensing an approaching peril, altered its direction and waddled back toward the water's edge.

I sat back upon the bench and relaxed. The sun was high, its direct rays very warm. All at once I find myself in Grasse, France, in the time of Napoleon the Third. I am a wealthy man. I am sitting on my balcony, smoking my pipe and sipping a glass of grenadine syrup and mineral water, while across the clear blue sky whistling swallows streak and plunge. My brother-in-law, Bernard, is sitting with me and I am gently but firmly refusing to lend him the money to buy a restaurant in Toulon. I have made my money in the shipping business in Marseilles, and though I am only fifty-four, I am semiretired as I wish to make good use of my later years and not die with a pencil behind my ear and a manifest in my hands. I have bought this stone house on the side of a hill, together with three and a half hectares of olive and apricot trees, from the heirs of a tile manufacturer who died of liver disease. My wife does not like it here and quarrels with me often. She would like to return to Marseilles, but I have decided to remain here for a long time—perhaps until I die.

My sister Catherine, Bernard's wife, died three years ago, and since then he has lived with us in a spare room, first in Marseilles and now here. I like to have him around because he is quite poor, and a rich man can better appreciate his wealth if he has near him always someone who has no money at all, and should that someone be a relative, so much the better. That is the real reason for my refusal to give him the money for the restaurant, though I am telling him, of course, that it is a bad risk and would never show a profit because it is in a poor location.

Many years ago, in 1837 to be exact, when Bernard and I were both young and with few prospects, I offered to include . . .

"Bow-wow, bow-wow!" said Randolph. "What's your name?"

I sighed. It was early but I decided to go to the library.

"What's your name?" he repeated.

"Bolide, my boy. Perry G. Bolide. I'm an astronomer," I said, getting up. "But I have to leave now."

"Where are you going?"

"I have to go and catch a falling star and I'm late. It was due in a minute and a half ago. I don't even have my mitt. You don't happen to have a catcher's mitt with you, do you?"

"I have one home," the boy said. "It doesn't have a strap though. My sister chewed it off."

"No, I guess I'll have to catch it barehanded. I hope it's a meteorite and not a meteorong. I once got struck on the forehead by a meteorong."

Randolph stood on his toes to study that part of my skull with obvious interest. "Did it hurt?"

"Oh yes, indeed. Fortunately, it was rather a small one. I was out of the hospital in less than a year. Well, good-bye, Randolph."

"Quack, quack."

4 ᣂ

UNTIL FAIRLY recently I was an artist. I suspect that I was born an artist, but if that is not the case, then surely the gift was bestowed upon me at a very early age.

My mother died when I was seventeen. While engaged in cleaning the apartment, I came upon three corrugated-paper boxes in which were neatly stored thousands of drawings and

water colors that I had done in my early childhood. Most bore
dates upon their obverse sides—some carried a few lines describing the circumstances under which they were conceived
or a proud maternal comment. I have never been one to under-
estimate my accomplishments, yet the sight of these remarkably mature sketches amazed me. The trees and houses that I
produced at the age of two were harbingers of eventual genius.
There was nothing infantile about these creations. The view
was fresh and naïve but the understanding of line and space
and the accuracy of detail was nothing less than witchcraft.
At three, I drew dogs, cats, birds, horses, flowers and sailboats
on the Charles River. I did sketches of the interior of our
apartment and of my mother and some portraits of my Aunt
Marie. At that age, too, I made an excellent drawing of the
bronze Garrison statue on the mall near Dartmouth Street. But
words do not convey the sureness and vitality of these works
nor can they explain the existence of such skill in someone so
young. At the age of four, I became obsessed with our cat, and
there was a shoebox filled with drawings of this animal that
would have done credit to many of the budding Rembrandts
who strut each year from our schools of art.

We moved to Gloucester Street when I was nearly five, and
there, from my bedroom window, I could look down into the
exercise corral of the Boston mounted police and fill my hungry
eyes with the glorious sight of prancing chestnuts and cantering
Morgans. Ah, those lovely creatures remain vivid in my memory today. Perhaps I have never loved anything with the
intensity that I loved those horses of my childhood, and when
one looks at the drawings they inspired, all that fierce ardor is
clearly evident. They are beasts that would put Pegasus to
shame, make Bucephalus look like Rosinante and reduce the
steeds of Rhesus to nags and hacks. There they all were, these
magnificent animals, delineated in bold strokes on brittle sheets
of cheap yellow paper. Fiery stallions gallop past, their coats
sleek and shiny, muscles taut and sinews tense. Or aroused
horses that stand upon their hind legs and paw the sky, snorting

in anger with bared teeth and foam-flecked lips. Or beasts that stand quite motionless, their strong straight limbs and noble bright-eyed faces as peaceful as if composed of stone. There is pride—more, majesty—in their bearing as they gaze from the page with their ears erect and every strand of their sable manes and tails expressing grace and beauty.

And with what deftness did I draw them! The foreshortening is very nearly as fine as any I could manage today. No animal, except man, presents such a challenge to the artist, since no animal, except man, surpasses the horse in the variety of its elegance. Nor can any other creature, not excepting man, convey such a sense of strength and movement. Later, when I was older, I was to travel throughout the city searching for horses to sketch, and to this day a glimpse of one of these graceful animals will quicken my pulse. My eye runs delightedly from fetlock to forelock while my hand instinctively wanders to my breast pocket for the soft pencil that is no longer there.

But perhaps I am boasting, and that is not my way. I am no Rodomonte. I am no gascon. Vanity is not one of my defects. Suffice it to say that I drew many things at that tender age and all skillfully, and that of these things, organic or inorganic, animate or inanimate, real or hyperphysical, my horses were most remarkable.

5 ख

I DEFINITELY do not like the look of that fellow Beels. There is something about his eyes that can only be described as spooky. He is forever drawing me into conversation, but conversation of a peculiar and irritating sort, crowded with innuendo, veiled gibes and ambiguous threats. What can he be after?

He came shortly after I killed the twin. I'm sure of it. It was toward the very end of last winter—a clear, sanguinely sunny day, scented with the subtle, though unmistakable, fragrance of the spring to come. Small patches of crystalline snow clung to the yellowed grass but there was little likelihood that they would survive till sunset. I had been gloomy, my mind darkened by the murder, and this sudden return of blue sky and bright light had done much to dispel that gloom. I remember looking at the little gnarled tree whose name I did not know, and thinking that its chartreuse buds, the first to appear each year, would soon be adding their delicate color to the scene. Then would begin the resurrection of the beeches, the tea crab-apples, the willows, the magnolias, all the elms, the Chinese Scholar tree and the ginkgo.

I remember thinking that my friend Faber (my only friend, now) would soon be packing his easel and paint box into the rear of his little red automobile and be running off to the countryside to capture the spring on canvas. A good artist, Faber, and a kind and gentle man.

Yes, that was the day. I reveried in Gades, that morning. I was a young man selling green plums in the market and I shouted to all who passed to come and profit by my youth and inexperience, while my brother, who was selling chickens across the road, crowed and cackled so loudly that I wondered at the strength of his lungs and marveled at his stamina. Business was good but I was annoyed by the bees that hovered about because of the flower seller beside me. Each time this man sold a bouquet, he would shake the bees from it before handing it to his customer, and the bees, unhappy with this treatment, buzzed angrily about my head. I had been stung once and had called it to the flower merchant's attention, but he only laughed, showing me a fine mouthful of black teeth. These people who gather the flowers in the wild fields are not noted for their intelligence. I look over the heads of the people to the masts of the ships in the harbor and wonder what it is

like to be a sailor. Then my eye is caught by the daughter of
the onion and garlic seller, and though she has seen me, she
pretends that she hasn't. I shout, "Profit! Profit!"

I returned from this little drama to find an aluminum wheelchair parked next to my bench, indeed, no more than a few
inches from my elbow. Behind it a tall, broad-shouldered,
grim-faced man in a form-fitting black overcoat stood, looking
like those hearse drivers one sees waiting patiently outside a
funeral parlor. But it was the contents of the wheelchair that
occupied most of my attention. It appeared to be filled with
a variegated bundle of woolens topped with a narrow-brimmed
tweed fedora. It was some seconds before I noticed that a thin
trickle of blue smoke was seeping from a point a few inches
below the hat, giving the entire mass the aspect of a miniature,
debilitated volcano. Presently the bundle moved. A hand, small
and very red, emerged, ducked beneath the fedora and re-
emerged grasping an Italian cigar. A great puff of smoke followed this movement, erupting from the volcano with such
vehemence that I expected to see next some tongues of flame,
a shower of hot ash and perhaps a dribble of steaming lava.

"A fine day," a voice proclaimed, and since it was apparent
that the giant behind the chair had not spoken, I was forced to
conclude that the pile of clothing in it had.

"Yes," I replied cautiously.

The hat suddenly tipped back, revealing a youthful, though
somewhat pinched and wrinkled, countenance with a thin nose
and lips and small bright green eyes. The forehead was hidden
by the hat and the chin was concealed in the folds of an ox-
blood scarf. The eyes examined me swiftly.

"My name is Beels. I'm in the insurance business," he asserted. His voice had the cracked and dissonant quality of an
adolescent youth but he used it in a most forthright manner.

I looked at him more closely and saw that the mound of
wool was composed of a thick tweed overcoat, glaucous-green
in color, a suit of cocoa-brown flannel, the scarf and a heavy

green plaid blanket—this last fabric being spread unevenly over his legs and lap. As I studied him, his left hand came into view. It contained a newspaper. With the aid of his other hand, which still held the twisted stogie, he opened the paper, though only enough to expose the upper half of the first page.

As I had made no answer to his pronouncement, he spoke again, saying, "That's Beels, B-e-e-l-s. What's your name, sir?"

The newspaper proved to be a French one, *Le Figaro*.

"Barber," I replied.

"Very happy to meet you," he said. "This big fellow behind me is Johann." He uttered a few words in a foreign language and Johann bent forward and straightened the blanket on Mr. Beels' lap. "He speaks only German, but he's worked out very well. Are you in business, Mr. Barber?"

"No," I said, thinking to smother the conversation in its infancy.

"A pity, if I may say so. The business world is as instructive as it is fascinating. I do not believe that I could survive, were it not for the endless delights of commerce. It is both vocation and avocation to me. My business is my pleasure, and my pleasure, my business. A happy condition, don't you agree?" he said, and I noticed that his speech was marred by an accent, though I was at a loss to identify it. Some words he pronounced like an Englishman while others were tinged by the modulations of the Romance tongues and still others—those that contained fricatives—had a curiously Slavic sound. There were even a few melodic intonations reminiscent of Chinese.

"Don't you agree?" he repeated aggressively.

"I don't know," I answered, still considering the problem of his accent.

"You don't know? Why not? Are you stupid? I can understand your agreeing or disagreeing but not your inability to do either."

I was startled by this sudden attack. A desire to get up and slap him on the ear came over me but was immediately dampened by the thought of Johann in the background.

"Well," I retorted contemptuously, "do not hold me responsible for your poverty of comprehension."

His green eyes darted about in their sockets. A cackling noise rose from the folds of his muffler.

"Well spoken," he said. "Repartee! I like repartee. You have a quick mind. I did not mean to speak with asperity, I assure you. My tongue is sometimes sharper than my intention, I fear. I am short of temper this morning, having spent a half-hour in lively telephonic debate with a student of Harvard University who had sought to cancel a policy he has with me. I convinced him of the folly of such a course, to be sure, but it was trying, very trying. I insure quite a few university students. It's always been something of a specialty with me. Johann, here, was a student when he took out his first policy with me. Oh yes, I travel to New Haven and Hanover and Ithaca, as well as Austin and Urbana and Berkeley. I have many young scholars under my wing."

He cackled again, put his cigar to his mouth and produced a swirling cloud of tobacco smoke.

As I offered no response to this inane piece of oratory, he resumed speaking, his general theme following closely that of his previous remarks. He delivered an encomium upon life insurance which suggested that it was more important than life itself. To be without a policy, it seemed, was immoral, irresponsible and unpatriotic. Though he did not actually say it, he implied that people of such improbity and improvidence should, after death, be denied the use of hallowed ground and be buried at the crossroads with stakes driven into their heretical hearts.

Though I found his discourse poor entertainment, I grew increasingly curious about this outlandish invalid and his peculiar articulation.

"Tell me," I said, when he paused for breath, "what is the place of your birth? I have never heard English spoken with such a bizarre accent. You are not an American."

It was a moment before he answered, but when he did, he displayed no resentment toward me for my interruption or for the directness of my remarks.

"I am not an American, Mr. Barber. You are quite right. Still, I have a little American blood in me," he declared, while a twisted smile formed on his thin lips as if to imply that he had only just quaffed a tumbler of that precious fluid. "I am of mixed ancestry: my forebears were a polyglot group and I, the last of the line, have an easy familiarity with a host of languages. Frontiers mean little to me, sir. I have associates in every nation, many in positions of great influence. I have business affiliations—not merely in the assurance field but in securities, real estate and banking—in every corner of the globe. Even as I sit here gossiping with you, my wealth is increasing. You, Mr. Barber, if you will forgive my presumption, do not appear to be a wealthy man."

"I am not rich," I replied, but my thoughts were drifting, for I had espied the first balloon peddler of the season.

"Have you no desire for wealth?"

"None," I said, getting up from the bench.

"Leaving so soon?" he said, his voice dropping an octave midway through the question. "Stay a while. Only last evening I received an interesting piece of information, which, properly managed, could provide an intelligent fellow like yourself with a stepping stone into the world of comfort, even opulence."

I walked away. I could see Randolph approaching from the opposite direction, his frog, Sebastian, waving its webbed paw in greeting. I bought a sausage-shaped balloon, translucent cerise in color, and handed it to the frog, who clutched it eagerly and asked, "What's your name?"

"Barber," I answered. "I'm very big in the market, you know."

"Quack!" said the frog.

"Bow-wow!" I replied and continued on my way to Copley Square, while Randolph continued on his, staring reverently at the red dirigible that floated above his head.

6 ❧

I WAS fourteen before I received any formal art training. At that time my mother sent me to a painter named Matthews, who charged a dollar for two two-hour lessons a week, but my stay there was short as the poor fellow, having only six students, was soon obliged to close his academy and seek some other form of labor in order to feed his family. When I asked him where I might find another instructor whose fees might be comparable to his own, he thought a while and then, laughing as if at a private joke, suggested a Mr. Loupa in the South End. He added that he was a difficult man but that he knew more about art than anyone else in Boston. I took the address and went there the following day.

The Loupa residence was a battered tenement on Tremont Street. As I entered it, a plump gray rat dropped from the rim of a half-covered garbage can and raced away along the hall wall. I found the apartment with the help of a frowsy middle-aged lady who called me "dearie" and smelled of beer. I knocked, the door opened and there was Mr. Loupa.

Perhaps the rat had unnerved me or perhaps the general appearance of the building—its dirt, gloom and smell—had ignited my anxieties. Whatever the cause, the interview proved a shattering experience. This sage artist was a man well into his fifties, with a huge, broad nose, bright black eyes (whose gaze,

I have no doubt, would have mesmerized Medusa) and a head of yellow-gray hair that, in its chaotic abundance, resembled an abandoned haystack. He was obviously well lined with drink, though he listened to me patiently enough until I mentioned that I had brought no money with me. At that point his manner changed dramatically. He began to shout at me in explosive Italian, embellishing his remarks with the most terrifying grimaces and most hostile gesticulations that I had ever witnessed. Suddenly he stopped, studied me a moment and then, realizing that I could not understand him, translated his philippic into an English that by comparison made Billingsgate sound like Bowdler. Meanwhile, his black eyes, like shotgun muzzles, riddled me with alarming glowers. In the face of such a barrage, I thought it best to retire. I went back down the stairs in great haste and grand confusion.

But I was eager to be an artist, and so the very next day found me knocking once again at Loupa's door. This time I had brought the dollar and I clutched it in my perspiring hand, like a talisman. And I was received warmly—almost paternally—and offered a seat in a worn and stained wing chair. A smile lit his face. He relieved me of my damp dollar, hung my coat on a nail on the back of the parlor door and bade me wait a moment while he obtained some materials from another part of the apartment. I could hear him talking to his wife in Italian in a distant room, then a great silence fell upon the place. This endured for more than an hour; I squirmed and fretted in the dirty wing chair. At last, unable to restrain my impatience any longer, I leaped up and searched the apartment. It proved to be large, filthy, crammed with junk and pervaded with an unidentifiable, though trenchant, aroma. All about were spent wine bottles like empty artillery shell casings at the site of a recent battle. I discovered broken plaster figures, some half-finished oil paintings, a bench covered with pots of dried paint, a sad-looking canary, but no Italians of either sex. I returned home without my dollar but bent upon repayment or revenge.

On the following day, however, the sharpness of my anger was soon blunted by the wily Mr. Loupa, who before I could speak expressed grand astonishment at my lack of patience in not waiting, and my crass incivility in departing without saying good-bye. But he was comparatively sober, and having cleared the table with a swipe of his hand, he began his instruction.

I was told at once that I must always call him "Maestro" and that when he spoke I must remain silent and listen, and when he ceased to speak, it was because he was thinking and I must be quiet out of respect. All this, he said, was part of the Italian Method, which had produced the greatest art the world has ever known. He then placed before me a green wine bottle and a large brown onion, handed me a pencil and a sheet of wrinkled paper and told me to draw them. I set to work happily and confidently, regretting only that the subjects were not more worthy of my skill. Despite this limitation, I worked carefully, taking pains to reproduce the two objects with exacting verac-ity, so that I might immediately impress this curious foreigner with the magnitude of my talent. While I worked, the Maestro sat quietly opposite me, his face softened by a smile that was surprisingly cherubic. At last I finished the sketch. It was a truly fine representation. Glowing with pride, I passed it across to him, whereupon he gave it one swift glance and rewarded me with a rap on the ear which has to this day made me slightly hard of hearing.

He then commenced a vocal flagellation, generously enriched with both English and Italian profanity, which lasted for half an hour and left me feeling that I was not only ignorant of the most rudimentary aspects of drawing, but that I was a creature from some other world who had never before seen a bottle or an onion. When he had finished singing this lively ballad, he bade me turn the paper over and begin again. A tear or two watered the page and my injured ear seemed to contain a boil-ing tea kettle whose whistling was very distracting, but my desire to prove myself was strong and I set to work once more, albeit, I must admit, with a much greater respect for the

"Italian Method." Looking back on it now, I have little doubt that the sketch was not all it could have been. After that one resounding blow, however, he never again struck me, though he often raged like an elephant with an earache when I made a blunder. The reason he hit me, he explained some time later, was that he could see at once that I had the hand of a master and that I was squandering its strength in weak, stylistic efforts.

The Maestro's first name was Angelo, I learned, for that is what his wife called him, but he preferred to be known as Seraphino since "it means the same and is more beautiful." He came from Tuscany, a town outside Livorno being his place of birth, but had lived in Boston for nearly ten years. His principal ailment, if it can be so designated, was red wine, but he would sometimes garnish this staple with yellow cheese, black olives, hot green peppers, white garlic, pink *prosciutto* or even a bit of chicken or veal. He would accept spaghetti or any other *pasta* only if he was near death by starvation. He had a vast contempt for Americans and all other nationalities excepting Italians from Tuscany.

There were few finished works of his in the closets of his gloomy flat—he had sold everything to satisfy the vintner—but what there was, left no doubt that he was an extremely fine artist. Greece and Rome, Byzantium and the Renaissance were all present in his paintings. He had selected what was best from the great ones of Florence, Siena, Venice and Milan and blended with it his own originality. He was a Mediterranean painter, to be sure, for there was little of the Flemish, German or Dutch influence visible in his pictures, but a Mediterranean who, for all his eclecticism, was modern in the very best aesthetic sense.

As for his knowledge of art in general, of the tools and materials of the artist, of decoration and of metalworking and the minor crafts—there were none in this country and few in the world, I am certain, who could match it. It was he who showed me how to make my own paints and who warned me against commercial preparations.

"If you want real color, use real colors. Don't buy those salad dressings. In a hundred years they will have as much color as a basin of dish water," he advised.

I was shown what to look for when buying linen canvases, and how to stretch them properly on their wooden supports and how to prepare the surface to receive the paint. The Maestro was a firm believer in imprimatura or underpainting and had no misgivings about using reds, browns or grays for this purpose or even, on occasion, intense shades of yellow, pink and orange. I learned how to select the right brush, how best to hold it and how to wield it to realize the finest effects. The mysteries of tempera were revealed to me along with the secrets of concocting firm, tough varnishes from hard resins that were not soluble in spirits but had to be fused in oil at high temperatures. I was instructed in the old technique of applying these varnishes with the ball of the thumb, a method that produces a smooth, almost glassy finish.

My arrival aroused him from a torpor that had gripped him for several years. He continued to drink but rarely to the point of total apathy, and though he was far from being a happy man, some of his bitterness left him. His love for art, long enfeebled but far from dead, was quick to reassert itself once the familiar smell of turpentine and new canvas reached his nostrils. He knew many people and was always able to find a church that desired a fresco, a monument maker who had a superfluous piece of marble or a foundry that would let us cast a bronze figure. Though his hand often trembled, his eye was infallible and his mind could grasp all the facets of the most involved problem with such speed and lucidity that he seemed more than human.

There was no boundary to his knowledge of art. He taught me how to work wood, stone and metal. Though always short of tools and first-rate material, we carved six-foot figures in oak at one time, and six-inch figures in ivory at another. He was skillful in the making of repoussé and could hammer wonderful figures and designs into sheets of copper and brass, finishing them by patiently incising the intricate details with a steel style. From him, too, I learned the fundamentals of the lapidary's craft, and when from some obscure source he procured a bit of coral, a piece of mutton-fat jade or an agate, the two of us would cut, grind and polish it with as much care as if it were the Kohinoor itself. Now and then some silver came our way and was quickly transformed into a tiny replica of Michelangelo's "David" or Donatello's "Angel with Tambourine" or some original conception.

"One day I will get some gold," he would say. "Yes, gold. One day soon. That is the king of metals. To work with it is like caressing a beautiful woman."

Unfortunately, the day never came. Many years passed before I was able to subject this majestic substance to the finesses Mr. Loupa had taught to me.

Only that was missing, however, for we cut cameos, carved peach pits (he swore that he once carved the twelve apostles in a single cherry stone and that it was now in a museum in Napoli), graved intaglios and embossed any pieces of horn or bone that we could get our hands on. Along with these activities, we created many elaborate mosaics. One, I remember, was so heavy that it required four men to carry it down the narrow staircase, while another was so beautiful that it caused an aged monsignor to weep like a child. This last one was of Jesus with a lamb and can still be seen at St. Athanasius Church in East Boston.

We did etching, lithography and woodcuts. The whole of one winter was spent in a blacksmith's shop in Dorchester, forging iron arabesques. The following spring found us pugging clay and pouring spill in a brickyard. The place was owned by a fat, jolly cousin of the Maestro's. I was taught the occult science of glazemaking, mixing and firing. Some of the plaques that came from the kiln at the end of this period might have been produced in the workshop of Della Robia.

We cast in plaster, lead, spelter, bronze and silver. We carved walnut, mahogany, oak and fruit woods and we gessoed, polychromed and gold-leafed all of the finer figures. In the backyard of the tenement we pounded away at slabs of marble and blocks of granite with such energy that the neighbors now and then summoned the police and we were forced to sneak through the basement to avoid an inane lecture on the zoning laws. But these efforts produced some excellent bas-reliefs, high-reliefs and four or five truly superb figures in the round, not the least of which was a rendition of the Venus de Medici that I made from a photograph and which the Maestro proclaimed *"Meraviglioso!"*—no small acclaim from a teacher who was chary of bestowing praise.

One day he brought out a coil of brass wire, a pair of pliers, a small ball-peen hammer and some soldering equipment, and while describing in grandiose terms the many ladies he had won by this minor art, proceeded to manufacture a series of very clever bracelets, chains, brooches and earrings. This pleasing pastime soon occupied our leisure time, and unlike most of our other undertakings, provided us with an easy income, as the gift shops on Washington Street were quick to buy our output.

There is someone at the door.

7 ❧

I AM always afraid when I open my door that a brawny policeman will be standing there in the hall, but tonight my caller was a wizened little old lady who was looking for the wizened little old lady who lives across the way, my enemy, Mrs.

Chakamoulian. When I drum with my slats in accompaniment
to my favorite record, "Le Coq d'Or" by Nicolai Andreevich
Rimsky-Korsakov, it is Mrs. Chakamoulian who makes such a
fuss. While I was telling my visitor that Mrs. Chakamoulian
had only yesterday moved to Baltimore, Mr. Barletty—the
building superintendent and a meddling busybody if ever
there was one—happened by and shattered my lovely fantasy.
The little old lady muttered a few unintelligible imprecations
before crossing the hall and disappearing into her friend's
apartment.

"How's the missus?" Barletty asked, eyes and teeth shining
brightly in his puffy face. He knew perfectly well that my wife
has left me. I have often thought that he was in the habit of
listening to our arguments. More than once, when I stalked
out, he would be hanging about in the hallway.

"Just fine, Mr. Barletty," I replied brightly. "I received a
letter from her Monday. She's in Badgastein at the moment,
but she's planning to go to Salzburg on Saturday and Wilkes
Land toward the end of the month—if the weather holds up."

"How nice. You must send her my regards when you write
her," he said. "Tell her everyone in the building misses seeing her."

"I certainly will. I'm sure she'll appreciate your thoughtful-
ness. Goodnight, Mr. Barletty."

I live in hopes that Mr. Barletty will one day fall down the
elevator shaft—from one of the upper floors.

WITH THE Maestro, all of these interesting and instructive activities were subordinated to our principal concern, the art of drawing and painting pictures. By far the greater part of my time was consumed by what seemed, then, endless lessons in the refinement of line, perspective, modeling, composition and the fusion of line and color. I was made to sketch and paint everything in sight, from the stately churches in Copley Square to the slavering chimpanzees in Franklin Park.

"To paint the whole thing," the good signore would proclaim, "it is necessary to know the little parts that make up the whole thing, even if you do not paint each of these little parts into your picture."

This dictum led to my climbing trees to discover the true aspect of the bark, branches and leaves and to my crawling about on my hands and knees on the Common, in order to observe the manner in which grass grows. We spent hours studying the waters of the Charles and days examining the sea at Castle Island. I was to make drawings and paintings of the sky in all its moods, my instructor one day ordained, and so for several weeks, in pencil, charcoal, chalk, pen and ink, aquarelle, tempera and oils I did little else. This led directly to the study of air and the action of wind and of the infinite guises of light and its brother shadow, and of the combination of air and light and shadow, the knowledge of which is essential to the creation of a fluid atmosphere in a picture.

But of all subject matter, the human face and figure were the ones most favored by the Maestro. For him, the representation of man was the supreme challenge, and those artists who had best portrayed humanity were the ones who received his loudest laudations. All else, fascinating as it might be, was mere decoration. Somehow, with little money, he was always able to secure models, who, though amateurs, posed very well under his astute direction. He seemed able to turn his poor command of English into an advantage, for the directness of its broken phrases was difficult to parry while his linguistic ignorance enabled him to understand only what he chose. By means of this two-edged sword and the ferocity of his ebon-eyed glare we gained entry into a medical school, three hospitals and the city morgue, which excursions did much to increase my knowledge of anatomy.

What a man was this Seraphino Loupa. He was a flesh and blood, bone and muscle, heart and brain artist—a vagabond Verrocchio, a misplaced Michelangelo, a Cellini born into a churlish era.

In his youth, all of Italy fell under his inquisitive eye; he roamed from the snow-chilled villages of the Alps to the sun-baked stones of ancient Syracuse, ingesting all the wonders on his way. Then on across the blue Ionian Sea he sailed to the birthplace of beauty, Greece.

"Italy was my mother and father. Ancient Greece was my *enamorata*. Those white stones were like flesh to me," he said, his black eyes clouding with memory.

In a transport of love, he wept before the Parthenon, embraced the caryatides of the Erechtheum and kissed the floor of the Propylaea, where the foot of Phidias had trod. He tramped the dusty roads of Hellas, haunting the ruins and the museums like a man in a beautiful, vivid dream. One night, in Olympia, after nearly a year of wandering, he looked out of the window of an inn and saw Zeus standing in the street watching him. He swore that his heart stopped at the sight.

"What a figure—two meters tall, if not more. He was like a Corinthian column with his long wavy white hair tied with a

fillet, and his curly white beard and his eyes! There was a
chlamys over his shoulders, dark in color—purple perhaps—
but bordered in gold that shone in the dark. His legs, *ragazzo,*
were—well, each was as thick as your body but stronger-
looking. He was very stern and looked directly into my eyes.
I am not weak, yet those eyes of his nearly ended my life.
At last he raised his hand and put a sign on me. I wanted to
call out to him but my heart was not even beating and I could
not move my tongue in my mouth. When next I came to my
senses, he was gone. If I could have asked him only one question. But I was hardly alive."

What question would he have asked? He never would tell
me, since, as he put it, he did not believe that I would know
the answer. The sign put on him he took to be a command to
return to Italy and do great things. He left Greece the next
morning.

What happened after that was never very clear to me. From
his own words, and those of some of his friends, it appears he
produced some wonderful works during a period of nearly
twenty years. He had a large studio in Rome and counted
the wealthiest citizens of that metropolis among his patrons.
When drunk, he would rave about a bronze equestrian statue
that he had done in Apulia that was "second only to the Col-
leone" and, also, of a Carrara marble St. John that "breathed"
through quivering nostrils. In those days, he said, he would
work for twenty-four hours without sleep, lighting his studio
when it grew dark by means of a gigantic chandelier that held
thirty kerosene lamps. In a place called Rossano, he
painted a Paradise on the walls and ceiling of the sacristy of
the church that was a marvel. If a man was unhappy, he was
told to "go to Rossano and look upon Paradise." Unfortunately, the church burned to the ground a few years later. The
people said the Devil set the blaze because the picture was
converting the sinful.

He had always been fond of women and drink, in quantity, but it was the latter passion that eventually degraded the excellence of his art. After his fortieth year he began to drink more and work less. Never an even-tempered man, he refused to admit any decline in the quality of his productions and soon alienated his customers, benefactors and friends. Then, suddenly, he left Italy and came to America. The reason for this abrupt journey is obscure, but he once hinted at an act of violence—of breaking someone's head, to be exact.

Drunk or sober, he was an impressive man. Though not above average height, he had a wide and deep chest, muscular arms and the strongest and (when not shaking) cleverest hands of anyone I have ever encountered.

His wife, Nina, was as fat as a squab and wore nothing but black. Her interest in the wine bottle matched that of her husband. When the old man was not too intoxicated, he sometimes beat his wife, and when he was too intoxicated, his wife sometimes took the opportunity to beat him.

He taught me for seven years. I arrived one morning in the winter to find Nina screaming and the Maestro lying in a pool of blood in the kitchen. He had suffered a stroke and was dead. Littleboy was with me that morning.

9 ಇ

EVEN WHEN he is sitting half the Garden away from me, I can feel Beels' eyes upon me. Sometimes his ghastly laugh rocks the air and I know that it is me he is laughing at.

And his servant, Johann, is like a walking dead man. He never speaks. What a pair they are! Perhaps they will leave when summer ends, since the old rascal has such a horror of the cold.

Mrs. Dandelion, too, is a nuisance. Whenever she passes me, she glares fiercely and bares her teeth. Usually I feint a hostile movement in her direction and she scurries off fearfully.

I have considered moving to some other location—the embankment or the mall, maybe—but the reveries come in so clearly here, and it is so convenient for me that I am loath to make a change. I really should not permit these perfectly harmless people to make me anxious.

But all will soon be resolved. This morning, in the library peristyle, I contemplated athanasia. It was very pleasant, very pleasant indeed. That is, it was until this ancient old woman sat next to me and began to cough in my ear. I believe that I would have beaten her if I had had a stick with me, preferably one with a nail in it. But I am only joking.

One isn't safe from fools even in a library.

10 ॐ

MY FRIEND Benjamin Littleboy looked exactly like the soldier who carries the pennon in Simone Martini's "Jesus on the Way to Calvary," a lovely work which, as it is in the Louvre, is known to me only through colored photographs. Littleboy possessed the same straight nose, the same down-turned mouth and the identical prognathous jaws as this gonfalonier. The sole difference between them lies in the eyes. In keeping with the grim task he is performing, the standard bearer's eyes are filled with malevolence. Benjamin was incapable of so evil an expression.

We met at the Boston Fine Arts School—Littleboy, Leo Faber and I. Since we all adhered to those principles of art that have currently fallen into disfavor and desuetude, we were looked upon as academic reactionaries. We painted what we saw, while they looked at one thing and painted another. After the first year Littleboy and I, feeling that we were being crammed into a Procrustean bed, left. Faber remained for the full two years. The three of us concentrated on painting the human figure, and each, in a different way, became highly competent in this labor. Leo took the nude and placed it in a sylvan setting, where amidst shimmering sunlight or the silvery mists of morning, it assumed a dreamy, sensual quality. I used it as a basis for classical groups and portraiture. Benjamin combined this skill with an uncanny understanding of animals and birds and put the whole into wonderful parables.

Littleboy belied his name, for while not very tall, he was heavy. He ate and drank enthusiastically and avoided exercise. I would guess that his weight approached two hundred and fifty pounds. His body was big, as was his heart, his spirit, his intelligence and his perceptivity. A most comical storyteller himself, he loved humor in others and would reward it with a laugh that I am certain has more than once left its mark on the graphs of nearby seismometers.

Like me, he was an artist and, like me, a very good one. His skill in drawing figures—both men and animals—was extraordinary. Some of his pen-and-ink sketches were so filled with movement that they could bear comparison with the etchings of Rembrandt. There was a fullness and naturalness about his creations that quite convinced the eye. As he grew older he was gradually able to transfer this adroitness with the pen or pencil to his brush, and the result was paintings of a high order.

Many of the great artists of the past have had a passion for fantasy. The fabulous animals of the Greeks, the dragons of the Chinese, the monsters of the medieval cartographers

and the serpents of Yucatan are all manifestations of this affection for the bizarre. Leonardo delighted in such things as
did Michelangelo, Dürer, Breughel, Bosch and Goya. But I
doubt if any artist enjoyed such work more than Littleboy. On
a piece of foolscap, he might draw fifty or sixty of the most
cleverly contrived freaks without any two bearing the slightest
resemblance. His imagination was rich with these chimeras
and a few, at least, were certain to appear in anything he did.

"Ah, Benjamin!" I would say to him. "Why have you put the
head of a pig on that beautiful stallion?"

"Why? Because it adds to his beauty," he'd reply with a
smile, "and does wonders for the pig, as well."

Sometimes he would create phantasmagorias of remarkable
intricacy and invention. There would be scowling donkeys,
winking cobras and smiling vultures. Feathered cows, web-
footed cats and men with faces like fish would add to the confusion. All these creatures would leap, run, climb, wrestle or
cavort in the most engaging way. I recall one picture, "The
Skink's Funeral," in which a hundred or more of these attractive monsters danced about with such vigor that it gave me
vertigo to view it for any length of time.

These exercises did much to sharpen his technique. So
strong was his love for drawing that even while in the midst of
a conversation, his pencil would race back and forth across his
pad, producing laughing heads, swimming girls, trumpeting
elephants or leering demons. It was a pleasure to watch him.
There was a kind of magic to it.

When he sketched human beings, he was never satisfied with
conventional poses. His models were asked to stand on one
leg, or to crouch, or raise their arms in curious attitudes or
twist about like circus contortionists, and since this was far
from the comfortable postures they were used to, they rarely
returned. Anatomy intrigued him while foreshortening gave him
the joy of a game. What little money he had often went on
second-hand medical books with good anatomical illustrations,

and one of his greatest treasures was a massive veterinarian handbook that was filled with colored diagrams of all the domesticated animals.

His paintings were usually small, but they contained so much that one did not notice this. It was like looking out a small window at a crowded street. There was always such a lot going on that the sensation aroused was one of expansion rather than contraction.

Benjamin also delighted in decorating his works with odd bits of writing or printing. As he wrote beautifully and employed these inscriptions judiciously, they in no way detracted from the overall harmony of the pictures. This calligraphy took the form of a single word or a brief sentence depicted on a banner, scroll, book, sign or newspaper—always legible but not often comprehensible. These were Benjamin's little mysteries. What, I wonder, did "The pomegranate spilt its foot" mean? And what was meant by "Glistening Ensilobotomy"? What was the sense of "The moribund padlock has learned to swim," or the alliterative "Coughing softly, the cowboy climbed the cotton," or "Down, devil clock!" Once, after he had doused the fire of his thirst with about a gallon of beer and was feeling quite merry, he translated all the notations on one of his paintings for me but that was the first and the last time he made such a revelation. A ram, wearing a jockey's cap, carried upon its back a white scarf bearing the word "Hellilium" and this, Benjamin said, meant "Destroy" since "Dis" was the Roman hell, and "Ilium" was Troy. Another figure sat reading a letter, the back of which revealed the sentence "Paper torch, the scales sang," and this, I was told, signified "Spill the ruler's blood," as a paper torch was a spill, scales were rulers and "sang" means blood. The word "Portalpick" was "Adore all" from a door and awl. There were others but I cannot recall them. An art historian of the future will someday decipher all of them, I venture to predict.

In the hands of a lesser man, all this might have become no more than a bit of harmless sport, but Littleboy was a power-

ful draughtsman with a passion for detail and an uncanny feel
for movement. These unnatural pageants with their casts of
implausible characters possess a reality often found missing in
the genre paintings that crowd many museums. Although he
was never a strong colorist, he always achieved blends that
were subtle and inoffensive, relying upon light shades of relatively low brilliance. He was a hard worker and proclaimed
often that art was not his profession but his vice. If there was
sufficient food in his house and a bed to sleep in now and then,
he could work continually for as long as a month, without once
setting foot on the street.

Few people appreciated Benjamin's skills, however. His
paintings were called "comic strips" by the punch-sippers and
the eyebrow-elevators, and since denigrating witticisms are
more valued than genius in this unfortunate age, the dealers
refused to handle them. My friend was never slow to repay an
insult; he made many enemies. Under such circumstances, he
found few customers for his pictures and was, therefore, always
poor.

I see that I have failed to mention Littleboy's great love
for rats—an infatuation that began when he had a part-time
job in a research laboratory at the Harvard Medical School,
not far from the museum. Since no portrait that omitted this
tenderness could make any claim to accuracy, I must correct
this oversight at once. Truth must forever be in the vanguard,
even if it becomes necessary to prod it now and then with the
prickly end of a halberd.

At the time that he was attending art school, Benjamin lived
in a loft on Dartmouth Street, just beyond the railroad station.
This area is riddled with alleys, and the earth beneath the
broken asphalt of these alleys is riddled with the labyrinthine
runways of the brown rats, whose city, crowded and cheerless
like most suburbs, lies only inches below our own. Equipped
with a pair of battered binoculars, Littleboy spent many an
evening watching the activities of his long-tailed neighbors by
the wan light of a streetlamp. His fondness for these rodents

led him to dispatch indignant letters to the Boston *Chronicle* (with copies also to his congressman and the local S.P.C.A.), complaining about their plight.

"Why," he asked, "is this country squandering huge sums on armaments for Latin-American dictators, Middle Eastern intriguers, Far Eastern despots and European revolutionaries and free-thinkers, when in the alleys of Boston—the cradle of liberty—American rats are reduced to eating from garbage cans? Why, only a short distance from the road along which George Washington once rode in stately splendor, must these unfortunate members of our society—whose ancestors may well have come over on the *Mayflower*—be forced to battle like savages over grapefruit rinds and moldy boulkie rolls?"

There was a good deal more in a similar vein, but the newspaper, alas, lacked the courage to publish these egalitarian epistles and neither the member of the House nor the S.P.C.A. evinced any willingness to mount a crusade. Undaunted, Littleboy carried on alone. From his meager supply of cash he allocated a fixed portion for oats and birdseed, which simple yet wholesome fare he served each evening in flat dishes along the rear of his building. A chipped jardiniere was made into a watering trough. On Sundays and national holidays he enlivened these meals with a morsel of cheese or bacon if he could afford these delicacies, or some bread soaked in milk if he could not. When the people of the neighborhood grew curious about this odd custom, Benjamin glibly assured them that the grain was laced with deadly ratsbane. Once poisoned, he explained, the rats developed a fearful thirst and the bowl of water was to lure them from the building so that they would not die in the walls or beneath the floor boards. He was warmly praised for his civic-mindedness and there was even some talk of putting him forward for the city council, an honor that Benjamin, with touching modesty, firmly declined. Those who saw him chasing cats and dogs from the alley knew that he did so to keep them from the poison, although a few wondered about the severity of his methods and the zeal of his pursuit.

Littleboy once swore to me that the rats wagged their tails when they saw him coming.

His paintings, therefore, contained many of these rodents. He drew one in pen and ink, I recall, that was almost as fine as Dürer's famous rabbit.

11 ৡ৶

MISERY IS fortuitous and gratuitous.

As a happy child of nine, I was on my way to school (the fifth grade it was), clutching my little lunch in one hand and my black and white speckled composition book in the other. That was how it was that day on Fairfield Street.

I had arrived at the corner and was dutifully looking in both directions before venturing out in the street, when a woman rushed from the doorway of one of the buildings. She was a heavy woman, with a round, pale, fleshy face and great breasts that wobbled as she ran. An orange bathrobe was wrapped tightly about her, the tasseled ends of the sash dragging along the ground.

It was a clear autumn day. There were acorns and rust-colored leaves in the gutter. Her mouth opened and closed in an oddly infantile manner, as if she sought to speak words that her lips had never learned. She looked at me. I had never seen that expression before. When she had approached to within three or four yards, there was a sound like the snapping of a circus-master's whip and she fell onto her side near a black-and-yellow-painted fire hydrant.

A husky blond man came down the two marble steps of the

building. He wore a gray sweatshirt and carried a small pistol in his freckled hand.

As she clung to the hydrant, trying to rise to her feet, he shot her in the face. A little red hole appeared in her fat white cheek, as if by magic. The whip cracked, and another jumped into being in her temple, an inch from her slightly mascaraed eye. Again that terse, crisp sound lashed the clear air and one nostril of her platyrrhine nose became a bloody pockmark. She ceased to move. With the muzzle of the gun he pushed aside her hair and fired a last shot into her ear. Then he walked back into the building.

"What did she say?" the policeman asked. "Then what happened, sonny? Did she scream? Did the husband say anything to her? Do you know what time it was, sonny? Didn't they say anything?"

No one seemed to believe that neither of them had spoken a word, that both had acted out the drama without dialogue.

It was three days before I returned to school. There was a boy in my class named Milton who enjoyed ordering me about. That first day back I hit him with a rock and gave him a concussion. There was a great deal of fuss made over it.

Can we say, perhaps, that savagery breeds savagery?

12 &

"DESTINY IS a door that hangs on the hinges of chance," says August Pfaff in his poem *Ogam*. Had I not been so poor that spring I would never have agreed to show my saints in that dingy gallery in Harvard Square, and if I had not shown them there, I would never have met Victor Darius.

The saints were six walnut-wood carvings that I had done the previous summer. They were inspired by illustrations of illuminated manuscripts that were the work of fourteenth-century Swabian monks and which I came across in an anthology at the Boston Public Library. I had changed the poses but had made a great effort to preserve the Gothic dignity of the faces. They proved to be the best wood sculptures I had ever done, and when Faber's dealer offered to buy them, though his price was fair, I refused to sell. It is also true that I was confident of obtaining a portrait commission from the widow of a banker at that particular time, and this expectation made me reluctant to part with my cherished offspring.

Needless to say, the portrait commission failed to materialize. By the end of the year I was in bad circumstances. I was living in a building on Marlborough Street that was so old, so dark and so dilapidated that it might easily have served as the setting for a work of Edgar Poe or Sheridan Le Fanu. My quarters consisted of a single large room, which being under the roof was uncomfortably warm in summer and dangerously cold in winter. There were two decent windows, however, and the landlady was compassionate; when one is poor, one is tolerant. I received four dollars a week for hauling the garbage cans into the alley, and when I was without food money, I could depend on either Faber or Littleboy to produce a dollar or two from their own meager supply. I subsisted on cabbage, carrots and the usual starchy foods of the indigent, with an occasional piece of fish or some chopped beef to thwart vitamin deficiency. McCoy, the art supplier, was threatening to deny me credit until I paid a little of the considerable sum that I owed him, and a department store was suing me in Small Claims Court for a debt that was more than two years old. Faced with these and other financial difficulties, I abandoned the luxury of sentiment and gave the saints to this fellow in Cambridge. Six weeks later I received a call from him on my landlady's telephone. An Englishman, he said, had bought four of the figures and paid three hundred dollars for them. Moments later I was trotting over the Harvard Bridge and down Massachusetts Avenue. The dealer gave me my two-thirds and told me that the customer had taken my address and might call on me, but with the money at last in my hands, I paid little attention to these remarks. The remainder of that pleasant day was spent in flying visits to my surprised creditors. In the evening I regaled Faber and Littleboy with a canned Dutch ham, a half-gallon of potato salad, two large Liederkranz cheeses, Russian rye bread, kosher pickles and a case of dark beer.

The next morning I arose a little later than usual but was working diligently at eleven o'clock when I was summoned to my door by a brisk knock. There on the landing stood a lightly built, finely featured young man, hardly older than myself and obviously English, since his hat, coat and tightly rolled umbrella could have been designed only in that quaint kingdom. He handed me an engraved calling card on which the name Victor Darius and a London address were discretely inscribed. I asked him in and thanked him cordially for buying the carvings.

"It is I who should thank you," he declared with great warmth. "They are very fine. They have a serenity rarely, if ever, seen in the work of today's artists. I did not, at first, believe what my eyes were telling me; the wood looked new but the craftsmanship was of an order that has long been gone from the earth. The Tyrolese, even the very best of them, are mere whittlers by comparison. You are a modern *imagier*."

I protested that the figures were not completely original in that they had been drawn from a series of fourteenth-century manuscripts. He listened attentively as I gave him all this information and explained my attempts to retain the purity of the old features while modifying the attitudes of their bodies.

"Ah. I know those saints, I believe. I have seen the manuscript in Darmstadt," he explained. "But what you have done is really quite original, nonetheless. You have been obliged to render those faces in depth. You have had to add a dimension. Why, those pictures in Germany are separated from your works by all the many distinctions that divide painting and sculpture. It is one thing to paint drapery but quite another to cut it into a piece of wood."

Our conversation became more general, and I learned, with pleasure, that his father operated the Matthew Hedges Gallery in London and that his uncle was the Mr. Pope of Pope-Debre, Ltd., the auctioneers. Other impressive affiliations were casually mentioned—Millbank-Carr, the New York collector, Riefenstahl in Vienna, the Galerie Mistral in Paris, the legendary Gunther Mithradatas, probably the biggest dealer in art in the world—names that bemused my senses. Darius said that he had come to Boston to negotiate the sale of some Ingres drawings to a collector. A friend in London had asked him to deliver a book to a cousin at Harvard, and it was through this happy chance that he had stumbled upon the basement gallery and discovered the statuettes.

"The newness of the wood was the only indication that they belonged to this age. There was a moment when I feared that they were really old carvings that some fool had sanded and polished in a misguided effort at conservation, but when I inspected them closely, I saw that this was not the case. Before yesterday I would have denied the possibility of a genuinely Gothic face appearing on a modern work. When a modern artist attempts an antique face, he invariably dilutes it with twentieth-century sentimentality, but these saints of yours are as bold and powerful as any at Rheims. I was quite overwhelmed," he told me, and my heart swelled with pride.

As he spoke his eyes traveled eagerly over the many finished canvases arrayed about the room, and more than once he faltered as if the sight of one of them had severed the thread of his thought. His hair was black and curiously devoid of sheen whereas his complexion was extremely fair, and this contrast, together with the delicate bone structure of his face, endowed him with that look of intelligent innocence that illuminates the portraits of the young early-nineteenth-century English poets. All his thoughts seemed inscribed upon his features as clearly as sentences upon a clean piece of paper. At last, unable to restrain himself any longer, he strode across the room and thrust his nose to within an inch of the surface of a painting that hung lopsidedly from a nail in the wall near the window.

"Incredible!" he exclaimed. "It quivers with vitality!"

This picture was one of the janitor's son eating from a bowl of red and green grapes.

"These are not modern paints," he said suddenly. "The colors are those of the old masters. Some are even rather coarse in texture. Where do you obtain such paints?"

"There," I replied, indicating the bench on which my mortar and my ball mill rested. "They are manufactured by me. I use no commercial preparations of any kind. I make my paints, my varnishes, my gessos—everything, in short, but the weaving of the linen canvas, is done by me."

"Ah-h!" he said softly, almost reverentially. "Who would believe that such an artisan still exists? Those eyes—if they blinked I shouldn't be surprised. How long have you been painting like this?"

I laughed in delight. "Ten years, perhaps."

"Does that small gallery handle your paintings, too?"

"At the moment no one represents me," I answered. "The local people consider me too far behind the times, I'm afraid."

"They are either blind or mad," he cried angrily. "What about the people in New York? Don't they know you?"

"A few have seen my work but they claim they have no customers for paintings done in 'that style.' The cognoscenti damn me as an anachronism."

"These cognoscenti are without cognizance. They would damn Rubens if he suddenly returned. I know them and they are a sorry lot. Never allow them to change you into a palette-knife painter or, worse yet, one of those monstrous, distracted abstractionists. I have looked at contemporary painting in most parts of the world and I have seen nothing that approaches the excellence of this work before me. May I see that one? Is it the entombment of Christ?"

He remained with me for several hours, examining one painting after another and displaying an understanding that was both broad and profound. Whatever was good, he recognized as such immediately; whatever was weak or failed in its aim was dismissed with a few gentle though penetrating observations. It was praise, however, that I heard most, that day. What was not declared to be "incredible," was "astonishing" and what was not "astonishing" was "staggering" or "prodigious" or even "miraculous." And since all these comments were delivered with such obvious sincerity and such sympathetic comprehension, I grew intoxicated from their potency.

Though I had but the one room, it was well stocked with the products of my labor. One huge closet was crammed with unframed paintings. A converted china cupboard held many small tempera pictures as well as some oak-wood carvings of Moses, Saul, David, Solomon and other Old Testament heroes. A steamer trunk contained several marble figures, two bronze busts and a number of mahogany panels depicting scenes from the Odyssey, done in low relief, while an aluminum suitcase accommodated most of my drawings and prints. Nor was this all, for beneath my bed and stacked against the walls were more canvases, more carvings and more sketches, etchings and woodcuts in neatly tied portfolios. Victor Darius inspected everything.

At last he sat back in my battered old armchair and sighed. I had given him a cup of coffee and he drank some of it.

"An heroic performance," he murmured, as if to himself, and then, looking at me in solemn wonder, he added, "You have created a world, my good fellow, an entire world, really."

"You are very kind. I hope that I deserve some of all that generous praise," I said. "Your words have made me giddy."

"These things are beyond praise. I am no less giddy than you. It is an exhilarating experience to look on such wonders. I know a few people here in Boston and more in New York. I lived there for a year when I went to Columbia. I had to study radiography and infrared photography." He laughed. "Nowadays one must be a scientist to deal in pictures. I am sure I can help you sell your paintings. Fortunately, there are still people in the world who have healthy tastes. There are several pictures I wish to buy myself, and I must have that marble maenad. I will have to cable London for more money, but it'll be here in the morning and I can return then."

"Take what you like, right now," I said. "I'll list the prices and you can send me a check."

He would not hear of this, however. "No, no," he said, "I will take nothing until I have paid for it." He then selected a portrait of an elderly man dressed in the clerical costume of the Italian Renaissance, a "Jesus in the Temple" done on an old oak board, and a very ambitious representation of Venus laughing at an angry Vulcan, done on canvas and framed with an elaborately carved molding. He said that my prices were too low; I said that I felt guilty charging him so much. In truth, I would have been glad to give him the things for nothing, so delighted was I by his gracious encouragement.

The next morning he arrived early with a Thomas Cook check, and together we put the four works into a cab. Clay and Dwyer, the shippers, crated them and arranged with Darius for their transfer to London. We then picked up his luggage at the Chester House, caught another cab to Back Bay Station and reached the platform just as his New York train was pulling in. He said that he would return toward the end of the summer.

That is how I first met Victor Darius. I was a happy man that day.

13 &

My sudden success brought happiness to Littleboy and Faber. I swore to them that I would conduct Darius to their studios on his very next visit so that they, too, might have a chance to stupefy a bona-fide English connoisseur. Faber, who kept abreast of all that happened in the art world, declared that Victor Darius was a prominent international authority on forgeries and frauds.

"It must be his father," I said. "This fellow is a youngster."

"No, no. It's the same one. He's considered to be something of a prodigy," Leo replied. "Do you remember the attempt by some Canadians to foist a fake Correggio on the Metropolitan? This Darius denounced the ascription and proved it bogus by showing it contained synthetic ultramarine. He shook the pundits."

"Ah!" I said. "No wonder he recognized my paints as being made in a muller. The man knows true colors. How many times have I told you both to abjure that catsup and mustard that you are always buying at McCoy's. You can't paint pictures with mayonnaise, you know! Maybe now that I am rich and almost famous, you will begin to heed my advice."

"Listen to him, Leo!" Littleboy exclaimed, smiling. "Success hasn't changed him a bit. He is still as peculiar as ever. He wants to make drugstore clerks out of us; we're to spend our precious hours grinding out headache powders in a mortar. We're painters, not alchemists. We don't paint with pestles."

"The true artist makes his colors," I proclaimed, waving my forefinger in his fat face.

"Does he now? And do you make the earths that you use

to make your colors? My Sunday school teacher once told me that they were manufactured by God."

"A poor job of it He did, too," I countered. "They are filled with grit and impurities. Given the proper equipment, I could make them better. It's not for nothing that we call the earth 'dirt.'"

Benjamin took great pleasure in provoking me on the subject of God. He well knew that I believe in a living, substantial Almighty, and this amused him. He knew, too, that I was not pleased with many aspects of the creation, that I thought it disorderly, ill-proportioned and often ugly and that I had, more than once, described my own conceptions of a perfect cosmos. And so we frequently joked about this, though I must confess it was not all jesting on my part.

14 &

ONE DAY, at least a year ago, I wandered into a very crowded, poorly lit antique shop on Charles Street. From floor to ceiling the single room was stuffed with a chaotic assortment of venerable objects. Chipped Colonial crockery mingled with Chinese bronzes and German steins on the scarred top of a French gaming table. Czechoslovakian glass goblets and Sandwich glass oil lamps sat precariously on a flimsy tiered table, which, in turn, rested upon a kind of music cabinet that was boldly decorated with intarsia. Every inch of wall space was covered by pictures, plaques, maps, samplers, sconces, crucifixes, hanging shelves and gilded mirrors. Crystal chandeliers, copper caldrons, moth-eaten tapestries and brass bird cages hung from the overhead beams.

It was several minutes before my eyes became accustomed to the gloom and a while longer before I could distinguish the shopkeeper, a small, white-haired, pale-faced lady of sixty or sixty-five, whose form, like that of a wild animal, blended elusively into the background. I was looking for amber, a substance that I used in the making of varnish and which I was sometimes able to obtain in broken necklaces for very reasonable prices from shops such as this one. From a rosewood lap desk, the old woman brought forth two strings of translucent brown celluloid that she called amber, but I rejected them at once. As I made my way to the front door, I rapped my ankle against one of a pair of massive andirons, and as I glanced down at them, I saw someone looking at me from a dismal corner of the room. A small, shiny brown face peered between an ancient coal scuttle and a dented tea chest and watched me even as I watched it. I must have flinched or cried out, for the shopkeeper asked me what was wrong. Even as she spoke, I discerned that the face was attached to some kind of box and that it was not flesh and blood but wood or metal. But I will not retreat an inch from my assertion that the little face, whatever its composition, contemplated me when I first discovered it, improbable as it may seem.

The old woman displayed surprising energy as she shoved and pushed a variety of dusty objects aside to gain access to the corner, and in little more than a minute she emerged with the shiny brown spectator, who proved to be an angel carved in high relief on the sliding door of an apothecary chest. I took the box and carried it to the door of the shop. Even in broad daylight it looked strangely alive. Somehow the sculptor had succeeded in endowing the lineaments with an expression that was vital and yet divinely detached. The face contained love and pity, peace and wisdom, inspiration and mystery. The eyes, which had pupils cut into them, were the most arresting feature, as I have indicated, but the mouth was very nearly as striking, for its full, slightly pursed lips seemed on the verge of speaking. The nose and brow were truly noble, the chin and cheeks quite feminine. Tight curls, finely incised, covered the head, while from behind the shoulders, which were just barely visible, the tips of two feathered wings appeared. The whole was enclosed in an oval cartouche and surrounded by imbricated oak leaves, except for a tiny space over the panel which contained a scroll upon which the name Louis Bourg was inscribed in swash letters.

"Louisburg is what it says," the old lady declared at my elbow. "A professor from Boston University told me that's a place in Canada that was captured by the Colonists during the French and Indian Wars. He thought this medicine chest might have been part of the plunder. That was in seventeen fifty-something. You can see that's very old writing."

The wood was mahogany and part of a living tree no more than seventy or eighty years ago but I made no effort to disenchant her. Her price of ninety-five dollars was low enough, however, considering that the carving was a masterpiece. I wrote a check and hurried home with my treasure.

There, I slid the door from its frame and placed it in the center of my mantle, where it has remained ever since. I never tire of looking at that bewitching expression; it is the last thing I look upon at night and the first thing my eyes seek when I awaken. There are times when I believe that it is not a representation of a human face but of a being from another part of the universe—an ultra-human. Indeed, I have some reason for so believing.

Who was Louis Bourg? I have spent many hours diligently searching but have never been able to discover an artist of that name. That Bourg was the artist and not the man for whom the chest was made seems to be confirmed by a second inscription, this in a kind of European hand, that I found on the reverse side of the panel. "Louis Bourg" is repeated—

beneath it is "La Rochelle 14-2-74." La Rochelle is a port in southwestern France and the numbers must signify February 14, 1874. That Monsieur Bourg is not mentioned in the art books of the world is incredible.

15 ?

LITTLEBOY MARRIED a girl named Danielle Grand, who spoke with a French accent and claimed to be a descendant of Alexandre Dumas. They had met at an adult education center in the North End where she modeled for a life class. On her part—though not on his—it was love at first sight.

Three days after this first meeting Benjamin answered a knock on his door and found Danielle, fragrant with sweet perfume, there on his threshold.

"I am your new neighbor. I take the place next door," she announced blithely. "You will help me with my few furnitures, no?"

These "few furnitures," Benjamin said, consisted of a chest of drawers fit for Pantagruel, a bed large enough to accommodate Bonaparte's Imperial Guard and an armoire in which Robespierre might easily have stored his guillotine. Each was polychromed and lavishly gilded. Cherubim and turtledoves were everywhere. He thought they were made of ironwood or *lignum vitae,* so great was their weight. But with the help of the janitor and Danielle's broken-English encouragement, he managed to haul, lift, drag and shove the monsters up four flights of stairs. In the end, his knees were knocking from exertion. Gessoed acanthus leaves, wooden grapes and the tiny fingers and toes of coy *putti* littered every step.

After she was settled, he frequently met her in the hall. Whenever he left his place, she was leaving hers. Chance seemed always to throw them together. And when he did not see her, the heady aroma of her perfume—which she used intrepidly—enabled him to smell her. So powerful was this scent that it easily vanquished the odor of paint and turpentine that formerly ruled the atmosphere of his apartment. It penetrated the walls with as little difficulty as if they had been made of silk. One day, however, he was blessed with a revelation. Having forgotten his wallet, he was obliged to retrace his steps to his apartment. When he approached the fourth floor, he became aware of an odd swishing sound, and when he turned the angle of the staircase, there before him was his cunning neighbor, busily spraying perfume through his keyhole. Not until she had finished the keyhole and sent a few blasts beneath the door, did she notice his presence.

"Ah, ha!" said he, affecting great masculine indignation.

"Ha, ha!" said she, after barely a moment's hesitation. Then like a wood sprite, she skipped into her apartment, but not before leveling her atomizer in his face and raking him with a parting shot. Her defiant laughter—which also had a French accent—assaulted the poor fellow through her closed door.

Against such an assault, it was futile to resist. There was a long and sometimes stormy courtship, but in the end they married. She was a dark, slender girl with large brown eyes and a gay, volatile disposition. Littleboy said that she was a Berber, though Danielle swore that she was a Parisienne. Tattooed in blue upon her thigh was some Arabic writing, but she glibly explained this as being *"un charme"* to protect her from evil, put there by her first lover (when she was but a schoolgirl), a wealthy Algerian from Constantine.

"But you speak Arabic in your sleep," Benjamin accused on one occasion.

"Arabic! What do you know of Arabic?" she replied. "I am

speaking Romany, perhaps. I have tell you that my grandmother has been a Gypsy."

"An Egyptsy from Cairo," he answered, laughing.

"No Egypt. Paris, *mon petit canard.* My great-great-
grandfather has been Alexandre Dumas, as you know."

"Yes and my great-great-grandfather was George Sand,"
Benjamin said.

"O-la-la! Pas possible," his wife shrieked, throwing up her
hands in glee. "You are a naughty person!"

Along with powerful perfumes, she wore elaborate jewelry
and heavy make-up. Her earrings were like chandeliers, her
necklaces bibs of multicolored beads. These, together with an
assortment of bangles of brass and silver that bedecked her
arms halfway to the elbows, gave off a pleasant jingle whenever she moved, and as she was constantly in motion, there
was never any silence in her vicinity.

Ah, Danielle! How happy it would make me to hear the
music of your walk and your broken English laughter. Time
moves on and takes all things with it.

16 ও

THE POINT on this stupid pencil persists in breaking. Objects
often seem guided by a malevolent intelligence.

About a month after his departure Victor Darius sent me a
letter with a check. I was to send him "Hercules Strangling
the Nemean Lion," "The Reunion of the Dioscuri" and a
"Portrait of Two Girls in Red Cloaks." He asked, also, if I'd
be willing to consign paintings to the Matthew Hedges Gallery
on a continuous basis.

They are certain to attract buyers [the letter continued]. You must elevate your prices, however, for these customers know value only in pounds, shillings and pence. I have sold the "Venus and Vulcan" and my profit was outrageous. There is a Belfast Irishman panting for the "Jesus in the Temple" but he is trying to force my price down. He will pay, though. The collectors are like people in love and their passion makes them weak as water. Still, they like to pretend they have a will of their own. But my conscience is clear, for they are buying that which they could find nowhere else on earth at twice the sum. One day their descendants will sell these paintings and realize a profit far greater than mine.

If you have not sold the other two carved saints, please hold them for me until September. I should have bought them all that day but I was in such a whirl. I have been speaking to everyone here about you. It may seem strange to you but there are often opportunities to conduct trans-Atlantic business, so to speak. There is one chap who is keen to have a portrait of his dead mother done from photographs, and a Glasgow lady has been after me to arrange a painting of Mary of Scotland and Darnley. This is labor that will produce little satisfaction on your part, no doubt, but it will bring in money and put you before the public eye. Even dead old ladies can be made into works of art, you know, and with a brush like yours that possibility becomes a sure thing.

The check was most welcome, though I had not fully consumed the previous one. I wrote at once, telling him that I would be delighted to send as many pictures as he wanted; he need only tell me which ones he had in mind.

It appeared as if my fortunes were definitely in the ascendant. Within a week of the arrival of Darius' letter I received a visit from a dealer from Detroit who was interested in Biblical subjects. After looking at everything, he bought a painting of Hagar and Ishmael, an oak carving of David loading his sling, and an ivory plaque of Saints Peter and Paul, mounted on red velvet and set in an oval frame. I stained the ivory with tea to accent its intricacies, and it was an impressive piece though barely two inches square in size. This oriental coloring technique subdues the brightness of the raw ivory and gives it what some people mistakenly regard as an age patina. The dealer must have concluded that I had done it for that purpose, for in a very confidential manner he asked me if I would be interested in executing some paintings on old canvas for him. I had received more than one such proposal in the past, usually from antique merchants who were looking for a ready supply of early American portraits or naval pictures. I had no interest in such nonsense. To paint on old canvases, I told the dealer, was not merely dishonest, but degrading and disgusting to anyone who considered himself an artist. The fellow was taken aback and quickly changed the subject. He paid me $280 for the painting and the two carvings and left well pleased with his acquisitions.

I decided to open a bank account and save for a trip to Italy.

17 &

THERE IS no question in my mind that those pigeons are up to something. Right at this moment there is an ugly-looking gray brute with his beak pressed against the windowpane and his burnt-orange eyes fixed upon me. Just a bird, perhaps? He has a look about him that belies that conclusion. What's more, none of these treacherous creatures has eaten any of the poisoned bread that I prepared for them. Isn't it because they know? Ah well, maybe I am hopelessly mad. I'd better write of something else. Let me write of someone who is really mad.

Visiting the Public Garden daily, as I do (except Sundays and holidays, of course), I have, willy-nilly, become acquainted with some of the other quotidian denizens of the place. One such is a man in a shabby black homburg who spends the better part of each morning sitting with one leg over the other, covertly eating something from a wrinkled paper bag. Another is a very old woman who wears pince-nez and clothing forty years behind the fashion. She sits for hours reading paper-backed western stories which she holds at near arm's length. There is a man who listens to dance music on his portable radio each afternoon, and two middle-aged ladies, who are almost always to be found on the bench near the water fountain, interminably exchanging their views of the world. And there is Randolph, of course, and Mr. Beels and Johann.

Mrs. Dandelion, however, is perhaps the most consistent member of our coterie and it is she whom I wish to introduce now. There are people whose skin is extremely pale—sick people usually—but never have I seen skin as pale as Mrs. Dandelion's—at least, not on someone who was breathing. Her complexion is similar to that of the underside of a fish, and this in spite of her being out of doors all day long. I would guess her age to be forty but I would not be surprised to learn that I was wrong by more than a decade. She is a very thin lady with hardly any distinguishable projections from her body for bust, hips or buttocks, and if I were to say that her figure was composed of four parallel planes, that would be an exaggeration but not a very great one. Even the knees and ankles of her legs conform to this plan, for they are ill-defined and scarcely recognizable as joints. Really, she is like a figure drawn with a ruler! Her face, too, is thin and her hair falls to her shoulders though it is strawlike in both color and texture. Summer and winter she wears a high-crowned, broad-brimmed hat, the color of tarnished brass.

This grotesque person comes to the Garden every day in order to feed the pigeons. I have known for some time that she is not what is called "normal," but until a few weeks ago I did not realize how far she deviated from the mean. Each morning she appears with a large bag of birdseed and proceeds to wander up this path and down that, strewing grain to her greedy, scrambling entourage. Sometimes she performs this ambulation in serene silence, while on other occasions she talks to herself in soft, even, conversational tones. But there are days when her soliloquy is thoroughly violent and the air around her is filled with curses, snarls, grunts, shouts, growls, squeals, moans and hideously mordant laughter. None of this, of course, disturbs the pigeons who flock around her regardless of her state of mind. The gluttony of these birds defies belief. Notwithstanding the generosity of their benefactor, who sprays the walk with thousands upon thousands of seeds, they seem as hungry at the end of the meal as they were at the beginning. And how they leap, hop and fly about to secure the greatest possible share of the food!

Even from a distance it is easy to discern this lady's mood, for when she is calm, so, too, is her gait, but when she is disturbed, then her pace quickens into an aggressive stride. The birdseed is flung fiercely about, striking the pigeons and bouncing from the asphalt path in fountain-like plumes, while her quarrel with an invisible enemy is sustained with unnatural jerks of her head, wild grimaces and threatening gestures. Then it is that she violates the peace of the Garden with her unbelievably virulent cries.

As I have said, it was only a few weeks ago that I came to improve my acquaintance with this woman. We had a conversation, a curious, if not prophetic, dialogue.

"Aren't you a little early today," she asked, and her voice and manner were as reasonable as anyone could wish. "It is a lovely day, though, and it's a good idea to get out early. But you are busy, aren't you? I've noticed that you are always very busy. I don't want to disturb you."

When she approached me, I was sitting with my hands in my lap and my eyes set unwaveringly on the green flank of Washington's horse, which was just visible through the leaves. To any other spectator, I would have appeared as idle as the sphinx, yet this Cassandra could see that beneath my placid exterior I was far from being unemployed. Until her words broke the spell, I was on the banks of the Lena, helping to unload pine logs from a barge, and since there was fear of the river freezing over before the job was completed, the foreman was short-tempered and goaded everyone with sharp words. Though I was muffled in heavy—and foul-smelling—woolen garments and working strenuously, I was very cold, and when I found myself back in the summer warmth of Boston, I was not displeased.

So I replied civilly and with a smile. "Yes, madam, today I am both early and busy and I agree that the day is lovely."

I was dismayed to see that these few words were interpreted as an invitation to further conversation and that she immediately sat down upon my bench, albeit three to four feet away.

"Yes, yes. Just lovely. And everyone is out," she declared, watching me closely. "Even Mr. Sally was out on the front steps when I left the house and he's been very ill, as you probably know. Mrs. Sally is always complaining because he isn't well, but, after all, she does have two children. They're probably mine, too, especially Helen, who looks just like my sister Nancy when she was that age. But I was even earlier than you, you know. I've fed all the locals and a dozen or so of the strangers and they were all very good today—but that's to be expected when the sun is shining. When it rains, that's something else again."

She halted and looked at me intently. Her pale face bore an expression of eager expectancy, though what she expected from me, I was unable to guess.

"The rain can be very trying," I asserted solemnly, after an awkward pause.

"It certainly can. But I come out in it anyway, no matter how wet I get. They're not going to keep me in. My husband complains, but then he's always working, so what difference does it make? He's a meat cutter and he makes good money, but he has to work sixty to sixty-five hours a week and he's always tired. He's been working like that for the last nineteen years and no wonder I don't always feel well. He wants to become meat manager but that's why we never had any children, and when he does get a vacation, it's down to Weymouth he goes, to see his mother. Sundays he sleeps and reads the paper and I've got to keep the coffee pot on all day for him, and he says that the house is never clean and that I'm crazy. Can you imagine a man saying that to his wife? How many hours are there in a week? I thought you didn't know! One hundred and sixty-eight! He makes a lot of overtime, though. You don't work, do you?"

"No," I said, wondering how I might best effect a smooth departure.

"Ah-h!" she said, as though my reply explained everything. "By the way, what's your name?"

I searched the more tortuous corridors of my brain and answered, "Scopas. Myron Scopas."

"Is that an American name?"

"English—but the family's been here for some time. Left England for America back in the time of Henry the Sixth."

"Wonderful! I love old families. You would never guess my name, so I will tell it to you. My last name is Dandelion and my first name is April! Isn't that the prettiest name? April Dandelion! I often think it's the only reason I married my husband—just so I could be called April Dandelion. Now my husband's first name isn't nice at all. His mother named him Valentine. I've always felt that Valentine Dandelion was ridiculous."

My head began to whirl.

All at once she said, "Shush!" and threw a crafty, conspiratorial look in my direction while surreptitiously pointing with her thumb toward a seedy-looking man who came trudging, head down and hands in pockets, along the path. She watched him very carefully as he went by, and there was no mistaking the hostility of her expression. No basilisk ever glared with more ferocity.

"He doesn't fool me at all," she whispered when he was barely out of earshot. "You don't know that man, do you?" she added a moment later.

"No, I've never seen him before," I answered, involuntarily lowering my voice. "Who is he?"

"One of the H.C.," she replied slyly. Again she looked at me expectantly, but as I had somewhere mislaid the sense of her remarks, I was unable to make a suitable contribution to the conversation.

"Come now, Mr. Henry," she exclaimed at last, her voice rather loud. "You're no fool. You've heard of it—don't pretend. You couldn't sit here all day long and not notice them; they're all so obvious."

I was mystified but exasperated as well, for I was anxious to fathom the murky depths of this strange discussion.

"I give you my word, madam, I have never heard of it or them," I said with some force. "Of whom are we speaking?"

"If you don't know, how do you know you've never heard of them?"

"I am forced to that assumption from the nature of your hints," I retorted as I began to feel that I was up to my ears in a quagmire and in imminent danger of disappearing completely.

"Hints?" she exclaimed. "It's not a question of hints. I'm not afraid of them." She looked over both shoulders, moved closer to me on the bench and whispered, "The Homicide Club!"

I was expecting something bizarre but I was nonetheless startled by her words and by the sudden shiver that ran through her whole body.

"What is the Homicide Club?" I asked, though I was not at all sure that I wanted to know.

"It's the biggest organization in the whole world, that's what it is. It has millions of members—and in every country. They're all over the United States and in Asia and Europe and Africa. They're in the big cities, the little towns and out in the country, too. Why, there are even children who are members! I know a nine-year-old boy who killed a kitten; he admitted to me that he was a member and said he had to do it or they would have put him in the box. No one knows exactly what the box is, he said, because no one ever comes back after being in it. They're clever, but they don't fool me. They fool everyone else, but not me! All their tricks and disguises and that invisibility machine and the voice gun and the telephone torture and the rest—none of it deceives me for a minute. And that one, just now, pretending to look at the ground while he was watching every move we made. I saw him the minute he came in the gate, and he knew it, too. He's the one who tried to step on one of the local pigeons last week, but he wasn't fast enough." She stopped abruptly, glanced over her shoulder again and said, "Well?"

"Well," I repeated stupidly, since my brain was fully occupied with trying to sort out the information it had been given. "What do they do? How do you know them?"

She moved a foot closer to me on the bench. The lack of color in her face was unbelievable.

"Everything! That's what they do! Everything that's evil and wicked and mean and nasty. Everything that hurts animals and people and makes them miserable. All the sadness and hunger and pain and fear and crime—it's all their doing, every bit of it! But what they do more of than anything else is commit murders. That's their specialty. That's how they got their name, you know. They kill old people, young people, men, women, children—even babies—it doesn't matter to them. And they love to kill animals, too. They destroy the birds. Where are the bluebirds that used to come here? Every year there are fewer ducks and robins. They've killed nearly all the horses; only the police have any now. If you go out into the country, you never see any sheep any more and they say all the animals in the forest are being slaughtered.

"Why, don't you even read your newspaper? It's all there, every single day. A girl strangled in Chelsea, a man stabbed in Revere, an infant suffocated in Winthrop, someone thrown out of a window in Framingham, or shot in Lexington, or beaten to death in Brighton, or drowned in Marblehead, or run over in Everett. Who do you think is doing it all? Who do you think poisoned the girl on Boylston Street and all the others? I don't have to tell you all this. You know. Everyone knows, but they're all afraid to do anything."

Her words were making me uncomfortable, but I sat and listened because there was always a chance—slight though it might be—that she really knew something of consequence.

"The Homicide Club is at the bottom of it all," she went on, tugging at the broad brim of her hat in a nervous gesture. "Take my word for it, they're everywhere. Listen. They have different colored eyes. One day they're blue, the next they're brown; it's a dead giveaway. Most people aren't quick enough to notice something like that, though. It took me a while to spot it, but once you get used to looking for it, you can catch them every time. The women always have those freckles on their arms and the backs of their hands, and the men always walk with their hands in their pockets—sometimes one hand, sometimes both. I wrote to the President and the F.B.I., but that was a waste of time: they never answered my letters. There's not much chance of getting at them that way. I know that there are Homicide boys down in the State House, so why shouldn't there be some in Washington, D.C., I'd like to know."

She stopped, compressed her lips to indicate that she was finished speaking and folded her skinny arms across her flat chest.

"Well, I'm glad you told me about this," I said, while I thought to myself that it had to be a lot of nonsense. Still, the most insane utterances always contain a modicum of truth, and her mentioning the girl on Boylston Street and "the others" had disturbed me. Despite her bravado, it was obvious that she was afraid. Perhaps this Ophelia was a sibyl in disguise and with those pale eyes saw something that was invisible to me. Not likely, I decided. She is only a lunatic, pursued by phantoms and obsessed by fearful fantasies. There was little intelligence here, and her lack of coherence was certainly not assumed. However, there was this close relationship with the pigeons. I determined to probe further.

"Aren't you afraid that they'll be after you, since you know so much about them?" I asked.

"Ha! After me? After me? They've been after me for years. Not a day goes by that they don't try to get me. Only yesterday afternoon one of them chased me to Park Street. He had a gun, all wrapped up in a yellow paper, but I hid in a phone booth until he went by and that's how I escaped." She laughed, and I could see that she had very even teeth, though small and ochroid. She moved another few inches toward me on the seat, pulled her hat and continued. "They nearly got me on Arlington Street one day. A taxicab came right at me, but I ran and ducked behind a tree and then the man in the cab looked back at me and said something awful, but I just yelled right back at him, the murderer. I keep my eyes open, you know?

"See the man in the wheelchair?" She pointed to Mr. Beels, who was sitting not far from the Chinese Scholar tree. "He's in charge of the whole Commonwealth of Massachusetts. He

admits it, the fool! He asked me to go up to his apartment
to see his parakeets, as if I'd be as stupid as that! I keep my
wits about me at all times. Why, they even tried to get me one
day when I was with my husband. A big, fat, red-headed man
aimed a gun at me from the roof of the Tilton warehouse.
I had to hide behind an automobile. My husband just stood
there, like an idiot. I tried to get it through his head later
that they were after me, but all he kept saying was that I was
soft as a grape and should be in Mattapan. But that's Valentine. I thought he was going to hit me again.

"The only one in the whole house who understands is Mrs.
Feeney, on the third floor, but she gets the Homicide Club
mixed up with the anarchists and the Masons, but it's because
she's very old. I wanted her to go with me to the Police Headquarters on Berkeley Street about the taxicab but she . . ."

Suddenly she stopped and began to scrutinize my face carefully. As she stared, her aspect changed from uncertainty to
distrust and from distrust to outright fear. I looked directly
into her eyes and laughed evilly. She leaped from the bench as
if it had suddenly been charged with electricity. When she had
put fifteen or twenty feet between us, she turned and shouted
defiantly, "You didn't fool me for a minute. I knew you! I
knew you!" Then, baring her teeth like an angry alley cat, she
marched sideways toward the lagoon, looking back as she went.

Having grown suddenly weary of her talk, I had put my
hands in my pockets.

TRUE TO his word, Darius returned in September. His enthusiasm had diminished not a whit. To hear him talk was, for me, like drinking a bottle of smooth, though heady wine. I had sent him seven paintings during the summer, which he had consigned to two very reputable London galleries, and three of these having been sold, he presented me with a check for $850. During his absence I had completed a number of works and he pored over these with his customary eagerness, making the most astute comments from time to time. The principal painting, a representation of a furious Othello on the point of killing Desdemona, he purchased unhesitatingly. He was quite enraptured by two small canvases as well. The first, "Diana with a Hind," was scarcely ten inches high and seven wide, while the second, "Persephone's Abduction," was only slightly larger. He also bought a tempera painting of St. Jerome, done on a piece of cherry wood that I had cut from a shattered blanket chest that I discovered one day in the alley.

In addition to all this, he informed me that he had secured a commission for me from a Dutch financier. This man had been reared by his grandmother after the death of his parents from influenza. The old woman, herself, had died many years before, and now the grandson, grown sentimental with age, wanted a portrait of her. Darius had four old photographs that I was to work from, as best I could. Fortunately, these pictures were rather good; the lady had a charming face, and with her white cap and collar, looked like someone out of a Pieter De Hoogh interior.

But Victor's visit this time was a brief one. I had hoped that he would accompany me to Littleboy's and subsequently, perhaps, to Faber's place, but as he was flying to Cleveland that same afternoon, this was not possible. He thought that he would be back in Boston before the year ended, since he had promised to attend the opening of a Kipstein retrospective in New York in December. I would hear from him before that, however, he assured me. I promised to begin the portrait immediately.

19 ?

I WAS disappointed when Darius could not come to see the paintings of Littleboy and Faber. I had not the slightest doubt that he would recognize their ability. As things turned out, however, Faber achieved a brilliant success that November. Invited to take part in a group show at a Greenwich Village gallery, he captivated the New York critics who pronounced him a "new Corot." By the time the exhibit closed he had sold fourteen paintings, one of which went to the Museum of Modern American Art. Previously the Boston savants branded him an academicist and termed his paintings "calendar art," but now they began to see him in a new light.

I do not wish to become involved in the tangled skein spun by today's interpreters of painting. I cannot attack them for I do not understand them. When they speak, it is in a language that defies translation. Where is the Champollion who will tell us the meaning of "conventional assemblage projections," or "implosive transfigurations," or "the fusion of analytic mechanics," or "manipulation of arcane formalism," or "the visual unity of metamorphized ambient identities," or—but I will spare you the sight of any more of these atrocities. What they missed in Faber's case was that he was, purely and simply, a most accomplished artist with a style that was both original and strong. The New York critics, who are exposed to a greater variety of art work, detected this pearl among the pebbles and Leo was on his way.

A diligent and careful worker, he had been able to support himself for several years by doing art restoration work at Lord's, and it was by working with the fine landscapes of other eras that he acquired many of his techniques. He became a very good restorer, in time, adept at cleaning, patching holes with canvas and beeswax, re-lining, transferring paintings from old canvases to new ones and, above all, the repainting of missing segments that had fallen victim to mildew, rough handling or other catastrophes. He could replace a piece of clear blue sky or cream-white forehead and no one could tell where the original ended and his repair began. In the end, however, he abandoned this lucrative trade, for it left him with no time to paint his own pictures, and the desire to create was, with him, an irresistible influence.

Leo is about six feet tall, thin, somewhat awkward of movement, soft-spoken and even-tempered. Much of his time was (and is) spent in the countryside that surrounds Boston, where, palette in hand, he has been forced on more than one occasion to flee bees, wasps and angry bulls. He is addicted to coffee and will drink fifteen to twenty cups a day, either at home from a samovar-sized coffee pot or in the field from a thermos that holds a gallon. He is an avid photographer and a great collector of reviews, programs, posters and other oddments of the art world. He has scrapbooks that go back to his childhood, boxes of correspondence and piles of magazines and art books. I do not believe he owns a garbage pail, for he has never thrown anything away.

The New York success was followed, a year later, by an even more auspicious occurrence. One of his early paintings, a picture of three adolescent girls bathing naked in a stream, was sold to a man named Bernard Lisbon, who lived in Brookline. Lisbon was a collector and owned a Millet, a Bonnat, two small Rodin bronzes and a variety of competently painted landscapes from the early years of this century and the latter part of the last. About the time of Faber's exhibit in the Village, this wealthy man died of a lung disease. To settle his estate, his collection was sent to Fraser-Philips in New York, to be auctioned off, and Leo's picture eventually found itself upon the block. Now, though this particular painting is far from being Leo's best, it is a good one and possesses a voluptuousness that is more Titian than Corot. These three young ladies triggered an emotion in the onlookers, particularly the male onlookers and more particularly the middle-aged male onlookers, that was as powerful as it was occult. At this auction the dealers and collectors present were carried away by what Faber called "a Sybaritic frenzy" at the sight of the painting, and the bidding became ferociously competitive. When the hammer finally fell, "Summer in Salem," as it was called (though it was done outside of Essex), fetched $24,000. From that moment on, Faber had no difficulty selling his paintings.

His fame now is well established and his pictures hang in the museums of Chicago, Los Angeles, St. Louis, Dallas and numerous Eastern cities. He travels about a good deal giving lectures on art at schools throughout the country, and there are few magazines in the field that have not carried at least one of his articles. Of the three of us, he alone truly succeeded. I must confess that I do not think him a better painter than Benjamin nor do I believe his art the equal of my own, but he is a wonderfully good painter, nonetheless, and a very fine man.

I must buy a pen. My thoughts are sometimes so intense that they cause me to lean too heavily on my pencil. I have sharpened all of them now so often that they are difficult to grasp. What has happened to my light touch?

20 &

WHEN I was a boy, I wanted to see God. I believed that if I walked straight down Commonwealth Avenue, He would be there at the end. When I discovered that the world was round and that such a promenade would only bring me back to my starting point, I was chagrined, but only for a while. I determined to walk down Commonwealth Avenue but not to follow the contour of the earth. I would walk straight, straight —on into the void, past the sun and the planets, past the stars and the nebulae and, without the smallest deviation, right to God. What Columbus did to my first scheme, Einstein did to my second. Still, I have not lost my desire to see Him. In those days, however, I had a great love for Him. Now I would like to ask Him some questions.

21 &

THIS MORNING, as I sat in the Public Garden, I reveried in Japan during the revolution of 1867. The soldiers of the shogun came to our village looking for food, but we had been warned of their approach and had hidden our poultry. The soldiers were angry. They discovered my brother's empty dovecote and asked him what he had done with the birds. At first my brother said that he had sold them at Mito, but when the strangers threatened to tear out his tongue, he became frightened and led them to the cave where he had hidden the doves in a basket. The leader of the soldiers ordered them to kill my brother, who, hearing his words, tried to run away, but his feet were blind with terror and he tripped over a stone and fell. This made the soldiers very merry and they laughed loudly as they beat him to death with their staves. I did not wish to watch my brother die, so I ran further into the woods and wept. I could hear the sound of his cries and of the blows upon his body.

When I returned to Boston from Honshu, I was surprised to see how crowded the Garden had become. The sun was very hot and seemed to be no further away than the tops of the elm trees. The walks were filled with lightly clad, camera-carrying tourists and the swanboats well manned with boister-ous children. I had hoped to go in search of a restaurant with a sugar bowl but the heat precluded this mild ambition. If there is one, I decided, it will be there tomorrow.

Randolph suddenly appeared from behind a lady with a baby carriage. On his left hand was Sebastian the frog, while in his right hand he held a ball the size and color of an orange. In fact, as he drew nearer, it became evident that it was an orange.

"Good morning, Mr. Vermicelli," he said.

"Mr. who?" I asked in bewilderment.

"Aren't you Jacopo Vermicelli the famous engineer?" he asked. "The one who was going to build a canal from the Baltic Sea to the Black Sea?"

"Oh yes! To solve the traffic problem in the Dardanelles. No, I'm not the one," I replied. "That's my older brother. There is a strong family resemblance, of course. I am Giacomo Vermicelli, the famous Italian navigator. Poor Jacopo is in Odessa, at the moment. He has run into some difficulties. The Germans are afraid that the canal will set the greater part of Europe adrift and that it might float out into the middle of the Atlantic. The Russians, on the other hand, are afraid that it might not. The French insist that it will not float away but that it will sink, drowning half a billion men, women and children and leaving England as the foremost nation of the region. The Italians feel the whole thing is an insult to Venice and have declared my brother an outlaw. No doubt Vicomte de Lesseps had similar miseries when he wanted to dig at Suez."

Randolph began to peel his orange. Sebastian lay draped over his shoulder, watching. "What's a navigator?" the boy asked.

"A navigator? You don't know what a navigator is?" I exclaimed in mock astonishment. "Have you ever heard of Christopher Columbus?"

"Everybody's heard of Columbus," he answered contemptuously.

"Well, twice as many people have heard of me. He was a navigator. Navigators go around looking for places to discover."

"What places have you discovered?"

"None, actually, but I've done a lot of other things. I was the first man to sail around Pantelleria counterclockwise and the first man to swim the English Channel . . ."

"No, no!" he interrupted. "Lots of people have done that."

"Underwater," I concluded witheringly. "I was also the first to discover that the earth travels around the sun and not the other way around, as some other people were saying."

"Copernicus!" Randolph said.

"What?"

"Copernicus was the first to discover that the world travels around the sun in fifteen hundred and something," he declared stoutly while looking me squarely in the eye.

"All right, so I discovered it second," I said. "He was a Pole, you know. I don't know which Pole he was, but it's certainly easier to see what the earth is doing if you are a Pole, especially if you are the North Pole; you don't even have to raise your head. But your friend, what's-his-name, never went to the moon, which is something I did only last winter while in New Hampshire. I fell asleep in a ski lift, went past my stop and woke up right in the middle of what's-his-name's crater. I made the trip a second time for the National Seleno-graphic Society. Nearly got killed by a moon baboon, that time, but I was just able to shoot him with a knife. There's not much on the moon. It's about as barren a place as I've ever seen. A jejune moon, you might say.

"What, my boy? It's very simple, really. It's a gun that shoots knives. That's the only kind of gun you can use up there because loud sounds are liable to cause avalanches. Moon mountains are made of penuche or peanut brittle and will snap off if you so much as blow your nose. I once saw a moon baboon get killed instantly by a falling mountain, after he sneezed. It wasn't a very big one, either—hardly more than a molehill, in fact—but it struck him on the forehead and that was that. Do you know how many balls of string you'd need to reach from here to the moon, Randolph?"

The child looked at me with great seriousness. One cheek bulged with unchewed orange while his skinny legs oscillated beneath the bench. "Five hundred and eighty-three," he pro-nounced gravely after a moment's cogitation.

"No," I said. "Just one—but it would have to be mighty long."

He groaned and raised his eyes to heaven.

"All right, I'll give you one more chance, me lad. Which is heavier—a half moon or a full moon? What? Certainly not! A half moon is heavier because a full moon is lighter! I don't know what they teach in the schools these days. Why, when I was your age I had already begun my calculations for the Vermicelli Scientific System of Stationary Navigation."

"The which?" asked Sebastian the frog, who was now drawn snugly over one of Randolph's sticky hands.

"You heard me," I said.

"How does it work?" the frog inquired in his squeaky voice.

"Simply, like most brilliant conceptions. You are aware, I hope, that the earth spins on its axis, like a top." The frog nodded his head vigorously. "Well, with my invention you make use of this phenomenon to provide the masses with comfortable, inexpensive transportation. If for some curious reason you choose to leave Boston and go to Chicago, Illinois, you simply stand still and let Chicago, Illinois, come to you. It's really the only way to get about. No seasickness, no air-sickness, no sooty railway carriages or stuffy buses. And it's very swift too, you know."

The frog hopped onto my knee and looked up into my face with big, sad eyes. "How do you do it?" he squeaked.

"Do what?" I asked.

"Stand still. Every time I do it, I don't go anywhere."

"Ah! But that is where the invention comes into it. You have to have a patented Giacomo Vermicelli Immobility Kit. It contains all the necessary apparatus—the heavy weights, the resin for the fingertips, the drogue chute, the push-button portable air brake, the billiard chalk for the shoes, and so forth. Of course, the actual function of all these devices is enormously complex, involving long division and fractions, so I won't touch upon that here, but it is important to be familiar with the equipment before you use it. One of my field engineers made a miscalculation and had a serious accident. This fellow was in Milan, Italy, and wished to have Geneva, Switzerland, come to him, but he made a blunder in the routing and got bashed by the Matterhorn."

Sebastian clapped his webbed paws in glee. "I'll bet it hit him in the forehead," he said.

"Yes, as a matter of fact it did," I admitted. "It gave him a fearful headache and prevented him from putting on his hat for the next eleven months." I paused and took a deep breath. "You, Sebastian, are a very perceptive, percipient, perspicacious person."

"I know," Sebastian said.

Then Randolph suddenly jumped up, leaped onto the bench and commenced an energetic Indian war dance while making the sort of unearthly cries one might expect from a coyote full of peyote. I flicked a piece of orange pulp from my trouser leg and departed for the library.

22 ଛ

> The daylight has a deadly glint,
> The air, a tomblike smell;
> And doors and windows seem to hint
> That therein demons dwell.

SO RUNS the bit of verse that I wrote a few months back, in an effort to express my feelings about Sundays and holidays. I have always disliked such days, and of late I have grown to hate and fear them. I am sitting by my window watching the gray buildings, the gray thoroughfares and the gray clouds that conceal the sky, and I can feel the odylic influences tugging me. Really! Electricity, magnetism, cosmic rays, radio signals—the atmosphere is charged with all these things and more. None of them can be seen and some cannot be named but they can be felt by anyone with the least sensitivity. Sundays and holidays are their days to cavort. I no longer set foot out of doors at such times. With so much at stake, why take chances? I don't go out after dark, either.

Since the rain has driven away the pigeons and it is quiet except for the occasional peal of a church bell, it would probably be best for me to go under my bed, where there is com-

fort and seclusion afforded by the sheltering mass. Psychiatrists
and other people of limited comprehension are apt to consider concealment beneath a bed as the action of a disturbed,
or even badly distorted, personality. These dwellers in the
basement of the house of knowledge insist that such behavior
springs from a deep-seated desire to return to the safety of
the womb. Certainly, the area beneath a bed is a refuge but
why a womb? For them, I have come to believe, most things
look like wombs unless they look like pudenda. Genitalia
should be their regalia.

Let us suppose, for a moment, that you are out walking
one day along a steaming track in the monstrous jungles that
border the majestic River Zaire. Let us further suppose that
while in the midst of this promenade you espy a gigantic lion,
whose blood-chilling snarls and nervously twitching tail clearly
indicate that he is on an anteprandial prowl. Would you not
make an instinctive dash for the nearest bush and conceal
yourself beneath its thick foliage? Just so! And are not beds—
having straw-filled mattresses, cotton sheets, wooden frames
and tendril-like springs—far more like clusters of shrubbery
than like wombs? Unquestionably! Ah, how overcome with
sadness I am when I contemplate the many luckless people in
the world who are denied the solace of an hour's rest beneath
their beds each day, safe from the insatiable carnivores of
civilization, simply because a few fortunetellers have made a
bad guess.

The space beneath my bed is no more than twelve inches
high, though the bed, being double, is very broad. Once beneath it, I can't twist or turn, but this lack of space has the
advantage of enforcing immobility, which, as the wise men of
the East well know, is essential for the attainment of true
relaxation and ataraxia. Then, too, the tightness adds to the
feeling of security, for there is no room for an enemy. Yet I
still have a choice of position, for I may lie upon my stomach
and contemplate the narrow ruts between the oak floorboards,

or, feeling perhaps in a little gayer mood, slide under upon my back and enjoy the busy pattern of the box spring. Both positions are admirably suited for the inducement of a tranquil state of mind, I have found.

Truly, I believe that to be under a bed is the nearest man can come to paradise here on earth. That cozy space is a room within a room, a world within a world. It is a magic mantle of invisibility, a catacomb, a secret chamber in the haunted house of society. Who knows? In the end it may well be the last refuge of humanity. How wise, then, is man to bring into his home, in the center of a sprawling metropolis, one small bush from the jungle! If, as Plato avers, there is a perfect bed in heaven, then I am sure that God spends a good part of His time beneath it.

23 ❧

I SCRIED this evening in my crystal globe but it seemed very, very dark in there. Sometimes it's like a bowl of clear water; tonight it was murky.

My phonograph needle isn't functioning properly. It can't be worn out; it's not that old.

I PAINTED the "Mona Lisa," you know. Not the original, to be sure—that was done by that other fellow—but a copy. I was doing a St. Sebastian (sooner or later every artist does—it's like St. George and the Dragon) and things began to go wrong. A superbly emaciated fellow from the Boston University pool of models was posing for the picture and doing very well, but somehow my conception of the martyr—which had been clear and strong at the start—had deteriorated as the work progressed. My head was cluttered with the arrow-pierced images of all the other St. Sebastians, while my own image of him grew ever more indistinct.

I stopped working, at last, and spent two days drinking coffee and reading an odd volume (L to N) of an old encyclopedia that I had bought for fifteen cents at Morgan Memorial. On the third day, in order to amuse myself and to further detach my thoughts from the elusive saint, I set to work painting "La Gioconda," inspired in part by the article on Leonardo in my displaced tome, and in part by a large colored reproduction of the work that I discovered among a portfolio of such things that Leo had lent me many months before. This print had been made in Germany and was remarkably fine. It quickly became evident that if I was in no mood to paint a St. Sebastian, I was in an excellent humor for painting a "Mona Lisa." I all but finished the thing in four or five days, adding a few final touches three weeks later after it had congealed somewhat. During the interval I returned to my saint and polished him off without further complication.

Strange to say, I was prouder of my copy than I was of my

original. I had caught that lovely portrait on the very tip of my brush, and stroke followed stroke with such facile precision that it hardly seemed possible that I had been imitating another. All facsimiles are notoriously labored, but this refreshing little exercise was free as the wind. As I had never seen the original and since even the best reproductions are unable to retain the true colors of the archetype, my rendering of these hues was only an approximation. Years before, the Maestro had lectured me on the techniques of Leonardo when he was teaching me chiaroscuro, and I remembered the colors, set upon the dark imprimatura, that he had concocted to show me the nature of the pigments used in the Louvre masterpieces of that mysterious artist. This knowledge, added to my general familiarity with the paints of that period, enabled me to make a good guess at the lady's actual coloring. As far as line was concerned, with one exception my rendition was very faithful. The eyes, the nose, the exquisite hands, the clothing, the eerie background—all was as it should be. The single exception, of course, was the famous smile, which I had replaced with a toothless grin. This juxtaposition of incongruities made the portrait irresistibly comical. One evening, when both Littleboy and Faber were at my atelier, I announced the completion of a major work, and after a suitable pause to heighten the suspense, I brought forth my merry gentlewoman.

"Ah!" Littleboy exclaimed, leaping from his chair to have a better look at it. "It has soul! Carloads of it, in fact! Doesn't it have a lot of soul, Leo? It's also very human and naturalistic but in an ethereal sort of way. I like it. It has a haunting quality. More, it's downright spooky. The model seems familiar. What do you call it, anyway?"

"I thought 'Mona Lisa' would be a good title," I replied, going along with his travesty.

"Very good. Very, very good. It has something—a lilt. It's catchy," said Benjamin, stroking his chin. "What do you think, Leo?"

Faber lifted his gaunt frame from my sofa, wrinkled his brow, pursed his lips, scratched his ear and said, "'Mona Loser' would be better."

"Funny, Leo, but a little unkind," Benjamin said.

"Well then, how about 'The Gioconda' for a name?" I asked, setting the picture on one of my more rickety easels.

"I like that one, too. It's lyrical. Sounds a little foreign but so did the other one, for that matter. What do you think of 'The Anaconda' for a title, Leo?"

"Better," said Faber.

"No, no, no!" I protested. "Gioconda, not Anaconda. Gioconda is the model's name."

"Of course!" Benjamin exclaimed, slapping his thigh. "I knew I recognized that face. How is old Max Gioconda these days? I must say you haven't flattered the old boy in this portrait. The least you could have done was to give him time to put his plates in his mouth. I see he's still got that place near the river."

There was a good deal more of this bantering buffoonery, but when the joke was finally exhausted, both inspected the painting closely and offered serious comment.

"You know," said Faber as he studied the sleeves of the gown, "you really do handle a brush the way those old Italians did. Signore Loupa taught you well."

"The eyes and the temple there—they're pure Leonardo," Benjamin declared. "And you do know something about mixing colors. I said it was spooky and it is. The play of light and shade makes the flesh seem alive. It's as if the old boy's hand reached from the grave to direct your own. What a pity you couldn't get the smile," he concluded with a laugh.

"Seraphino's hand is in it, too," I said. "He used to say, 'This is how Leonardo da Vinci painted flesh,' and then, in a few strokes, produce a forehead or cheek as good as any made by nature. As for the smile, I didn't avoid it because it was difficult, but rather because I was weary of looking at it. My gaping maw at least has the advantage of freshness. Without it you would have had no opportunity to exercise your dazzling wit. Besides," I added gravely, "had I copied the smile, think of the confusion that would result in a hundred or two hundred years. With this painting well aged and the three of us dead, who could tell the original from the imitation?"

"Ah! No one would call you self-deprecating," Benjamin said, raising his eyebrows.

"This painting is bigger," Faber said. "What's more, the original is done on wood."

"So you see, you had better get rid of those fancy ideas," said Littleboy. "With your limited knowledge of the more mundane aspects of art history, you would make a pitiful faker. You might make an exact copy of the Venus of Milo but you'd probably use green marble. In short, you would make a poor desperado, Leonardo."

25 &

WHEN I put the Bourg angel on my mantel, I placed the apothecary chest in the bottom of my clothes closet. One Sunday, when my wife was out of town, I dragged it forth, set it upon the kitchen table and commenced a leisurely inspection of its contents. The box itself was a handsome object, rich in swirling grain and smooth as glass. A cast-brass handle adorned the top and brass plates served to protect the corners. The interior, I found, was divided into four sections: one large compartment which contained movable racks; one small compartment which held an old, dried rubber syringe, an eyecup and a roll of yellowed gauze, and two little drawers filled with pencils, string, safety pins, pen points, broken tongue depressors and dusty balls of cotton.

I removed the racks, which were the repository for three or four dozen stoppered vials, the two drawers and the debris, and with the help of a flashlight, scrutinized every inch of the interior in the hope of finding further clues to the article's provenance. There was nothing at all. Disappointed, I began an idle examination of the vials. Of these, there were two sizes —one half again as large as the other. In letters of gold leaf and black paint, each jar proclaimed its content. It was impossible not to feel like a medieval alchemist while reading such impressive labels, for words like *Resina Mastiche, Alum Pulversat, Castor Fiber, Acacia Catechu, Sulphas Magnesiae, Pulv:Fol:Belladonae* and *Sanguis Dracon* reek with the effluvium of sorcery. The vessels themselves contained powders and crystals of various colors; chunks of rocklike substances; hardened brown residues; pieces of bark, dried leaves and bits of twisted roots. I mixed a few of the powders together in a saucer and tried to induce a mild explosion by the cautious application of a lighted match, but without success. Then Mitya wandered into the kitchen, obviously looking for something to eat.

This Mitya was a Russian Blue cat that Veronica had bought a few months after our marriage. He was nearly lavender in color and had eyes like wet, shiny pennies. I do not have a blind affection for cats but I must admit that I found this beast to be most attractive. His legs appeared a little too long for his body but in all other respects his proportions were perfect. His coat was magnificent both in color and texture and his easy, graceful movements were a joy to the eye. In the beginning we were close friends, this cat and I; I never forgot his meals nor neglected to change the sand in his box; I patted him occasionally and allowed him to rub himself against my trouser leg as often as he desired. Time and familiarity, however, soon impaired our friendship. When I left off painting, much of my day was spent at home with Mitya, and this circumstance did little to encourage my tolerance of him, or his of me. One day, when the animal seemed to be forever under foot, I flew into a rage and punched him in the face.

The results of this blow were two in number. First, Mitya developed a profound hatred of me and would bite or scratch me at every opportunity and, second, one of his eyes became slightly displaced in his head so that he always seemed to be looking in two directions at once. If this Slavic feline had been an irritant before this unfortunate occurrence, he was now an out and out menace. Wherever I placed my hand, he would be lying in wait to perforate a finger or two with his needlelike teeth or to etch a precise pattern of parallel wounds on my wrist or forearm with his claws. And woe be unto me if I went about barefoot or in shorts. No Bengalese *shikaree,* out for a man-eater, moved more gingerly through the jungle than did I on my way to the bathroom for my morning shave. In addition to this sanguinary solicitousness, the vengeful creature would glare at me for hours. Whenever I raised my eyes, I could be sure that he would be there, searing me with a most deadly stare—one eye transfixing me by the shortest route, the other cleverly turning my flank and coming at me in a wide arc. There was no escape.

I continued to feed him, nonetheless, but with due caution. I filled his saucer with water and changed his sand but the pats and the leg rubs were a thing of the irretrievable past. We were enemies. Then, as I have said, he wandered into the kitchen while I was playing at "mad scientist" with my vials of medicines.

I am not a cruel man, really, but Mitya's unremitting guerrilla warfare necessitated some form of retaliation. In the course of my rummaging, I had come upon a bottle labeled *Nux Vomica,* and as my recollection of Latin indicated that this meant vomit nut, I thought it would be a good joke to sprinkle a soupçon of the stuff on my foe's bowl of milk.

Perhaps, I mused, he will be purged of his viciousness. I poured the milk and stirred into it a little of the chemical, which being white, disappeared at once. I then put it on the floor. Mitya, always a trifle greedy, went to it immediately and began to drink, but after a series of rapid laps, he made a face and stalked indignantly away.

"You're wise, aren't you?" I said to him as he left the room. "Maybe when you're a little hungrier, you'll change your mind, Dmitri."

I returned to my examination of the intriguing pharmacopoeia and thought no more of him. Ten minutes later I felt his eyes upon me, and turning, saw him crouching on the sideboard in the next room. The sight gave me a frightful shock, for not only was he treating me to his most potent, cockatrice glare, but he was grinning broadly as well. Alice's grinning cat on a printed page is undeniably amusing, but believe me, it's a different matter altogether when you come upon such a phenomenon in the flesh. The animal's smile seemed to expand even while I watched, until it split his face like a wound. His eyes, meanwhile, gradually closed in the process, emitting from their disoriented pupils an almost tangible ray of concentrated hatred. I sat spellbound, the hair rising on my nape. As the pink lips of the creature stretched ever wider, his small, sharp teeth, wet and glistening, came ever more into view, and I could see that they were tightly clenched. One of his ears twitched nervously and his whiskers vibrated from the tension of his facial fibers. Suddenly his head jerked back and he stood up. His tail became rigid as a length of a broomstick and his four long legs extended stiffly, making him appear abnormally tall. A moment later he toppled from the sideboard onto the floor.

His fall brought me to my feet. Cautiously I entered the dining room. The little lavender body lay quivering on the beige Chinese rug.

"Mitya," I whispered, awed by the spectacle.

Saliva dribbled from between his grinning jaws and muffled squeaks escaped from his taut throat; his back began to arch, not in the normal convex fashion but concavely, until he was sway-backed. Every muscle in his body was flexed by an enormous spasm that stretched him into a totally unnatural attitude. Even his claws were thrust out from his opened paws. He lay thus for some time, then, as suddenly as the attack had come, it just as suddenly departed, leaving the cat wild-eyed and panting. I returned to the kitchen for a dish of water, thinking that it might help to revive him.

There have been times in my life (being a city dweller) when I have been awakened in the night by a cry that combined the most dreadful features of both human and animal vocal expression—the howl of a battling tomcat. Such a wail came from Mitya as I reentered the dining room, causing me to drop the saucer of water. A new paroxysm had overtaken him —this one more violent than the first—and when this, too, had exhausted itself, it was followed by a third. In fifteen minutes the fits finally ended. The cat was dead.

I ran off to the library that afternoon, where I learned that *nux vomica* is the somewhat misleading designation for that most lethal poison, strychnine. I owned a jar full of sudden death. Later I was to put these innocent-looking crystals to more serious use—but I did not know that then.

My wife wept when she saw the dead Mitya. Although we were not on very good terms at the time, her tears moved me to offer a soothing explanation.

"It was a sudden seizure," I said, "without suffering. I saw it happen and it was over in a matter of moments. The attack was probably brought on by the injury he received when the wind blew the bathroom door shut and hit him in the head, months ago. He took an awful knock that time. No wonder it made the poor fellow cross-eyed."

I am not at all sure that she believed me. She said not a word.

Victor Darius' visits to Boston became more frequent, and with each visit, my bank account grew. Virtually everything that left my studio went to him. He even took seventy or eighty old canvases that I had stored in a warehouse in the fens, though some of these were rather weak productions. I continued to work at my place on Marlborough Street but I transferred my living quarters to a more comfortable two-room flat around the corner on Beacon. At this time it was not uncommon for me to work from sunrise to sunset, with no more than a ten-minute interlude for a sandwich at lunchtime. A twelve-cup electric coffee pot provided me with an adequate supply of that indispensable stimulant during the long day, and when the pot was empty and the light fading, home at last I'd go. All in all, I do not believe that I have ever worked better than I did during that period. Later I might have done finer individual pieces, but for overall quality in abundance, that stage in my life was the best. And I was happy. The world seemed to be opening up before me, revealing all the treasure and glory that I had dreamed of since childhood.

Darius, too, was advancing in the stubbornly serried ranks of the art world. I saw little of him when he did come to town; he was forever being invited to the homes of bigwigs. Milton Prender would have him to dinner or he'd take tea with a group of Harvard panjandrums in Cambridge or cocktails with Baxter Sawyer at his town house. Faber would send me clippings about Victor's activities and I was always amazed by their variety. He attended meetings in Rome or Stockholm, or auctions in Paris or New York, or a private sale in Mexico

City, or a seminar in Heidelberg. One article said that he was the prime mover in the sale of an important Velasquez to the National Gallery, while another stated that he was the confidential agent for an Arabian king. During one of his sojourns I managed to get him to Littleboy's, but though he was cordial enough, he bought nothing. I was bitterly disappointed by Victor's lack of enthusiasm. Benjamin, however, accepted his rejection with philosophic indifference, remarking only that "the Englishman seemed to be in agreement with all the other authorities." Nor was Darius impressed by Faber's abilities when I brought him to meet Leo. We spent a pleasant hour chatting, and though there were compliments on both sides, they were civilities only.

About two years after the beginning of our acquaintance, Darius secured for me a most interesting portrait commission— one that promised rich remuneration and a fair measure of prestige. The thing came about more by accident than design.

Some months earlier I had sent him fourteen finished canvases; these he was to transship to galleries in Amsterdam, Barcelona and Rome, where, it was hoped, they might attract the attention of one or two influential critics, if not the specie of the more discriminating dealers and collectors. This "Continental exposure" was to be one means of accelerating my rise to international prominence. The pictures were assembled by me at my studio and duly fetched by two men from Clay and Dwyer. Not long afterward I discovered to my dismay that the best of the lot, a moving portrayal of "Jesus and the Blind Man," had unaccountably been left behind. The shippers insisted that they had packed and forwarded fourteen paintings. I was a little upset and more than a little puzzled by this odd event, but there was nothing to be done until the crate arrived at its destination and its contents were verified.

A month later the mystery was solved when Victor wrote to me and thanked me for my amusing caricature of the "Mona Lisa." "But," he asked, "where in the world has 'Jesus and the Blind Man' got to?" I hastened to write and apologize for the blunder though he was not really put out by the substitution. Indeed, in a subsequent letter, he confessed that he had grown quite fond of the lady and had startled more than one dignified graybeard by suddenly exposing them to the potent charm of her toothless grin. One of these sedate gentlemen happened to be a Florentine Marquis, who was greatly shocked by my whimsical treatment of what he considered to be a sacred object. This man, whose name was Tomaso Seganti, resided in London and was a member of the Italian diplomatic corps. He was well known for his boundless love of Leonardo.

On his next visit Victor related the tale. "At first he was rendered completely speechless; his face became quite crimson and I feared that I had gone too far and that the old boy would have an attack right there in my rooms. But he recovered quickly and was soon sternly lecturing me on the irreverence of youth, but in the nicest way imaginable. Before long, however, he was asking me the name of the artist, for he was astonished to see how well the painting had been done. When I told him that it was the work of an American who had never seen the original, he was flabbergasted. '*Lo sfumato!*' he cried. 'How has he done it?' You would have been very pleased to hear him. He was positively lyrical. Actually, you know, it *is* a virtuoso performance and deserving of his lavish praise."

This man was very wealthy (his property included half the countryside between Florence and Fiesole) and much of his fortune had been freely used in support of projects whose aim was to preserve Italy's massive art heritage. A passionate admirer of Leonardo, he spent at least one month of each year in Paris so as to be near the brilliant conceptions of that fertile mind—though the sight of these Italian masterpieces in a foreign museum dimmed some of his pleasure. He was once the center of a stormy controversy for having remarked in a radio interview that Leonardo was a greater man than Jesus Christ. The argument split his native land asunder, with the Vatican on one side and the free thinkers on the other. In spite of his close connections with the Church, he refused to retract the statement.

"The debate eventually abated," said Victor, "for though most of the people of Italy thought the Marchese was mistaken, they believed he was not mistaken by very much."

At one time this noble nobleman had headed a syndicate which offered the equivalent of more than a million dollars for a Leonardo in the possession of a prince, but the offer was refused. He did, however, acquire several of his idol's sketches; one of these—a red chalk head of the Virgin—was a cartoon for the "Virgin of the Rocks": it now occupies a prominent place at the Pitti Palace.

"This, then, is the chap who thinks highly of your work," said Darius. "I do not believe you could find a more discriminating admirer anywhere in the world. You are only the second painter that he likes."

We laughed. "And he wants me to paint his daughter? Has he seen any of my other portraits? Or perhaps he would like me to make her look like the Gioconda," I said.

"You are not far from the mark. He has seen your portrait of that blond beauty—the one in the satin dress with the pearls—and pronounced it excellent. As for his daughter's picture, he wants you to do it just as Leonardo would have done it. Quite simple, isn't it?"

"Ah, simple, yes. Simple to say. Simple to dream about. But to realize such a fantasy is far from simple. It might be simpler to exhume the signore from Vinci and ask him to do the job himself. Does he really believe that I can make his daughter the rival of 'Mona Lisa'? Have you see this ambitious model? She probably has a face like a Pekingese lapdog."

"No, no," he protested quickly. "She is a lovely girl. If you were to seek a Leonardo type, you would look far before you came upon one as suitable as Lisabeta. Really—it's true! The Marchese is a man of sensibility; he would not initiate something of this sort if it could only result in embarrassment for his daughter and himself. You see, she looks rather like a Leonardo and her name is Lisabeta. When he came upon a man who could simulate the Master's style, it occurred to him that he might have his own 'Mona Lisa.' "

"Do you mean this girl really looks like the 'Mona Lisa'?"

"Not at all, but she has that kind of oval, sweet, spiritual, intelligent countenance that Leonardo was partial to. Understand, the Marchese does not expect a masterpiece—he would be horrified to learn that any painter could duplicate the feats of his hero. He wants a portrait of his daughter dressed in the attire of an early cinquecento gentlewoman of Florence and done in the manner of Leonardo—as near as that is possible. He will pay three thousand dollars for it."

"Well then, that's settled," I replied. "For three thousand dollars I would go to Milan and do another 'Last Supper.' "

"Who knows? If this turns out well, you may be offered that opportunity," Victor answered with a smile.

"When do I begin? Am I to journey to London?"

"No—as it happens, she is coming here."

"Not this summer, I hope."

"Yes—in June. Why?"

"You've forgotten my tour," I said. "I'm going to Europe with Littleboy and Faber this year. We sail the ninth of June."

He placed his hand to his forehead and a look of distress came over his delicate face. "I'd forgotten it completely! Good God! I've all but guaranteed the thing."

"I'll be back the end of August. The month of September would provide time enough, I should think."

"Too late. She is coming in June and will spend July and August with some relatives at their country place in the State of Maine. At the end of that period she is going on to Mexico and an extended tour of South America. I reasoned that you could run up to Maine and paint her there. Your trip totally slipped my mind. Somehow, I thought it was on for next year—

not this one. The worst of it is that these titled people are sometimes a trifle difficult if they think their dignity is being abused. I'd be very sorry to lose the thing altogether. Do you suppose that you could leave a month later, perhaps, and then join them?"

"I would miss a great deal—Greece and Venice. We've worked out our whole itinerary."

"Perhaps you could stay on after they return and go to Athens then," he suggested. "I do feel that this is an important commission, one that might do much to advance your career. The Marchese is a quixotic character, but his patronage is not to be treated lightly. I would say that of all my acquaintances only he has access to all the truly influential fine-art people in Italy—and that is no small virtue. And, of course, three thousand dollars is an excellent fee."

In the end I agreed to consult my friends. That night, at Benjamin's, we talked long into the night. I believe that if I had made the decision by myself, I would have forsaken the three thousand dollars and gone with them; but neither of them could counsel me to abandon such a chance, much as they would miss my company. We revised our plans. I would fly to Milan and they would meet me there. I called Victor at his hotel the following morning. He was pleased with my decision.

27 ઙ৯

I AM wearing buskins. They are not in the best of condition (my big toe protrudes from one of them) but they are of doeskin and soft as velvet and I can move about like a wraith when I am wearing them. The house is still but for the snoring of Burgher Knoop. This even (and reassuring) rumble filters through the oaken planks of the ceiling, telling me that I have not disturbed my unsuspecting host and that I need make no incautious haste. The darkness of the room is almost total.

"If Ivo has not lied to me, the cupboard should be just there," I say to myself, thinking in a whisper.

Like a grim grimalkin stalking a sparrow, I move slowly forward, feet and hands probing for unseen obstacles. Thus my bare toe encounters a solid surface. I halt. Warily my fingers creep through the air and touch a smooth, cold, rounded article. It proves to be a cheap stoneware stein—a half-liter mug—standing on a table, the leg of which had met my foot. I change my course, pause, listen, then continue my stealthy progression.

A flickering light shines through the cracks in the shutter behind me and my heart begins to hurry its beat. With my breath thick in my throat, I wait, and soon the sound of voices reaches my anxious ears and I know that it is the watch and that if I have not fastened the shutter properly, or (worse yet) if I have been seen by that widow across the way, then the alarm will be raised and I must take to my heels. The swinging lantern sends its tongues of light licking through the narrow chinks. A longing to crouch comes over me but I resist it. They can see nothing of me from the street. They are abreast the window, the creak of their boots clearly audible. At last they pass. The light and the sounds diminish and I release a noiseless sigh.

Moments later I am at the cupboard. My fingers seek and find the line of the door and the position of the lock. With my knife I commence to cut the wood, slicing slivers of the cherry frame from around the mortise of the bolt. It is slow work but it produces no sudden loud noises since the knife is very sharp and I know well how to use it. Above me the snoring goes on like the beat of a distant drum. Shreds of wood stick to my perspiring hands and my fingers begin to ache. As the minutes pass I can feel the iron bracket against the knife blade. Gradually the staples loosen, but I must not grow too eager. One pull would free it, but one pull might cause a shriek that would fetch Herr Knoop back from his dreams. Finally the thing is in my hands. My fingers itch to pull open the doors, but I repress this anxiousness and rest for a minute. I wipe my knife and replace it in my belt. After dripping some linseed oil onto the hinges, I most slowly open the two panels. I must see with my hands, so complete is the darkness.

Ah, what a happy sensation! My fingers run over the silver tankards, the candlesticks, the plates and porringers. They caress the graceful goblets, the ornate salt, the ladle, the gravy boat and the napkin rings. There is a charger, polished to the smoothness of a maiden's breast, and on the lowest shelf a chest of flatware, each piece sheathed in chamois. Oh, the darlings! No pewter here! My hands well know that argentine feel! I will have kuchen at every meal, I tell myself.

Into the bag they go, a piece of rag twisted about each to insure its silence. I cannot have them crying out and waking the good burgher!

Ivo, what a comrade you are! I think. I will give you an excellent share of the spoil, my friend. Not as much as I promised, of course, but a handsome portion all the same. One should reward true friendship. What is more precious, after all?

Once the bag is filled, I strap it to my back beneath my cloak. If I am seen, I will appear to be a hunchback—but I do not plan on being seen. Big as the sack is, I am forced to leave behind several tankards and a dented pitcher. It is as well, perhaps, since my bundle weighs as much as half a hogshead of black beer and I am nearly bent in two by it. I make my way back across the room, taking care to avoid the table, and I am at the window surprisingly soon. No light comes from without and the only sound that I can hear is the even rattle in the bedroom above. Cautiously I pull the windows open. Gently I unlatch the wooden shutters and push them outward. The street is filled with comforting darkness. I am not one to attempt such gambols by the light of the moon! I pull my cloak tightly about me, and straining beneath the load, step over the sill. It is as my bare toe touches the chilled cobbled pavement that I hear the growl.

Out the window I fly, like a boy of ten, but before I can close the damned shutters, the beast is upon me and snapping at my throat. I swing about to flee and my pack of plunder hits the animal's muzzle, knocking him back into the room. Down the street I go, cursing that fool Ivo for failing to know there was a mastiff in the wretched house. I have a lead of a dozen yards before the creature gets through the window, but I am no match for him in running. He is baying, barking, snarling and yelping alternately. Now I see my shadow on the wall, which means the night watch, with its lanterns, pikes and cudgels, has joined the chase. More lights appear in windows and the cries of men join those of the dog. It is Walpurgis Night on the Brocken.

I cut the thongs and let my treasure slip from my shoulders, hoping that this will appease my pursuers. Free of this burden, I double my pace. Still the mastiff is close behind; his great pads beat the stones with rapid and persistent regularity. Suddenly the church looms up before me, dancing in the light of the guards' lamps. There are the three familiar arched doorways with their blackened, nail-studded doors. I make for the center one, anxious to put its bulk between me and the monster at my heels.

The horror! Oh, the misery! I push against it with all my strength but the treacherous thing is bolted from within! What kind of church is this that locks its doors? If it would keep out sinners, it will have a small congregation, indeed. But I have little time for such musings. I turn to try the door on the left, but before I can take a step in its direction, the beast comes hurtling toward me. The square head is agape and

bristling with pointed teeth. The eyes are embers. I come back
to Boston. My body is covered with perspiration and I am still
very frightened. I sit quietly until my heart ceases to pound.
Mrs. Dandelion walks by and spits on the ground at my feet;
some of the spray lands on my shoe. But I am too spent to
become angry. I wonder why I am not afraid of the dark in
my reveries.

28 ❧

"LIFE INSURANCE? How can you insure me against life?" I
asked Mr. Beels this afternoon. It had been an easy day and
my mood was one of mild buoyance and tolerance. My inter-
rogator wriggled about inside his cocoon, trying to get comfortable. One of his small red hands pawed at the blanket.
It looked like an exotic crustacean stumbling about a green
plaid beach.

"No. I regret that I cannot insure you against life, Mr.
Barber," he replied in his cracked, adolescent voice. "It's too
late for that, you know. It is death that we underwrite."

"Then would it not be more accurate to call it death insurance?"

"It would. Indeed, it would. I agree wholeheartedly, my
good sir. I would like nothing better than to rename the profession but, unfortunately, custom prevents the change. Death
is a splendid word—a vigorous Anglo-Saxon word, superior
to those designations derived from the Roman language. A
fine word for a majestic concept. I confess a certain partial-
ity for death, due, doubtlessly, to the nature of my work. Ed-
ward Young called death 'the crown of life' and I find that

both accurate and beautiful. But there are few who take this view. There is a general hatred of death—a hostility induced by fear, to be sure—even by those who benefit least from life. To be candid, it is death who writes most of my policies. He is the super-salesman of the insurance business; he is the irresistible personality, the grand persuader. I think of him as a pleasant fellow, tall, with broad shoulders, a ready smile and powerful dark eyes—eyes that captivate the whole of mankind. From the depths of one of these somber orbs flows the murky light of inscrutability, while from the other streams the hard gleam of inevitability. That is how he appears to me—but perhaps you find me fanciful?"

"Not at all," I responded amiably, "but I do wonder how you can insure me against death. Can you provide me with a policy that ensures everlasting life? I have little desire to meet your broad-shouldered agent with the ready smile."

"Alas, I cannot promise you such an endowment at this time. But who knows? The industry is progressive and I may one day be able to satisfy your request. I need not tell you, I'm sure, that the premiums will be out of the ordinary." He produced a short dry chuckle. "Do you have reason to fear death at this particular time, Mr. Barber?"

I did not like the tenor of that question but I parried it lightly. "Yes, insofar as I am alive at this particular time. A hundred years from now I'll be less concerned, I imagine."

Again he chuckled. It sounded as if someone down inside his throat was crumpling a paper bag. It was a feeble manifestation of merriment, and following it he fell silent for a time. Behind him, Johann's huge form loomed as still as a statue; he seemed hardly to breathe. I took my right leg off my left and crossed my left upon my right. A large fly zoomed past my ear, buzzing belligerently, and somewhere overhead a jay or starling was complaining about something. I could see Mr. Beels' feet beneath the lower edge of the blanket. They were no bigger than those of a child of seven and were shod in shiny brown laced boots, the toes of which were slightly curled. As I looked at them, the blanket dropped a few inches and they disappeared.

"Have you no responsibilities?" he said at last, and his foreign modulation seemed now more evident in his speech. "Are there no loved ones to be provided for in the event of your demise?"

"None, I am pleased to say. I have given no hostages to fortune; I belong to myself alone."

The hat tipped back unexpectedly, revealing his thin lips, pinched nose and glistening green eyes. "I might still be of service to you, nonetheless. There are many policies that would bring you numerous benefits in your later years. What is more, should you be without resources at the moment, there is even an agreement that gives you what you require in your youth and you need not begin payments until you are old and prosperous."

"What if I should meet your broad-shouldered, hypnotic friend before I've had time to reimburse you for your kindness?"

"There are always certain risks that we are prepared to assume, Mr. Barber, though our actuaries are usually dependable. Would you like me to bring you a prospectus tomorrow?"

"No, thank you. All your coverage is so obviously benevolent that I should feel as if I were victimizing you if I were to avail myself of it."

"Ah, you are a difficult client, sir. Have you no desires? Money buys contentment, love, power, wisdom and health —contrary to the stupid adages of the moralists. Have you no wish for these fruits of life? Are you without ambition?"

"Not entirely."

"I am pleased to hear it," he said.

"I do have one ambition."

"Only the one? A great pity, if I may say so. You should not limit yourself. Your mind should abound with ambitions. As you satisfy one, two more should burgeon in its place."

"Only one," I said, holding up my index finger to emphasize the quantity.

"Well, Mr. Barber, one is surely better than none at all. It is a beginning. From such a single scintilla, a great flame of aspiration may one day be born, filling you with fiery desires. What might this lonely ambition be?"

"I wish to be God," I said lowering my finger.

This time I was treated to a far more elaborate display of hilarity. Beels drew one of his crimson hands from his nest of garments and slapped his knee. Then, having located the other hand, he brought that out also and attacked the other knee. Simultaneously he splintered the drowsy summer air with unearthly laughter. Within this uproar, I was able to identify the braying of an ass, the barking of a dog and the grunting of a pig. In addition, there were some strains from a rusty calliope and the sizzling sound of frying bacon. But these were only a few of the elements of this attempt at mirth; the others elude comparison. The old lady with the pince-nez, who was seated a bench away, glared at us in indignation and then departed. The clamor ended abruptly with a finale that was like the smashing of a large, thick plate-glass window.

"You find that amusing, then," I said.

"My dear sir," he croaked after several desperate gasps. "You are the absolute limit! As a jester, you are without a peer. Yes, sir, you are matchless. Upon my word, I'd have made your acquaintance long before this had I known you were such a sparkling wit. Only the one ambition. Superlative! 'I wish to be God.' A staggering line! That Frenchman has nothing better, nor Aristophanes before him. I'll not want for humor while you're about. What a pity Johann can't understand you. He'd enjoy the joke at least as much as I do."

"But," I pointed out, "I'm entirely serious."

"Are you now? Better and better! And if by some unimaginable ruse you achieve this goal, what then would you do with your predecessor?"

"I've thought about that. First I would make him mortal."

"And then, Mr. Barber?"

"Then I would kill him, of course."

Once again the atmosphere was shaken by his grim laughter. He roared. I looked down into his woolen burrow and saw his little face wrinkled with glee. The wheelchair made a clattering sound as it vibrated in sympathy with its occupant.

As it was getting dark, I arose, waved my hand in farewell and walked toward the gate. A fat squirrel, alarmed by the racket, scrambled up the bole of an English elm.

Intermission

I do not know why I am writing this all down. Who could be interested? There are no knee-knocking, spine-tingling, nerve-shattering, blood-curdling, teeth-chattering, hair-raising, heart-stopping actions to titillate an audience. At least, not yet. But I am only halfway through with my account—maybe even less than that. What follows is of interest, I believe.

Not everyone can begin his narrative with ghosts wandering about a battlement, or shipwrecked sailors in the Pacific, or creepy voices calling across a moor. Even that most august of volumes, the dictionary, does not hit its stride until nearly half its pages have been turned. As every college freshman knows, it is only at the letter L that the tempo picks up, with such intriguing adjectives as lascivious, lecherous, leporine, lewd, libertine, libidinous, licentious, lickerish, lubricious, lustful and the like.

Nevertheless, I may have begun badly. What kind of tale can possibly evolve from such a gallimaufry of trivia? A dreamer on a park bench, a dim-witted bird fancier, a dead cat, an eight-year-old boy, a picture dealer, a handful of pigeons and an insurance agent—hardly the cast of *War and Peace,* I must agree. Still, I'll go on with it. This ugly duckling may yet bloom into a graceful swan. Have I not mentioned a marquis? That, surely, is a step in the right direction. What's more, if things progress as I hope, I will bring onto my humble stage a Personage of such importance that by comparison Tzar Aleksandr the First of Russia and Emperor Napoleon the First of France will seem of less significance than Punch and Pierrot at the parish fair.

If only my pen were not so scratchy. The niggardly point refuses to part with its ink.

Yes, I am sure that the things that have happened to me are of interest. But what will the end be? That, I do not know.

THREE WEEKS after Leo and Benjamin sailed for Europe, Victor Darius and I boarded a train for Camden, Maine. Victor had come to Boston only the day before and we had little time for consultation before our departure. Our journey was a long one, however, and during it I was given additional details concerning the task before me. The Marchese had become very excited about the project and would have crossed the ocean himself had not pressing affairs prevented him. It seemed he had found a fifteenth-century carved wood frame in an Aretine antique shop several years before, and as it was a thing of incomparable beauty, he wished to use it as the setting for the portrait. Letters had been exchanged with his staff in Italy and Victor was informed that the painting would have to be eighty-three centimeters high and fifty-three wide. This news was disconcerting, as I had provided myself with two seasoned walnut panels but both fell short of the larger dimension. Victor was confident that we would be able to get what we wanted at our destination since the area was rich in forests. I was not so sure. The wood could not be green, for such a panel would certainly shrink and in a few years cause the paint layer to buckle.

"He has made another request, even more unreasonable," Darius said. "He does not want you to use any pigments that were not in use in 1500. I didn't argue with him, of course, but I do think such an instruction is a bit too much. I made the mistake of telling him that you did not use modern paints,

and that convinced him that the success of the copy was due
to this."

"The only thing that I have in my case that could possibly
be termed modern is zinc white, but I have lead white as well.
I believe there is some Scheele's green, also, but I won't really
need that either. I'll paint it the way he wants it," I said. "However, I'm glad he couldn't find time to come over. I'd get little
accomplished with him watching my every move."

He laughed and replied, "It could be worse, I suppose. What
if you were commissioned by Julius the Second?"

We chatted for a couple of hours, discussing art and artists,
and the time till lunch passed rapidly. Afterward the railroad
coach became extremely warm. Victor dozed off while I perused
a large, lavishly illustrated biography of Leonardo which I had
bought a few days before. We arrived at six in the evening. A
slender, florid-faced man, who introduced himself as Buster,
met us at the station and directed us to a glittering new automobile. We drove leisurely down the main street, avoiding the
bare-legged, sunburned tourists who were scampering about
in search of a good, though inexpensive, evening meal. In moments we were out on the highway. The air was thick with
heat and dust, and though the ocean was visible on our right,
it provided no cooling breeze.

I suppose that I had visualized our new lodgings as an Ital-
ianate palace or, at least, a cozy villa; great, then, was my surprise when after a drive down a private road we swept around
the base of a wooded hill and beheld the most ill-proportioned
building imaginable. Victor clutched his head and gasped. I
laughed. The thing was very large and sprawled upon the ground
like an ungainly giant. Among its more notable features were
a Romanesque dome, a pair of castellated turrets, a spire
equipped with a lightning rod, several bartizans, a couple of
hideous wrought-iron balconies and a rich assortment of gables.
The façade of the principal structure was disfigured by an
enormous porch whose pitched roof was supported by alter-

nating pilasters and Tuscan columns of painted wood. Windows abounded and utilized many forms, being square, round, triangular, hexagonal, octagonal and trefoil. Two huge mullioned windows presided over the lot, like proud parents. The walls of the place were chiefly of fieldstone, though there were wings clothed in siding and a tower, which was either a campanile or a silo, that was made of red brick. The roofing material varied from common asphalt shingle to pink pantile and green slate. One tentacle of this octopus had a number of Tudor arched doorways and another had half a dozen different chimneys.

"It looks like the fun house at Nantasket," I said.

We were to discover later that the interior was no less quaint than the exterior. Darius proclaimed it the Palace of Minos. A patent-medicine tycoon named Morris Potter had had it built to his own specifications half a century before. Buster said the medicine was called Potter's Potion and that its prime ingredient was muscatel wine. The old boy had lived in his dream house for many years and then died of a liver ailment.

The present tenant, our host Anthony Grassi, met us at the door. He was an importer of wines and brandies and a cousin of the Marchese. In a soft, good-natured voice, with just a trace of accent, he apologized for the architecture, saying that he had come to Maine for some deep-sea fishing and was unable to find anything more suitable.

"It is not the Palazzo Vecchio but it is comfortable," he said, "and it remains cool all day."

A girl in a maid's costume showed us to our rooms, and Buster followed with our bags. After washing and donning fresh clothing we returned to the parlor and met Grassi's daughter, Nina, and Lisabeta Seganti. Nina was in her mid-twenties—delicate, pretty and bright-eyed. She bore no resemblance to her father, who was dark and stout, and with an array of gold teeth, resembled a successful Sicilian bandit. Mrs. Grassi, the mother, had gone back to New York the day before, in order to nurse an ailing sister. It was hoped she would return soon.

But, of course, it was in my subject that I took the most interest. Given the wrong model, my paraphrase of a Leonardo would sink to mere caricature. It is a sad fact that really good faces are a rare commodity in this age, for the value of a face depends on the quality of the expression, and modern countenances are either altogether devoid of character or endowed with aspects that are displeasing to the eye. The ancient peoples of Mesopotamia, Egypt and Greece produced majestic heads, whose grave and lofty expression was well suited to kings and gods; the later Greeks and Romans introduced sensuality and delicacy. It was not until the Renaissance, however, that the possibilities of human lineaments were fully explored and the results of that exploration applied to the portraits created throughout the greater part of Europe. All the passion, all the dignity, all the inner mystery of mankind are recorded in these works of the great ones of this fertile period. Donatello, the Van Eycks, Raphael, Dürer, Velasquez, Rembrandt and many others of comparable excellence gave to the world miraculous pictures and sculptures of living men and women, their visages clearly revealing the contents of their hearts and minds.

That was the zenith. Somewhere in the latter half of the eighteenth century, strength and nobility began to disappear as sentimentality crept into portraiture. By the end of the next century all was engulfed by simpering smiles and feeble affectations. Maestro Loupa was fond of calling it the *Scuola di Zucchero,* the Sugar School, and he blamed half the evils of the world on its appearance. This century has added its bit to the general deterioration, for today's faces exhibit uncertainty about the eyes and nervousness at the corners of the mouth along with the other weaknesses. Is this the fault of the artist or have men lost their vigorous aspects? A little of both, perhaps.

And this Lisabeta? Ah! A face from the past! A marvelous

face! Here was a face that would have captured every eye in the Cathedral of Florence on any sixteenth-century Easter Sunday. It was a joy—strong, serene, free of the blemishes of modern life, devoid of the shadows of anxiety, the lines of irritation, tension and bewilderment. I will not attempt to describe in words that which can only be rendered by the point of the brush. Her eyes were the most reflective that I have ever seen in the head of a woman; her lips were perfect; the curve of her jaw was one of the most beautiful arcs in art or nature. As I looked at her, I had to repress a powerful desire to dash forward and run the tips of my fingers over the gentle planes of that graceful countenance in order to verify the reality of what my eyes beheld.

That night, I retired early and dreamt that I had painted a masterpiece. It stood on a giant easel in the piazza before St. Peter's. The space between Bernini's colonnades was jammed with people who were pushing and struggling as they strove to get a glimpse of my picture. It was the first dream that had come to me since childhood. I haven't had one since.

The sun had barely risen the next morning when I was awake and busily sketching Lisa's face from memory. It was not until that afternoon, however, that I was able to get her to sit for me. The morning was spent in wandering about the labyrinthine mansion in search of the room best suited for a studio. I chose a corner bedroom that caught the morning sun from one side and the rays of the afternoon sun from the other. Two of its windows were triangular and overlooked the sea, while a third was a long oblong, divided into four sections that opened outward. With the help of Buster, I removed most of the furnishings, added others and unpacked and arranged my equipment.

As Lisabeta spoke only Italian, and since my knowledge of this language was limited to a few art terms and an assortment of curse words learned from the Maestro, Victor assumed the role of interpreter. With a charming smile, she declared her willingness to begin sitting at once. That day I made a dozen maquettes in pencil and colored chalk, my hand fairly leaping over the paper, so enthusiastic had I grown. She held a pose extraordinarily well and appeared to possess an even temper and a most gentle disposition. In the days that followed, I worked feverishly. When she was available, I posed her on a chair or couch in various parts of the room, and by adjusting the window draperies, gauged the shadows that formed about her graceful features. At other times I would follow her about like a dog, sketching her as she thumbed through a magazine or while she played cards with Victor and the Grassis or as she sunned herself on the shingled beach. She never became annoyed. After a while she hardly knew that I was there. Some of these drawings, I believe, were the best that I had ever done, and Victor was delighted with my progress. Besides these studies, I modeled her head in white plasticene—a work that I hoped later to transfer into some more durable medium. Between times I read my life of Leonardo and pored over the reproductions of his drawings and paintings.

One day, about a week after our arrival, Darius and Buster brought me a pine board to serve as a panel for the portrait.

"Pine? Is that the best you could do?" I asked, somewhat vexed by the nature of the material.

"They had no poplar, and oak and walnut in plywood only. I would not have believed it. These forests are all pine or elm," Darius said, shaking his head. "Still, this pine is well seasoned, as you can see, and perfectly straight and true. Look at it on edge. And it is free of knots and blemishes."

"I would have preferred something harder," I said, examining it carefully.

"The Venetians often used German fir," he assured me, "and through the years it has held up very well. When you have primed it, you will find it no different from walnut to work upon. The fellow cut it to size for us."

It was true that the surface was exceedingly level and smooth and the fibers well dried. Victor said it had been a shelf in a linen closet and that it was about forty years old, according to the lumber merchant who had salvaged it because antique dealers were always looking for such things for commode or table tops. I made no further complaint and that same day applied a gesso ground to it.

I found the household a very easy one in which to live. There was little formality. The evening meal was something of an occasion, but for the rest, all came and went with complete freedom. Buster's wife was the cook and produced excellent meals; a young girl came each day to make beds and sweep and dust. It was far from the aristocratic opulence that I had anticipated with apprehension and I was completely at ease. Old Grassi spent his days fishing with a group of cronies who came up from Rockland in a cabin cruiser each morning, while Nina was involved with a summer theater group. Lisabeta made daily trips to Camden but was usually gone for no more than an hour or two. Now and then the two girls would drive to Bar Harbor or Bangor. For the most part, however, Lisabeta was content with posing for me, or lying about on the beach, or listening dreamily to jazz recordings, or sitting in a deep upholstered chair lost in a paper-backed Italian romance. She never entered the water, for it was very cold. Her love of jazz was such that she always brought a small radio with her when she sat, and though I was not pleased with this in the beginning, it was only a short while before I ceased to notice the blaring saxophones and ululating clarinets. Darius reminded me of the legend that Leonardo had music played to keep Mona Lisa smiling while he painted her, but I denied that the radio served that purpose, insisting that I had a better model than he did. He remained in Camden only for the first two weeks, after which he was obliged to return to New York. A man accustomed to a hectic pace, he found life in Maine a rather tiresome business. He would return when the work was near completion, he said.

The day before his departure I began to paint. I had prepared all my colors before leaving Boston but I checked them again before I picked up a brush, to be certain that I lacked nothing. Paint is really composed of two elements, the color or pigment, which is a powder, and the binder or medium, which is a liquid and serves the dual purpose of facilitating the application of the color and holding it in place once the moisture has evaporated. The ancients obtained reds, greens and yellows from earths called ochres that contained iron compounds, and browns from manganese clays. Copper verdigris gave them turquoise blues and greens, and lampblack and lime supplied them with black and white. The binders employed with these pigments were many and varied. Egg white, egg yellow, pitch, gum arabic, cherry gum, wax, blood, animal glue, vegetable glue, cheese, human flesh taken from mummies and excrements were all tried. Until the fifteenth century the two principal methods of painting were tempera and fresco, although the latter is really a development of the former. Tempera covers all painting that depends on a water-soluble binder. With it you can achieve brilliant hues and an admirable flat quality, but as water dries very quickly, it is impossible to blend one tone into another. In the painting of frescoes, the color is mixed with water and then laid on wet plaster; when the surface dries, the color is fixed in the plaster. Fresco painting demands speed and precise conceptions but it is a rewarding labor, nonetheless.

Jan Van Eyck is said to have been the first artist to use oil as a medium, although the monk Theophilus mentioned it as early as the twelfth century. Oil dried very slowly, enabling the painter to blend his colors gradually and thereby produce effects never before known—not the least of which was the illusion of a third dimension. Oil paint requires many years to dry completely although the surface hardens in a relatively short time. Once dry, however, it is tough, impervious and permanent. Yet because of its special virtues, tempera continued to be used for two hundred years and oil was applied only for special effects. I, for one, rarely paint a picture entirely in a single medium since I find the combination superior to either alone.

I learned how to make these things from Loupa, as I have related. To him, any paint from a tube was toothpaste.

"The old colors are made of stone, iron and lead. That is their strength and why they last forever," he would say, laughing and showing his broken brown teeth. "Let the Sunday painters work with coal tar, *Figlio,* we will use the colors of eternity. That medicine they sell is too weak for the work. It cracks. It peels. It fades. You put your life into a picture and in fifty years it looks like the bottom of a river when the water is gone."

So we ground our colors and made our orpiments, siennas and cinnabars, and it was in colors such as these that I was to do Lisabeta's portrait. The Marchese had asked for a cinquecento palette and he would have it.

Victor Darius had purchased a silk gown from a theatrical costumer in New York, and Nina and Lisabeta had it altered to fit properly by a local dressmaker. It was the color of red wine with a little light shining through it—a deep, rich garnet that was a challenge to my skill as a colorist. The sleeves were long with nacre cuff buttons, the neckline square and adorned with veil-like lace. In this fine robe, then, I sat her upon a backless bench with her body turned slightly to my right and her head tilted upward and to her left, but very subtly. The eyes, too, glanced in this direction as if they rested upon a companion who was standing some distance away. Victor asked if I would attempt a smile; I said that I must see first how the thing progressed. I arranged her left hand in her lap and her right, with the fingers pointed upward, in the center of her breast, lightly touching the gossamer trim. I had drawn her many times in this pose, as well as numerous others, and it struck me that the inclination of the face would do much to reveal its marvelous expression. On a relatively dark imprimatura, I blocked her in and set to work.

From the beginning it went well. Never have I had a better model. A placid, almost languorous creature, she displayed in the grace of her movements and attitudes all the dignity of a queen. Once posed, she became as still as a figure of stone, her lovely face relaxed and tranquil. I was afire with inspiration. The preliminary shape was finished the first morning and it looked well on the panel. That afternoon I labored as in a dream. Everything fell into place. It was as if the brush knew exactly what it had to do. If the sun had remained aloft and Lisabeta not grown tired at last, I'd have finished it in one session—*alla prima,* as the Italians say. The following day she came early and sat for most of the morning, but in the afternoon she went to Camden and did not return until the light was too weak for work. After that we fell into a routine; she would sit in the morning and perhaps for an hour in the afternoon, and between these times I would work on other parts of the picture.

In ten days the portrait was very near completion. It was then that I decided to repaint the hand that held the lace, for it seemed stiff and unnatural. Before long I had transformed a bad situation into one a good deal worse. The fingers began to look like talons and all my confidence melted away in the space of a few minutes. I stopped painting, washed up and walked into Camden, where I dined sumptuously at the hotel. I spent the evening reading a detective story and went to bed early. The next morning I attempted the hand once more, only to find that I was clumsier than the day before. Once again I gave it up and told Lisabeta that I would not need her. Victor called from New York, and when I told him of my difficulties, he suggested a day's fishing with Grassi.

"Yes," I said derisively, "a bout of seasickness should work wonders."

"Well, then, take a trip to Bangor. Have Buster drive you. It's a very pleasant drive," he suggested.

"No. I think I'll return to Boston for a couple of days."

"Very well—but when are you supposed to meet your friends in Europe?"

"My airplane ticket is for the seventh of August. I still have two weeks. Once I regain my form, I can finish it in three or four days, I believe."

That afternoon I explained to Nina that I was going to Boston for a couple of days as the painting was going badly and I needed a change to revive my powers. She explained this to Lisabeta, who expressed her sorrow with soft sounds and rolling brown eyes. Before Buster drove me to town she kissed me on the cheek and bade me *ciao*.

30 &

THE NIGHT of my arrival in Boston, I slept long and deeply. In the morning, shunning my pencils and brushes, I sought the open air of Commonwealth Avenue and the Public Garden. With my friends gone, there was nothing for me to do but roam at will, refreshing my senses with the pleasant sights of my native city. It was brilliantly sunny, but as the air was clear and in constant motion, it was not hot. As the noon hour approached, I determined to have my lunch at a French restaurant just beyond Copley Square. Some duckling, perhaps, and a glass or two of white wine. At the juncture of Newbury and Dartmouth streets, a girl in a yellow dress came briskly around the corner and almost collided with me. I stepped aside, glancing at her face.

I am told that in the slaughterhouses of Chicago the cattle are led down a runway, at the end of which is a burly chap with a sledgehammer who as they emerge strikes them with all his might, so that—rendered unconscious—they might be more easily dispatched. When I looked at this girl, I experienced much the same sensation as a steer must feel when that massive hammer head comes in contact with his own. My wits flew out of my ears and I fell into a coma.

Not until I reached the opposite side of the street—with no recollection of the intervening passage—did I regain my senses. And with their return came a thrill of terror. There was I, wandering about like a demented dunce, while the creature was departing! Back across Dartmouth I bounded, the virile remonstrances of a cab driver assailing my ears, and along Newbury I sped. Midway down the block I overtook her, but not until I reached the next corner did I come to a halt. There I paused for a moment, looking innocently in a store window and regaining my breath, if not my dignity. A moment later I was retracing my steps, this time more leisurely. I walked by her a second time. She looked me squarely in the eyes, and my heart leaped up through my throat to the top of my head, where it remained for a few seconds before plunging to the heel of my right foot. A devastating beam radiated from her aquamarine eyes and enveloped me. As we passed, a spasm raced about my stomach, like a bolt of hot lightning seeking egress. My legs trembled. It was as if the bone had been emulsified. Then she was gone.

Not wishing to repeat my previous maneuver, since it had drawn some curious glances from a passing policeman, I walked as quickly as I dared back to Dartmouth Street and ducked around the corner. Once out of sight of the law, I picked up my heels and sprinted down the alley that separates the Newbury Street buildings from those on Commonwealth Avenue, emerged on Clarendon Street, and having described a complete circle, managed to pass her yet a third time. Again

I stared and again I was afflicted by those puissant eyes; again the locomotor ataxia; again the anguished agony. If anything, it was worse than before. Evidently, thought I—when thought was again possible—one does not acquire any immunity from previous attacks.

How long I remained in this deranged condition, I do not know, but when I at last returned to my senses and stole a glimpse over my shoulder, I was horrified to see that the yellow dress—together with its occupant, of course—was nowhere in sight. Reversing my direction, I commenced a frantic search of doorways and shop windows. She had disappeared. A numbing sense of despair flooded my abused heart. I tottered into a restaurant and planted myself at a table near the window, where I remained for more than two hours, gazing hungrily (though the table before me was loaded with uneaten food) out the plate-glass pane. Within me there was a longing to see this girl again, to speak to her and to get to know her. This longing was of a ferocity I would not have previously believed possible. It was an ecstatic sensation—thrilling, beautiful and violent. I left the restaurant and wandered about Newbury Street for another hour before departing, at last. I went home and drank coffee and thought.

She must work in the area. It was lunchtime and she had gone for a sandwich. At four-thirty I returned to my post. At six-thirty I gave it up and went into the restaurant for supper. By then I was convinced that she had only been a visitor to the area and that I would never see her again. The food tasted like ashes. I thought of putting a half-page ad in the morning papers. I went back to my flat and tried reading and then sleeping, both with little success.

At eight o'clock the following morning I resumed my patrol and a half hour later I saw her. I had just made my turn at the corner of Clarendon when she appeared from behind a group of other girls, midway down the block. Even at that distance my knees began to tremble. I was determined to speak to her this time, but as we passed I realized what folly such a determination was; I had all I could do to remain upright. But I did manage to retain consciousness. There was no time for a dash around the block, so I followed her. She crossed to the next block and then entered one of the stores. With feigned nonchalance I approached the place and looked in the window. It was Lord's, a gallery that specialized in American painting—primitives, seascapes, Hudson River School and the like. Staring past a gilt-framed storm at sea that was a feeble parody of Turner, I saw my quarry walk to a desk at the rear and put her purse in one of its drawers. Ah-ha, I thought, I've tracked you to your burrow, my elusive rabbit. She looked up, and I quickly lowered my eyes to the turbulence of the painted ocean. A moment later I strolled casually away and into a nearby snack bar. Over a cup of coffee and an egg, I formulated my battle plan.

Roderick Lord was a dignified old boy with full cheeks like a gopher's. He had been in the art business for more than fifty years and had been a friend of Sargent. Now in his seventies, he had a clientele that hailed from every section of the country, and so heavily did they rely upon his judgment, it was claimed that most of his sales were made through the mail or by telephone. Faber had worked for him on many an occasion doing restoration or, as the old fellow preferred to call it, conservation. Indeed, I once helped Leo to transfer a rather charming eighteenth-century primitive from a rotting canvas to a new one—a very tedious job but one that wholly delighted Lord, for he had about abandoned hope for the painting. This good will might now serve me well.

I got a haircut and went home and bathed and donned my best summer suit. At eleven o'clock I sauntered into the gallery. The girl was busy typing, but contrary to my hopes, the old man was not there. Beyond the clatter of the typewriter, a tapping sound told me that Lord's framer, Hugo, was at work at the other end of the building. I studied the paintings.

It was a group show of some sort—all seascapes—and I did manage to notice a fine small Ryder, but my heart was thumping and my head seemed filled with hot blood. I had the uneasy feeling that the thumping would shake one of the pictures from the wall.

Suddenly the typewriting stopped. "What do you want?" I heard her say. The voice was soft and canorous but with an edge to the words.

My heart stopped thumping; it became inert. My scalp tingled. The question struck me as decidedly strange. Under such circumstances, shop assistants generally approach customers with "Can I help you?" or "Lovely, isn't it?" "What do you want?" was a trifle abrupt if not altogether rude. While I considered this matter, my eyes still glued to the painting before me, she repeated the query and I saw that I would have to reply or flee the scene.

"I was admiring this Ryder. Have you any others?" I said in what I hoped was a reasonably normal voice.

She came out from behind her desk and walked toward me. Involuntarily I took a side-step in the opposite direction.

"The Ryder," she said, and her voice, though still melodious, now contained some strains of displeasure, "is on the other wall. You're not interested in Ryder at all. You've been following me."

I raised my eyebrows in a show of outraged innocence but it was an empty moue. What I really felt was a powerful urge to run out the door.

"Yesterday you passed me three times in a single block and leered at me each time," she continued. "I don't know yet how you accomplished it, but you did. What do you want?"

"Fantastic," I said, trying to pull myself together. "Three times in the same block? It doesn't seem possible. Are you certain?"

"Oh yes. That wild, disoriented expression that you habitually wear is not easily forgotten. You walked by me again this morning, mumbling. Then you followed me to the gallery and peered in the window."

"I wasn't mumbling."

"You were. What do you want?"

"Well," I began, feeling my poor dead heart going up in smoke. "Yesterday afternoon, you see . . ." But after this preamble my mind became a blank and the best I could do was cough a few times and run the palm of my hand across my feverish forehead.

She watched me dispassionately. "I hope that you are neither apoplectic nor epileptic. Your face is alarmingly red," she said, but her voice conveyed neither alarm nor mercy. "May I fetch a glass of water for you?"

"Not necessary," I croaked. "It is only a sudden rushing of the blood to the head. I get it now and then in the hot weather."

"The gallery is air-conditioned. Perhaps you should run along and see a doctor. There are some who even specialize in maladies of the head," she said with mock concern.

But at that moment I espied Roderick Lord making his way across the street and, emboldened, I cried, "Will you have lunch with me?" Ney was not more courageous at Waterloo.

"No," she declared, but with no pretense at surprise.

"Dinner, then?" I persisted fearlessly.

"Out of the question." She returned to her desk.

"I'll throw myself into the Charles," I began, but before I could elaborate on this romantic notion, the door opened and the old fellow minced in.

"Well, well, well," he greeted me, and we were soon discussing what I was doing, what Leo was doing, trips abroad, cities of the continent, and subjects in a similar vein.

She had lunch with me the following day. Two weeks later Victor came up from New York and dragged me back to Maine. Her name was Veronica.

While I was in Boston, I received a long letter from Faber and Littleboy. I also received a picture postcard from Benjamin in Athens, which read: "This is the hotel we are staying at. The room is spacious and sunny but somewhat draughty in the evening. Wish you were with us." It was a picture of the Parthenon in sepia.

I sent them a letter telling them that I would not be able to meet them in Milan, that I would have to come later. As it happened, I was unable to make the trip at all. The summer went before I knew it.

31 ॐ

I RETURNED to Camden in a daze. I had spent my rest period in Boston engaged in a most strenuous, nerve-shattering courtship, which during its course had unfolded before my startled senses the abyss of abject grief, the dizzying peaks of flaming rapture and all intermediary points between the two. I got little sleep and no rest but it did take my mind off the portrait.

Lisabeta affected to be angry with me for not returning sooner, while Darius, though very much annoyed during the journey, was greatly mollified by the sight of the portrait. His pale, fine features brightened at the first glimpse.

"God," he said, "it will set them on their ears!"

I spent two days rehabilitating my mind. The painting, which had been a vital part of me, had become an alien construction remembered as in a dream. I did some sketching and puttered about, giving Victor and the girl the impression that I was hard at work, and on the afternoon of the second day something quickened within me and the pretense became re-

ality. I tackled the offending hand immediately and in no time
at all it was as real as one of my own. The work then went
splendidly. My thoughts wandered to Boston frequently and
the nights were very long, but knowing that my return depended on how well I worked, I concentrated manfully on
my labors.

By the end of a week I had her face pretty much as I
wanted it. I had not attempted a smile but had essayed a
cheerful curve to the mouth that was an habitual expression of
Lisabeta's. The line of the lips, while not somber, suggested
concentration but concentration of a light-hearted sort. I believe I caught it as it was—without the restlessness of the modern mouth. The shadows about the eyes and the throat turned
out particularly well and the brows and the one visible temple
had the soft curves of reality. The modeling and the
chiaroscuro fused neatly in the manner called by the Italians
sfumato. The slight upward glance of the eyes had also proven
successful and the pinkness in the corners and the hairs of the
lashes were not at all bad. The black hair, which fell in front
of her ears as was the style in Leonardo's day, was not quite
so satisfactory. It required additional work, as did the sleeves
of the gown. I had always been an admirer of the backgrounds
of the three Louvre Leonardos; thus, in emulation, I designed a scene that featured a single deformed pine tree, the
sea and a towering rock outcropping containing a cavern upon
a somewhat misty shore. This, too, needed some repainting.
The tree and the rock were actually on the grounds of the
estate but the cavern was an invention. It was all quite
mysterious.

At this point Lisabeta caught a cold after being drenched
by a sudden squall that came in from the sea one afternoon
while she was on the beach. She was in bed for three days and
unable to sit for three more. Victor insisted I remain in Camden, though had I known the duration of her illness, I would

have returned to Boston nonetheless. As it was, I was preparing to leave when she appeared for breakfast on the seventh day, somewhat wan but otherwise normal.

Three days later the portrait was finished. I fiddled with it for another day and a half, but as I was well satisfied with my work, I made no significant changes. I signed my name boldly in the right-hand corner and called Darius in.

"A marvel! The best that you have ever done," he exclaimed, laughing excitedly.

Lisabeta was enraptured by it. *"Magico!"* she whispered. *"Miracolo!"* The Grassis, father and daughter both, appeared stunned by the sight of it. They spoke in hushed voices, as if in a church or a museum. I was altogether happy with the response of my small audience. All were sure that the Marchese would adore it. That night I wrote a lengthy letter to Leo and Littleboy, telling them of the successful conclusion of my task and giving them a word description of the picture as well as a rough sketch showing the pose and the background. I had to tell them that I had not yet made new reservations for my flight to Europe but I would write again in a day or two.

But it was the thought of seeing Veronica again that dominated my actions. I packed all my things that night and in the morning Buster drove us back to Boston. Before leaving I took a last look at my painting, knowing that I would never see it again. Lisabeta stood beside me and murmured something in Italian, and Victor laughed.

"She says that if you breathed on it, it would come to life," he translated.

I smiled. "I guess it's a success then."

"More," he answered. "It's a triumph."

After bidding farewell to the Grassis and *arrivaderci* to Lisabeta, who kissed me on the cheek and shed some tears, I climbed into the car beside Darius and off we went. The painting was left on its easel; Victor had given Mr. Grassi careful instructions about having it sent to New York in about a month, when it had dried enough to be transported. A Rockland mover, who handled most of the antique shipments in the area, had been hired to crate and carry it. The varnishing would be done in New York before the picture went to London.

We stopped at a small town called Kennebunk to have lunch, and an unfortunate event occurred. A portfolio containing the sketches I had made of Lisabeta was stolen from the back seat of the automobile. I was more than a little upset by this, for I had intended to show them to Littleboy and Faber; some of these drawings were very finished—one in particular, I had planned on framing. We notified the local police, who promised to write to me if they found them, but no word ever came. Perhaps they will one day appear in a Boston gallery or antique shop and I will have another chance to see again that lovely Renaissance face.

Darius gave me a check for a thousand dollars and said he would mail the balance to me in about six weeks.

32 &

MY REVERIES seem less vivid lately. This morning, for instance, I was prospecting for diamonds at Tejekem. At one point I was bent over the waters of the river, a large round sieve in my hands and my bare feet sunk in the ooze. The sieve was filled with mud and pebbles and I was dipping it into the coppery water to wash the one from the other. The earth was a rich sienna and the stones ranged in color from bright whites to pea-green and indigo, but as I looked at them, the colors faded and for several seconds all was black and white. Then it gradually reverted to normal.

This is the third or fourth time something of this sort has happened in the past week, and I am growing concerned.

My ordinary thinking, too, has become somewhat hazy. I can't seem to keep everything properly arranged in my head. I find myself increasingly annoyed by objects. This morning, because there was no hot water (that fool Barletty!), I kicked the bathtub so hard that I nearly broke my toe.

This will never do. Above all, I must preserve order and precision in my thoughts.

Did I mention that I have gotten a new phonograph needle? I drummed with my slats for about an hour last night, but very softly. I do not want Mrs. Chakamoulian calling the police, as she did that other time.

33 &

A FEW years back, there lived in Boston a man who claimed to be a Peruvian general, though his English was perfect while his Spanish, according to those who tried to converse with him in that tongue, was strangely barbaric. General Jorge de Reyna was what he called himself and he was possessed of great wealth which he was not slow to expend in the pursuit of his pleasures. I need hardly mention that this trait assured him of many friends. Like many another idle man of means, he was attracted to the arts, and with few to contradict him he was convinced that his opinions were axioms and his predilections, laws. He had some intelligence, a little wit (mostly borrowed) and a very grand manner. He lived in a three-storied Victorian house that overlooked the Charles River from Beacon Street, and it was here, in rooms with molded ceilings, crystal chandeliers and ormolued furniture, that he held court.

The art moguls, like pigs at a trough, shouldered one another aside to gain admittance.

The General was a squint-eyed, bulbous-nosed, thick-lipped specimen but he had a beautiful blond wife who did much to offset his own lack of comeliness. Rumor alleged that he had purchased this woman from her former husband, a real estate dealer who had been ruined by an unwise speculation in Florida shore-front property. The sum of money involved in this carnal transaction depended on the raconteur, varying from ten thousand dollars, as claimed by those who did not like the lady, to one hundred thousand, a figure strenuously put forth by those who did. This pair attended all the major events at the galleries, universities and museums, where, surrounded by sycophants, they expounded their empty theories with all the authority of oracles. Poor weak-minded, dabbling dabbers were sometimes declared new Tiepolos or Fragonards, while at other times a lifetime of original and highly competent painting was dismissed and damned with a borrowed bon mot.

Now, each spring the Tauchnitz Gallery held a charity auction, the proceeds from which were given to a settlement house in the South End. A prominent New York critic, Bernard Sylvane, attended one of these affairs and had the misfortune to drop down dead, halfway through the sale. It chanced that a painting of Littleboy's, "The Tower of Babel," was being held aloft at that particular moment, and de Reyna was later heard to remark, amidst much servile laughter, that this picture was the cause of Sylvane's seizure and that the artist should be had up for manslaughter.

A month after this auction the Back Bay Fine Art Society held its annual fete on the grassy plot of ground in front of the library, and again, led by the mayor himself, all the distinguished dilettanti gathered. Benjamin, though not a member of the society, had by some heavy persuasion succeeded in getting one of his works exhibited in the section allotted to invited artists. The painting was larger than was usual for him and the colors very sharp and eye-catching. It featured a donkey, who was dressed like a king but who was being dragged from his throne by an enraged multitude. His crown hung from one long ear and his ermine and purple robes were being ripped from his body. The scene was crowded with Littleboy creatures and Littleboy calligraphy. The principal banner, held by a rat-faced lady, proclaimed in beautiful script: "If he hadn't spoken, we'd never have known."

The fete had barely gotten under way, however, before people began to notice that the dethroned donkey bore an unmistakable resemblance to General Jorge de Reyna. This curious circumstance was soon the subject of all conversations and the source of much covert merriment. In so genteel an assembly, there could be no headlong rush to view the picture but there was a definite drift in its direction and anon a crowd had formed. The Peruvian and his wife, together with their entourage, joined this general movement without being aware of its cause. Littleboy, who had chosen a good vantage point to view the drama, swore that the sight of the jackass brought smoke from de Reyna's nostrils.

The society, now painfully cognizant of the trick played upon them, could not decide whether it was wiser to remove the work, and thus acknowledge the caricature, or to leave it where it was and pretend that it was in no way unusual. General de Reyna found himself in a like situation. Much as he wished to be away, he knew that a sudden retreat would confirm the asinine resemblance. He adopted an air of Olympian calm, but as the painting remained where it was (less because of a firm decision than for the lack of one) and the derisive laughter was less and less suppressed, he lost his aplomb, and squinting horribly, fled from the field—wife, myrmidons and all.

The painting was returned to Littleboy the next morning, along with some harsh words. His air of injured innocence, he said, would have honored a Garrick.

WHEN I received the second thousand-dollar check, which represented my fee less Victor's portion, I received as well a long letter describing the effect produced on the Marquis by my portrait. Such words as "captivated," "entranced," "ecstatic," and "sorcery," "prodigy," "masterful" occurred at frequent intervals. The nobleman's only regret was that I was not an Italian. I was gratified by these laudations and even more pleased by the news that I had been offered a second commission, this one comprising the fourteen stations of the cross. I wrote at once and advised Darius of my willingness to undertake this project. I was beginning to feel that I had at last found a Maecenas.

Along with these pleasant events, my pursuit of Veronica was progressing most favorably. I was afire with desire and burning with yearning, as the poets say, and few thoughts passed through my head that were not directly or indirectly concerned with this slip of a girl. What with lunches here, cocktails there, dinners hither and the theater thither, we were not often separated. In her little rose-colored German automobile, we rambled about the countryside, invading the Cape and Rockport and Concord and similar happy settings, on Saturdays and Sundays that she was free of Lord's. She, too, was a painter, and though we often brought our paints and brushes to these charming places, little work was accomplished. At that time she was a stipple painter, imitating Seurat. Before our meeting she had spent an entire year as an abstractionist and nearly half a year as a cubist. After a spell of Cézanne, she now found herself among the Impressionists. Later she was to adopt Delacroix. Even at that period, when I was quite mad about her, I had to admit that she executed all these styles with equal skill—but only to myself, for she cared little for criticism. Having graduated from Smith the previous spring, she had set her heart on becoming a great painter, "a Jane Austen of fine art," as she phrased it. I shivered slightly, but being the helpless slave of passion, added my words of confidence to her own.

Her father had died three years before and she and her mother had moved from a house in Winchester to one on Lime Street in Boston. Her mother was a dear old girl whose notions of an artist's life were a happy compound of *Trilby* and *La Bohème*. There was an older brother, who was a lawyer in Milwaukee, and an older sister, who was married to a textile mill owner in Woonsocket, Rhode Island.

One day, before a Caneletto at the Fogg, I proposed and she accepted.

35 ⮾

LEO AND Benjamin were both deeply impressed by what they saw in Europe, but of the two, it was Benjamin who seemed to profit most. His colors became richer and the attitudes of his figures grew bolder and more varied. He began to experiment with distemper, a medium he had previously rejected as impractical, and the results were exquisite. My ears were treated to all their experiences, so that I soon learned the shapes, colors, size and texture of the wonders they had seen. It was like hearing the words of the Maestro again. Both were disappointed by my failure to join them but both wished me well in my love affair.

It was that fall that Benjamin met Danielle and her rococo furnishings and that winter that they were married. We all got together occasionally, but nowhere nearly as frequently as in the days before the summer.

Leo continued to wander the groves and meadows of rural New England, painting his idyls with ever-increasing finesse. Now and then he would give a little talk at some art association or write an article for some struggling periodical. At Christmas he held a large dinner at which two dozen people gorged themselves on roast turkey and goose as prepared by the chef at the Westminster Hotel, who attended the feast himself and became very merry on *asti spumonti*. That January another show in New York added to Faber's fame.

And me? Well, I painted and carved and hammered away at various things, but my heart being elsewhere, they were not as inspired as they might have been. I did complete the stations of the cross, and both Victor and the Marquis professed delight with them; to me, however, they were lacking in strength, despite some clever contrivances. When the money for this work was received, Veronica insisted that I find a better studio now that I had achieved such success. Like children, we wandered about the city searching for an ideal atelier, and at last, when such a place seemed nonexistent, we discovered a fine, spacious, sunlit loft atop an office building on Boylston Street. It overlooked the Common and the Public Garden, and in the distance the gleaming surface of the Charles could be seen. Ah, what a happy day was that! I was a week transporting canvases and gear into the place and some time longer getting accustomed to working there. On Saturday mornings Veronica would come and paint views of Boston in the little dots and dashes that I called Morse code, for which flippancy I was roundly reprimanded.

I still rent that studio, though I no longer visit the place
and have not worked in it for nearly a year. It is filled with the
fruits of my invention. Stacked paintings, like an army poised
to conquer the world, cover half the floor. Some of these are
very old and contain corrective brush strokes by Maestro
Loupa; others were done just prior to my renunciation of art
and are paintings of power and brilliance. My masterpiece,
"The Shackling of God," sits by itself on a packing case against
one wall. It was my final painting. No one has ever seen it but
me; it is absolutely luminous. The bronze bust of Littleboy is
there and the "Flagellated Jesus" in the white marble of
Pentelicus and the walnut "Luther." The bas-reliefs dealing
with the Trojan War are there, including the large center panel
of Achilles and Hector; so, too, is the high relief of David and
Goliath and the carving in the round of Voltaire. My coffee
table there was a piece of scalloped gray marble supported
by a bronze Samson tearing down the temple. I had done it
for Veronica but she had tired of it and I returned it to my
workshop. This was also the fate of a wonderful mirror that
I had made for our bedroom. The glass is divided into many
sections and the frame and interstices are covered with gilded,
carved figures depicting the great loves of Greek myth. The
Daphne and Apollo tableau is truly arresting; its supple sinu-
ousness led Veronica to think it obscene. There, also, is the
chest I made for Victor, and never gave to him because of the
de Reyna business. It is of brass and weighs one hundred and
forty pounds. On the four sides are scenes from the life of
Alexander the Great while the bowed top shows the Battle of
Gaugamela. This was cast in sections, the whole finished by
hand with great care and then brazed together. But I could
continue this catalogue for twenty pages. It is a museum, my
studio, but a padlocked one that none can enter.

Victor came to Boston soon after the New Year and invited Veronica and me to dinner. A blizzard hit the city that

night, and while we dined handsomely at the Vendome, the
wind and snow beat upon the large windows. We had several
wines and Darius, who does not often drink and is therefore
not very adept at it, became very light-hearted and amusing.
His Byronic features, his British accent and the astuteness of
his mind completely charmed Veronica, and her beauty and
grace, it was clear, were not lost on him. When we finally left
the warmth of the dining room, we were unable to find a cab
and nearly perished from the cold. We saw Victor safely to
the Chester House and then tramped across the Garden to
Lime Street and home. I believe that Victor was the first, and
only, friend of mine that Veronica genuinely liked.

The snows of winter melted away, as Villon observed years
ago, and spring arrived. There was a great deal of hectic activity
and general perturbation, following which Veronica and I were
married. This event took place in Winchester, but the recep-
tion, a most sumptuous and interminable affair, was held at
the Crillon in Boston. We flew to Quebec City for our honey-
moon and a very different kind of life began for me.

36 ❧

AFTER MY marriage I saw less and less of my two friends. The
commissions obtained for me by Darius together with my new
social obligations left me with few free moments. When I returned from the studio in the evening, there was always an
aunt or an uncle, a cousin or a childhood friend or a college
chum expected, and when they were not visiting us, it was we
who visited them. On weekends we drove to Rhode Island

to see Veronica's sister or stayed the better part of Sunday with her mother.

I found all this gregarious activity amusing in the beginning, but it soon grew tiresome. Still, being in love, I continued docile.

37 &

IN SPITE of the excellence of his post-tour paintings, Benjamin was still unable to support himself with his brush. Danielle's modeling provided a steady trickle of money for a while, but she soon became pregnant and had to retire. Leo and I, when fortune favored us, were quick to share our wealth with Benjamin, just as he had shared with us in bygone years, but now he became irritable when money was mentioned and often refused to accept what was offered. He began to call Leo Croesus and me Crassus, and though neither of us minded these mild epithets we were both worried about his altered mood.

At the bottom of all this, of course, was his anger with the world for refusing to acknowledge his work. He knew that he was a good painter. He knew that if the dealers gave him a little exposure, success would quickly follow. And he knew that his current paintings were the best that he had ever done. Leo was forever prodding people in both New York and Boston to give Littleboy a chance to show, and I had used what little influence I had to get him in a gallery; but the dealers complained that they had forty artists to handle and there were only twelve months in each year, and you could not convince them that Benjamin was better than the whole forty together.

His poverty, then, being the offspring of his love of art, soon assumed a sacred position in his thoughts and he resented any attack upon it. He became increasingly shabby in his dress, wearing paint-stained clothing as if it were a uniform and permitting his hair to grow to wild length.

That summer Leo went to Texas to give a course in drawing, and Veronica and I spent three weeks of July at the Vineyard. Before leaving I had managed to give Danielle six twenty-dollar bills while Littleboy had his back turned, but it was not until late in August that I saw either of them again. The weather had been strangely cold for that time of year and there was no sun. I had been to McCoy's to buy some fine brushes and I decided to call on them while I had the chance. Their home was in a very narrow brick building on St. Botolph Street. There was a barber shop on the ground floor and single apartments on each of the other three above. A rickety stairway connected the floors amidst mustiness and gloom. Danielle opened the door and greeted me with a cry of delight.

"How are you? How are you?" she asked, throwing her arms about me and kissing both cheeks in rapid succession. "Benjamin! Come see who is here! You have the color of a cinema star. I 'ope the sea was more warm than it is here. Sit, sit! Give me your package."

From his workroom in the rear of the place, Littleboy made his appearance. "At last!" he exclaimed, laughing and clapping me on the back. "I was afraid you had drowned, wasn't I, Danielle? I said, 'He's probably at the bottom of Buzzard's Bay. Tried to paint a Nereid and became so involved with his work that he drowned before he noticed that he was underwater.' Isn't that what I said, Danielle?"

We sat and chattered for a while, then, while his wife made coffee, Benjamin led me off to his studio. In my absence he had completed a wonderfully active "Battle of the Minotaurs," using both tempera and oil.

"My Minotauromachy," he said proudly, "is not bad, eh? At night, before I fall asleep, I can hear their hoofbeats. But over there is something even better." He pointed to a corner of the room where the outline of a canvas could be discerned beneath a piece of green cotton cloth.

"May I have a look?" I asked.

"Not yet. It's not finished."

"What will it be?"

"It will be a masterpiece," he said happily. "That's what it will be. As to the subject—you will have to wait. But after Danielle, you and Leo will be the first to see it. Prepare to be confounded and amazed."

He was in good spirits though his face seemed thinner and his eyes brighter. While he was in this mood I offered him some money, but he refused, saying he really didn't need it.

"How do you manage?" I asked in perplexity.

"Ah, I have a new sideline. I've become a money-looker."

"A what?"

"A money-looker, Crassus. I wander about the streets in my spare time, looking for money."

"Are you serious?"

"Certainly, you dolt! It's a very interesting pastime. It all began when I found a two-dollar bill near the Y.W.C.A. last month. The next day I found a quarter on Stuart Street and a one-dollar bill on Huntington Avenue. Since then I've been a money-looker."

"How much can you possibly find? Certainly not enough to live on."

"More than you'd think. Oh, not huge sums—I don't mean that—but I did find a five in front of the opera. It's mostly nickels and dimes and pennies, with a quarter now and then and a half-dollar more rarely. In a way, it's fascinating—like a game of chance. Shall I walk on Boylston or Commonwealth? Near the curb or close to the buildings? This side of the street or that? And when you find something, it's quite a thrill—like *creation ex nihilo.* Parking meters and bus stops are the best places to look. I must take you with me sometime."

"You're crazy!" I said emphatically. "Why the distaste for my money—and Leo's? We've used yours often enough."

"You two have arrived," he answered, shaking his big head from side to side. He was wearing some kind of fur vest, an outlandish thing that was open down the front and swayed with his movement. "If I live on your success, I'll never have one of my own."

"Lunacy! It's only a matter of time before you'll be recognized. Until then, you must use our money. How can you work if you are roaming about the city all day long?"

"I don't do it all day long. As for the world, I've waited for it, let it wait a bit for me. Who knows? I might even find a solid-gold bracelet studded with rubies, or a diamond as big as a walnut. I have a recurring dream in which I see a man in an orange hat; then I walk a few steps and find a great wad of bills held together by a clothespin. Funny, eh? I sometimes dream it three or four times a night—how can it help but come true?"

"Leo and I could open an account for you and you could draw on it as you need it. You can't pay for paint and canvas with what . . ."

"No, thanks," he interrupted brusquely. He got up and walked to his picture of struggling minotaurs. After a moment he said, "How do you like the articulation? I may do a centauromachy as a companion piece. Perhaps after I finish the masterpiece there in the corner. I got a card from Leo with a picture of some Indians on it. Have you heard from him?"

The conversation drifted, and try as I might, I was unable to get him to talk about money again. But he had not become sullen; indeed, I believe he was glad to see me, for his mood was one of light-heartedness and joviality. When I asked him about his hair shirt, he made a most comical grimace.

"It's a cat skin," he disclosed.

"Cat skin?"

"Absolutely. Don't you recognize it?"

I inspected it closely, and sure enough, it was the yellowish-gray, black-streaked color of a tabby. Several skins had been sewn together and these seams were outlined by the white underbelly fur of the hapless creatures.

"Did you make it yourself?" I inquired politely, though perhaps a little warily.

"No, no, no. Danielle brought it from Paris. I had a little cough the other day, so she insists that I wear it. The French use them all the time. If you own a cat there, it is wise to keep him indoors."

"Then it's good for coughs?"

"Oh yes. And sciatica, bursitis, rheumatism, arthritis, pleurisy and the evil eye. Rather becoming, too, don't you think?"

"Very. Brindle makes you look thinner."

"Yes, but there are disadvantages. Three days ago I went out with it on and seven stray dogs chased me down Huntington Avenue."

"Come, now," I protested.

"Yes, it happened. I had to climb a tree near the Mechanics Building; they were snapping at my heels. In the end the Fire Department had to get me down with a ladder." He said all this with a straight face, though I was shaking with laughter. "It really happened, honestly. I was afraid to come down. It taught me something about perspective—trees are taller when you are looking down from them than they are when you are looking up at them."

He paused and allowed me to catch my breath. "The French are strong for home remedies, you know," he resumed, stroking his vest. "If I feel a little nervy or I've got a headache or indigestion, Danielle whips up a little tisane. It's great stuff. Only yesterday I had a lovely decoction of mistletoe, vervain and cinnamon. There aren't many sick people who wouldn't respond to that, believe me. Have you ever had boiled anise mixed with a Chinese herb called ginseng? Very good for arterial tension. For the skin I recommend cucumber milk, and if you are having trouble with your virility, a little oyster powder in water will set you aright in no time. Don't laugh. After all, Pasteur was a Frenchman and Avicenna an Arab, so Danielle must know what she's talking about. Her grandfather once felt a trifle bilious and began drinking tisanes of what's known as 'Paraguay tea.'" He stopped and looked contemplatively at his palette, which hung from a nail on the wall.

"Did it work?" I asked.

He looked at me in surprise. "I should say it did. The old boy lived to be ninety-one. What's more, three days after his death his liver was still functioning. Remarkable, eh? They had to beat it to death with a stick."

I found it impossible to control my laughter. Danielle arrived with cups of coffee.

"I've just been telling him about your grandfather, Achmed," he said to her.

"I have no such grandfather," she said to me, raising her eyes to the ceiling. "Never believe what he says. He tells untrue stories."

"I was explaining about tisanes—how good they are and how well you make them, *cherie*. There is an excellent one—radish leaves and daffodil petals boiled over a low flame for half an hour and garnished with a tablespoon of mixed lovage, borage, cabbage and foggage—that will bring instant relief to a man who's been run over by a steam roller."

"You're too much, Benjamin," I said, wiping my eyes.

"*Pas vrai,*" his wife cried. "There is no thing like that."

"There is. Why are you both so skeptical?"

"Oh, you liar!" exclaimed Danielle. "What a crazy one he is."

We drank our coffee in high good humor. Danielle was in an advanced state of pregnancy but it did not prevent her from wearing giant hoop earrings and a string of beads of great length and varied color.

When Benjamin went into the kitchen for more coffee, I gave her some money. As she took it she kissed my hand.

38 ❧

I'VE BEEN lying under my bed all day. Of course, it's Sunday, but even that cannot account for my enormous sense of anxiety. I am living in an aura of impending cataclysm. I suspect that the police are watching the house and following me wherever I go. I've been afraid to continue my sugar-bowl hunt, even afraid to go into restaurants.

And the pigeons are still around.

All imagination, perhaps. I'm alone too much.

Odd things are happening. Last night the doorknob came off my bathroom door. And this morning the water wouldn't boil for my egg. I gave up at last and had my breakfast on Charles Street.

I am growing forgetful, too. There definitely has been some change in the atmosphere, for nothing is as exact as it once was—neither within me nor without.

The screw for that ridiculous doorknob has vanished completely.

My reveries are faint and brief. I think there must be some sort of disturbance in the ether.

VERONICA'S MOTHER died after we'd been married about a year, and she inherited some property and a considerable sum of money. Though she continued to work for Roderick Lord, she now began to talk of opening her own gallery. I encouraged her in this. It was evident to me that she would never be a painter (she painted less and less after our marriage) and yet she was strongly drawn to the art world. The operation of a gallery, I concluded, would be well suited to her. It was not difficult for me to imagine her suavely peddling pictures to bejeweled dowagers and crafty collectors looking for sound investments. Moreover, I was pleased to think that Benjamin would at last have a proper place to exhibit his tableaux. Those of my own works that were not sold abroad were being shown at Gault's; he was a friend of Victor's, and though he had sold a few things, I was sure that he would not object to my trans- ferring to a gallery owned by my wife. In a very short time she had accumulated a list of artists for her "stable," as she called it. Most of them were mediocrities, but I did not interfere or attempt to force my views upon her since it was her money and her scheme and she was so obviously enthralled by the whole idea.

We were soon giving dinners and cocktail parties. Victor had promised to help her, and through his introductions, it was not long before she knew most of the dealers and museum people. Along with these, she had also acquired an assortment of well- dressed, well-mannered ne'er-do-well writers, musicians and theatrical types. There were endless discussions about the sort of gallery it should be, where it should be located, whether she should have a frame shop, what kind of openings she should hold, what kind of décor, whether she should hire a restorer, and so forth. At that moment it seemed there were no decent locations available on Newbury Street.

"It has to be spacious," she kept repeating. "These brownstone parlors are impossible. And it must have a large window."

At first I enjoyed it all nearly as much as she did, but as the social functions continued with no sign of abatement and the clever, though mindless, chatter palled, I began to long for a little peace and a few hours of tranquillity in the evening. I found, too, that my work suffered if I failed to get sufficient sleep, and this worried me. After a while I turned down some invitations. Veronica was displeased but accepted my decision. One night, however, she asked if I'd mind if she went to an opening alone, and, of course, I consented willingly, for I saw no reason for her to be deprived of pleasures that were inexpedient for me. Once having established this precedent, she was soon attending most of these affairs without me. We still entertained at home frequently, and these parties more than satisfied my meager desire for conviviality.

Faber came to a few of these gatherings but soon wearied of them. Benjamin came to one, stayed a half-hour, said he had a headache and then departed. He never came to another. I really couldn't blame them. The conversation seemed to be culled from the latest magazines, and the humor, even at its best, rang hollow since it lacked warmth and spontaneity.

ONE DAY, a couple of months after my visit, Benjamin called me and told me that he was the father of a boy and that the child was to be called Charlemagne. I congratulated him, sent a box of candy to Danielle, and a week or so later I went with Leo Faber to see them and the infant. The new mother was up, though she looked tired and wan. She brightened at the sight of the various buntings and infant's wear that we deposited on the living-room table, and after two glasses of the champagne that Leo had brought she was as gay as ever.

The proud father ushered us into Charlemagne's presence. The child was hairless, blue-eyed and chubby. His apoplectic features bore a strong resemblance to those of his father.

"Charlemagne?" Leo asked, raising his eyebrows. "Why not Julius Caesar or Alexander the Great?"

"We almost named him Napoleon," Benjamin replied. "I wanted to call him Haroun al-Rashid but she said it sounded foreign. We started with Oliver, then went to Roland and then soared to the heights with Charlemagne."

We had a pleasant time drinking champagne and eating cookies. Faber had won a grand prize at a show in Baltimore and we chivvied him about his rapid rise to prominence on the strength of bare breasts and dimpled buttocks.

"How's the *magnum opus* coming?" I asked Benjamin. "Have you told Leo about it?"

"Oh yes. He's been warned. I haven't finished it yet but it's marching well, as Danielle would say. You'll have a chance to see it before I announce its completion to the rest of the world. That way, you won't be trampled in the rush. It will make them forget the Sistine Chapel, even though it's not as big as that table top there. Wait and see! Someday, in the not too distant future, the three of us will be walking on Fifth Avenue or the Champs Elysées or in jolly old Piccadilly, and you'll hear someone say, 'Who are those chaps with Benjamin Littleboy?'"

We all laughed, though none as hard as Littleboy himself. Leo tried hard to elicit from him some idea of the nature of this new work, but he refused to reveal anything. Even Danielle said that she had been forbidden to see it.

41 &

A YEAR ago or so I began to devote much thought to God. The events of that period brought on this rush of theological concern, though, as I have mentioned elsewhere, it was a concern never far removed from my mind. God has always existed for me. As a child I dreamed about Him, picturing Him as an enormous, perfectly proportioned man surrounded by an aureole aura. When the Maestro spoke of seeing Zeus in Olympia, it was like an echo of my dreams. But in my childhood I thought of God as goodness—a beneficent Deity that maintained order and regulation throughout a happy and wonder-filled universe. Over the years my views altered. It became increasingly difficult to reconcile what I saw and what I experienced with these juvenile beliefs.

Once the Maestro and I passed through a children's ward at City Hospital, on our way to study a cadaver. There was a little girl of seven or eight lying in one of the beds. She had been to a birthday party the previous day and an older child had set fire to her flimsy dress with one of the cake candles. The doctor told us that she wouldn't live. Only her eyes were visible through the bandages, and these, with the lashes gone and the lids brown and cracked, were so charged with anguish and bewilderment that I couldn't bear to look into them for more than a moment. But the moment was enough.

Who would allow this to happen to a child? What right had God to use His power for such horrible purposes? What was the sense of it? What was the sense of the man shooting his wife that day? There are some outrages that cannot be permitted, some torments not to be borne.

I dwelt upon these things now and then, but it was not until a year ago that all these ideas came into sharp focus. A small accident in my studio started me on a complete philosophical investigation of God. I examined His wisdom, His motives, His justice, His generosity and His entire nature. My head became a furnace of flaming indignation.

Who was this clumsy Architect of the universe? Who was this insensate Scatterer of misery? Who was this liberal Bestower of pain and death, this feelingless Father, this demon Deity?

42 ?~

I VISITED the tenement on St. Botolph Street occasionally but I rarely caught Benjamin at home. "He is walking," Danielle would say, and I surmised that he was searching the streets for money. His absence, however, enabled me to give a few dollars to his wife without a lot of awkward sleight of hand. The baby appeared healthy enough, though the apartment, despite Danielle's attempts to brighten it, was a dilapidated, depressing place. There were few windows and the air seemed always stale.

"If he is out all the time," I asked her one day, "when does he paint?"

"Almost always he paints at night now," she replied. "It is necessary for this picture. It will be a great one, he says. Very different, you understand." She laughed self-consciously. "Maybe you and Leo will not have need of giving us money soon. Benjamin thinks the next year we will go to Paris. What do you think of that, eh? Not bad, eh?"

I told her how happy it would make me to see him become rich and famous and how sure I was that it would come about eventually. But his painting at night, though not unprecedented, was certainly odd. Something in the manner of Caravaggio, I deduced. When I did catch him at home, he volunteered no further information about this project, other than to say that he had been experimenting with painting by candlelight and that he had hopes of conveying flickering light onto his canvas.

I saw even less of Leo. He had taken another teaching job for the spring term at a university in Indiana. That summer Veronica and I spent two weeks in New York, wandering around the galleries and the museums, and another two weeks in the White Mountains. In September, Benjamin came to my studio one morning and told me that he had finished the painting. He looked weary and his movements were nervous and abrupt.

"Fifteen months I've been at it," he said, "and I'm not sorry it's over, believe me. But it's been worth it. Can you come this afternoon? Leo will be there. I want you both to see it at the same time."

I agreed to go. He looked about the studio for a while, offering occasional comments on my recent work, but his mind was quite evidently elsewhere. Then he left.

I went at two that afternoon. Benjamin was wearing a clean shirt and had his hair combed. Danielle looked very gay in a red print dress and a long rope of purple beads. I was handed a glass of sweet wine and a few minutes later Leo arrived. Benjamin's morning nervousness had vanished. It seemed likely that he had taken a glass or two before we came. His face was flushed and his general demeanor was that of a frisky young hippopotamus. While we talked, he kept urging us to finish our drinks and refill our glasses. At last he rose from his chair and beckoned to us.

"Come," he said, "and prepare to be confounded. The moment of revelation is here." He winked at his wife, who gave him a smile, and then led us to his studio at the other end of the apartment.

In the middle of the room stood an easel with a battered folding screen in front of it. We stationed ourselves before it. Littleboy then folded the two outer leaves in on the center and, with a flourish, carried the partition away.

"There!" he said, his voice strangely hushed.

On the easel sat a most astonishing painting. It was certainly less than three feet in length and barely twenty inches high, yet it surged with movement. In truth, when the screen was removed and my eyes first glimpsed it, I could have sworn that the central figure wriggled. The title of the work, emblazoned on a scroll at the bottom, was "The Birth of Death." The mall on Commonwealth Avenue was easy to identify as the setting. There were the brownstones, the old elms, the walk and the broad lawns. He had taken the liberty of placing a fountain there, however, and it gushed sparkling water quite realistically. It was night, but an eerie fluid light, utterly different from moonlight or starlight, illuminated the scene from a hidden source above.

The main figure, Death, had just hatched from a shiny blue-black egg in the center of the picture. He was not a large figure—scarcely half the size of the humans around him—but he dominated everything. The lower part of his body was covered with skillfully rendered olive-green hair, which as it reached the hips thinned to reveal freckled chartreuse flesh that glistened hideously in the strange, shifting light. His head was large and contained a pair of bulging round eyes, noseless nostrils and a twisted-lipped fanged mouth. The malignancy of the expression made my heart miss a beat. The projecting eyes radiated a palpable hatred, while the crimson mouth, sawtoothed and gaping, was as cruel a maw as any in the annals of art.

Surrounding this demon was a vast throng of people, beasts and people-beasts. Those nearest Death cringed in fear, while those further away fought and killed one another. The number of forms arranged on the canvas seemed almost infinite and the variety of faces and postures stupefied the eye. His coloring was bold, the draughtsmanship unbelievably fine. The picture seemed to draw you into it and make you a part of the dreadfulness—the unbounded terror and the merciless slaughter.

"What do you think?" Benjamin whispered in my ear.

"It's an explosion," I replied, my eyes still probing the intricacies of the scene.

"Everything moves," Faber said in awe. "It's the light."

"Yes," Benjamin agreed, chuckling, "and the shadows and the modeling and the color."

My eyes returned to the sinister figure emerging from the eggshell. Again that horrid countenance electrified me. His hands were on his hips, his elbows jutting out behind him like rudimentary wings. The shimmering light glanced from his vulture-like shoulders, his wrinkled forehead and his black-nippled breast. It danced upon the feathery down—all livid yellow, like a callow chick's—that covered his scalp and it glistened on his smooth long jaw and square chin. Each evil feature was caught and magnified by this scintillating noctilucence until the tiny creature assumed an impossible reality.

"He's a beauty, isn't he?" Littleboy said. "And what about all the others? There's more than twelve hundred of the little villains. And the composition—not too bad, eh? As balanced as a bird in flight. Everything where it should be, right, Leo?"

"It must have been difficult . . ." Leo began.

"Difficult?" Benjamin said, raising his eyebrows. "It was impossible. Look at them. Each one is a poem, an epic. Look at this pair locked in a death struggle. See the perspiration? You can almost smell it. And this harridan vomiting on the grass, can't you hear the sound of her retching?"

What he said was not far from the truth. The more I looked, the more convincing it all became. He had shown a prowess that he'd never revealed before. The picture was almost impossible. Everywhere I looked my eyes met vignettes of fear and fury. Men hacked limbs from women; dogs tore at the throats of screaming children; a piebald stallion stomped a bloody old man; a boy battered a gray kitten; a teen-aged girl cut the throat of an infant; a gryphon, its beak speckled with grume, fed on a struggling redheaded man; a monstrous snake, its scales reflecting the light like shards of glass, crushed a bawling calf in its coils.

Nor was the violence confined to the mall; the brownstones had their share of atrocities. Writhing forms filled the roofs and windows. Bodies were hurled from the heights along with furniture, bricks, crockery and steaming water. Two combatants, their hands fastened about each other's throats, plunged through space oblivious of their imminent doom. Even the trees held warring birds. At the base of one elm a tattered newspaper lay. Its two-line heading read: *Oh cursed be thou, devouring grave,/Whose jaws eternal victims crave.* A lemur, its stomach agape, dripped blood upon the words from a branch above. And over everything, the lurid, fluctuating light prevailed.

"What's the source of that light?" I asked.

"Ha! It's God," Benjamin said. "He's returning to heaven after hatching the egg. You'll notice He leaves his offspring behind."

"But how have you produced it? I've nothing on my palette like that."

He laughed and clapped me on the back. "A trade secret. And I don't grind my own paints, bear in mind."

Leo, his eyes still fixed immovably on the painting, remarked softly, "I've never seen anything like it."

"There isn't anything like it," I said. "Signorelli, Pollaiuolo—perhaps there is a resemblance to their works or to the 'Last Judgment,' but there is nothing that is really like it. A towering achievement, Benjamin, far better than your previous best. The drawing is as near perfection as a man could get. The lineaments, the faces, the fall of the garments are all truly marvelous. And the eyes! As minute as they are, they're alive. It's a masterpiece in the highest sense. I wish I'd done it. The figure of Death, alone, would testify to your genius. All those dynamic poses, all that movement—why, you have left nothing for the rest of us to invent."

"It's true," Leo said. "You have brought something new into the world—new and immeasurably strong. It's flawless. The color is brilliant and the drawing so smooth and precise that I am very envious. If you continue like this, we'll all look pretty tawdry."

"You are approaching the divine," I said. "Where it differs from nature, nature is at fault."

Benjamin smiled but did not reply. His eyes were very bright. I think he might have wept if we'd said more.

All afternoon we sat around drinking and talking. Now and again we would wander from the living room back to the studio to have another look at "The Birth of Death" while Benjamin would describe a particular difficulty that he had encountered or a particular moment of inspiration that took hold of him during the painting's creation. The day wore on and the room darkened eerily. The flat, freckled face of Death became still more compelling and the tortured figures yet more frightful. One woman reminded me of Masaccio's Eve. My ears waited for her cry of anguish.

Danielle prepared an elaborate dinner, the main course being a French dish composed of grains of pasta embellished with lamb and chicken and a delicious sauce. There were side dishes of red cabbage, cauliflower and spinach, and at the end, a fine cheese and apricot tarts. We ate like children at a birthday party.

"Well," Benjamin said when we had finished, "this has been a good day. I have heard things I never really believed I'd hear. Yet in all modesty I must say that I agree with you. After all, twelve hundred beautiful creations on a cloth no bigger than a pillowcase—that is not a mean feat. I have decided that I will not sell it for less than ten thousand dollars. Fifteen months of my life I've given it. I will keep it rather than take less."

Leo and I both agreed; it was such a remarkable accomplishment, we never doubted that it would find a buyer.

Later in the evening, when both Leo and Benjamin were at the other end of the apartment, Danielle asked in a low voice, "What do you think of it?"

"Your Benjamin is a very great painter," I replied.

"Yes, but that one is a bad picture. It is full of evil and the Devil himself is in it. He should paint beautiful pictures, beautiful people—not dirty beasts and *horreur*. He should paint like you and Leo. You tell him, eh?"

"No one can tell a painter what to paint, Danielle."

"He thinks it will bring us much money," she said, her dark eyes troubled, "but such a terrible *tableau* can bring only the bad luck. No money is better than bad money. You know, I have gypsy blood in my body. That is not a good picture." Her worried gaze shifted to the open door through which, two rooms beyond, we could see the slim body of Faber and the bulk of Littleboy. Between them, the electric light causing it to gleam, stood the painting. Even at that distance I could feel its madness. A chill passed through me. I refilled my glass.

43 &

"ONE OF my clients passed on yesterday," Mr. Beels said to me this morning. "That is the way with life. One day you discover that you have used up all your time."

What a tiresome prattler the man is. I try my best to avoid him but he's ubiquitous. There's no escaping his benefits, annuities and paid-up policies.

And his talk of time running out—what drivel! I'll have eternity, yet. But he bears watching.

44 &

LITTLEBOY INVITED various dealers to his home to see "The Birth of Death." All thought it a very fine performance but only one made a firm offer for it, and since his price was only a fraction of what Benjamin demanded, the painting remained in the studio. The next time I saw it, it was framed in ebony with a gold liner and hung in the center of the wall—a most striking picture that never failed to send a chill down my spine.

"I don't care if it ever sells," he told me. "It's my glory. Someday, after I'm gone, it will go for a million dollars. The dealers will bay like wolves at the sight of it. And after that it will have its own room in the Met or the Louvre."

Danielle confided that he had left off painting for a while but that he still toured the streets looking for treasure. Indeed, I met him one day standing in a doorway on Massachusetts Avenue. It was raining and very cold and he appeared thoroughly draggled. Over a cup of coffee he told me of a plan he had for a new painting. It was to be called "Cosmogony" and would surpass even his "Birth of Death."

"It will reveal everything," he said.

His face was flabby and his color poor but he spoke cheerfully enough until I tried to give him some money. He grew annoyed, then, and made some sharp remarks that angered me. I left him in front of Horticultural Hall; neither of us was in the best of humor. It was a couple of months before I saw him again. He was sitting outside the library.

"I've lost my touch," he complained. "It's all clumsy and labored."

"It happens to everybody," I said.

"It's never been this bad with me. I can't get back my rhythm. I want to start in on my 'Cosmogony' but I can't get going. Danielle wants a happy picture and this will be it. I've got it all blocked out in my head but my brush is like a barge pole. It'll come though and it'll be beautiful. Those who look at it will hear music—celestial melodies." He smiled but his eyes were worried. There was a stubble of beard on his jutting chin and his clothes were badly wrinkled. I was distressed to see him looking so shabby but there really was nothing I could do.

45 ❧

AS THERE were no suitable quarters for the elegant gallery my wife envisioned, she and her friends were soon discussing alternative plans. There was an excellent building for sale on Berkeley Street but the price was high and it would require some remodeling. Moreover, she had bought a Mercedes in the summer and a jaguar coat in the fall, and though by no means destitute, she was a little afraid to go deeper into her capital at that time. Someone suggested New York as a possible site and she took to it immediately. When I refused to even consider moving there, we had a quarrel. From then on, there was always a coolness between us. We treated each other with forbearance but rarely with cordiality.

Victor came to Boston twice that winter. I was astonished to see the deference paid to him by the local collectors. When he spoke, all heads turned toward him like heliotropes toward the sun. Wealthy men like Baxter Sawyer and Irving Gammage followed him about everywhere and Todhurst was hardly less attentive. All asked his opinion. If some work attributed to a master but lacking credentials was due to be put up for sale, Darius was besieged. If he said it was genuine, the bidding was sure to be furious.

But with all his new celebrity, he never ceased praising and encouraging me. Almost my entire production was sold through him. If I had a complaint, it was that I had nothing left to sell in my own country. Great as my reputation might be on the other side of the Atlantic, few knew me here. Veronica and I made plans to go to Europe and visit some of my benefactors, but, unfortunately, this trip, too, was canceled. At the

last moment Victor came up with a commission for a financier's chapel in Switzerland. As the work would have made it
necessary to greatly curtail our tour, we thought it best to
wait until the next summer.

On one of these winter visits I asked Darius to have a look
at Littleboy's picture.

"It's a tour de force. You must see it," I urged him. "Luca
Signorelli's 'End of the World' isn't as strong, I swear it. It has
all the versatility and ingenuity of a Rembrandt etching but
in glowing colors. Come see it. You will not be disappointed."

He was thumbing through some of my pen-and-ink drawings and he smiled. "What is it this time? Sodom and Gomor-
rah? The destruction of Sennacherib? Or, perhaps, the pit of
hell? Your friend is an excellent draughtsman and a fine anat-
omist, but really, my clients won't buy monsters and allegory.
No, a 'Hercules at the Feet of Omphale' or the 'Rape of
Lucrece' is more their style. You see how well Faber does
with his maids in the meadow." He looked up and laughed.
"Modern man wants no part of horror. He has lost the religious
and philosophic beliefs necessary to cope with it." Then, returning to the drawings, he asked, "Who are these gentlemen—Aristotle and Alexander?"

"Agamemnon and Achilles," I said. All further attempts to
lure him to Littleboy's were fruitless. He parried my arguments
gracefully but adamantly.

Great, then, was my surprise when Benjamin came to me
several months later and told me that Darius had bought "The
Birth of Death" for two thousand dollars. I was delighted to
hear of it but puzzled by my English friend's erratic behavior.
I had seen him only a few days before and he had made no
mention of his decision.

"He took just one look at it and offered me two thousand.
I wanted more, but he said that though it was worth more,
that was as much as he could offer at this time. He might be
able to do better, he said, if I was willing to wait, but I am

tired of waiting. I took the cash and let the credit go. It may be a foot in the door," Benjamin said.

He handed me a bottle of brandy, which I opened at once. I drank to his success and he to mine. Danielle had put the money in a bank but not before she'd bought her husband a new suit and a fancy sport shirt, and these garments, together with the pleased expression on his broad face, did much to improve his appearance.

After a few drinks he became pensive. "I'll probably never see it again. That saddens me."

"Ah, now," I said, "you'll come across it at the Tate someday."

This made him smile. "Maybe. But I do miss it. I was very close to that painting—very, very close."

"You'll do plenty of others," I said, refilling his glass. "When you reach Titian's age, you'll forget what this one looked like."

"I'll drink to that," he replied, chuckling.

46 ❧

RANDOLPH IS really a very bright little boy. Today, during the course of some buffoonery, I asked him if he could cross his eyes.

"I suppose I could," he said, his mouth on the verge of a mischievous grin, "but it's not right."

"Not right? Why is that?" I asked, all unsuspecting.

"You're not allowed to cross your i's. You're suppose to dot your i's and cross your t's. Ha, ha! Didn't they ever teach you anything at school?" he bellowed triumphantly. "You don't know your ABC's. You dot i's and j's and cross t's and x's."

He began to jump up and down on the pavement, filling the air with scornful laughter, but this frantic performance came to a quick end when he discovered that his root beer drops were flying from his pocket in all directions. He sobered at once and began gathering his scattered horde. "See what you made me do?" he said.

"Well," I answered mildly, "they are drops, you know."

He gave me a quick little smile.

47 ह॰

FOLLOWING THE death of Mitya the cat, I went to the library and read all I could find on strychnine. This deadly substance, I learned, is derived from the seeds of certain trees which are native to Cochin China and adjacent areas, and of these trees the most important is one called *Strychnos Nux Vomica*. It is of moderate size and has a thick, usually twisted trunk and ovate leaves. The flowers are tubular in shape and greenish-white in color while the fruit is no bigger than a lemon and consists of hard skin, white pulp and one or more disclike seeds.

The poison, strychnine, was first extracted from these seeds by two Frenchmen, Pelletier and Caventou, in the early part of the nineteenth century. It is an alkaloid, crystallizes in the rhombic system and has a melting point of 290 degrees centigrade. Three grains of the stuff will kill a grown man. A grain was originally equivalent to a grain of wheat. There are four hundred and eighty grains in a single ounce. This iota of poison will terminate the workings of an organism as large and complex as a human being in less than half an hour. It is a colorless, crystalline substance with a bitter taste.

The descriptions of its effects agreed well with my observations of Mitya's expiration. Ten or fifteen minutes after its ingestion the strychnine strikes; fifteen minutes later its victim perishes. During that brief period the body is racked with spasms of agony, the face wears a frightful smile and the eyes an expression of the most awful terror. It did not seem like an easy method of ceasing to exist.

48 ઠ્ૐ

ONE SUNDAY afternoon I met Benjamin, Danielle and Charlemagne in the Public Garden. Danielle was wearing a bright green dress and a broad straw hat and was obviously very happy. Charlemagne, resplendent in a lavender shirt and a yachting cap, toddled along with one chubby hand firmly gripping the stroller that his mother was pushing. Walking a pace or two behind them, Benjamin was quite the staid, respectable head of the family. He had undergone a haircut and his shoes were polished.

We sat together on a bench and talked for an hour or more, mostly about Charlemagne. Danielle made some incredible claims for the child's sagacity while her husband winked behind her back. I had little experience in such matters but it did seem that the boy, who was less than two, spoke very well.

Benjamin said that his painting was still giving him trouble but that it appeared to be improving a little. He had abandoned the "Cosmogony" for the time and was doing a small tempera of his wife and son. Danielle insisted that it was a beautiful picture, but he said it was without grace and "stiff as a Byzantine mosaic."

I had to leave them to go home and bathe and dress for a cocktail party that a Daughter of the American Revolution was giving at her cultural bastion in Louisburg Square.

"Don't let them lionize you," Benjamin cautioned. "And watch that high living, sonny. Remember what happened to Raphael."

I felt very happy about meeting them. It was delightful to see them outside the walls of their murky apartment and in the sunshine.

49 ͗

THE FIRST big opening of the new season occurred in the middle of October of that year and featured some puerile representations of the Berkshires by a Worcester woman whose husband was a celebrated writer of historical romances. My wife compelled me to accompany her to this gala, much against my wishes. There were two large rooms packed with overdressed ladies and stoic husbands. So brightly illuminated was the place, and so saturated with cigarette smoke was the air, that my eyes were watering five minutes after I came in the door. Veronica quickly disappeared into the gabbling horde. After a cursory look at the three nearest pictures I edged my way out into the hall. It was crowded there, too, but not so much so, and a cool, fresh breeze from an open window relieved the atmosphere.

"Have you heard of de Reyna's auto-da-fé?" someone beside me asked.

I turned. It was a man named Hartley—an art critic for a local paper.

"I'm not one of his circle," I replied.

"Nor am I," Hartley said. He was a blond man with a birthmark the size of a penny on one cheek. His voice was dulcet though tinged with mockery. "It took place at his birthday party —a Friday evening, the eighth. I received an invitation, so I went. Haven't you heard anything about it? Personally, I thought the General made an ass of himself, but his hangers-on thought it the height of hilarity."

"Oh? What happened?" I asked, but with no real desire to know.

"You haven't seen your friend Littleboy, then? Well, at the peak of this grand affair Jorge asked everyone to join him in the garden. He wished 'to present a small entertainment,' as he put it. It was mild that night. Earlier in the evening they had cooked a suckling pig over the barbecue pit. When we were all assembled, we saw that the fire in the pit was now out but something square in shape and covered with a cloth was fastened to the spit. A spotlight attached to one of the trees was directed on this object; it drew all eyes. You've been there, haven't you?"

"Just once, but I remember the garden. What's Littleboy got to do with it?"

"Wait. The General walked over to the barbecue pit and then made a little speech. 'Tonight I am unveiling my latest acquisition,' he began in that pompous way of his. Then, after a couple of heavy pleasantries, he said, 'I have bought a painting by a pig. You have heard of paintings by chimpanzees, I'm sure. There is even an abstractionist in New York who is said to have a snake as a collaborator. He dips the poor creature into a pot of enamel and lets him slither across a piece of masonite, and another masterpiece is born.' There was some laughter at this. 'But I am the first to have a painting by a swine. Yes, a swine, and here it is,' he said, and with a theatrical sweep he yanked the cloth away. Do you know what was there?"

I shook my head in bewilderment.

"It was one of Littleboy's paintings," Hartley said. "It was neatly wired to the spit. Every detail was clearly visible in the glare of the spotlight. It was a mad, strange thing with a devil coming out of an egg. But quite marvelous. There were some murmurs, while those in the rear strove to improve their positions. Those who knew Littleboy's work quickly shared their knowledge with those who didn't. All of them knew of Littleboy's practical joke in Copley Square.

"Then de Reyna went on. 'I am told,' he said, 'that it took the pig a year to do this thing. Was it not clever of him? A whole year. Who could imagine that a pig would have such powers of concentration? But, alas, there is no place in the world of art for hogs, I'm afraid. Here is the place for such animals.' He indicated the fireplace. 'And so, in the interest of aesthetics, we shall roast our second pig of the evening.' With that, he struck a match and dropped it into the pit. A vivid blue flame burst forth and enveloped the canvas in coils of fire. There was a gasp, followed by a little half-hearted applause. The painted figures—and there must have been hundreds of them—melted before our eyes, and in a few moments the thing was gone. One of the General's flunkies doused the fire and the still-burning stretcher. I was told that what was left was mailed to Littleboy the next morning. Then the old boy clasped his hands before him in a prayerlike attitude, smiled benevolently and said, 'What is a year in the life of a swine?' It got a few laughs but not too many. I thought it was rather sick, myself."

I began to move toward the door.

"Did you ever see the painting?" Hartley asked as he followed me through the press. "It was the best thing he's ever done. Absolutely brilliant. I never knew he could paint that way. I think de Reyna might rue the day he destroyed it."

Hartley's voice grew less audible as we became separated. "Don't behave foolishly, now," he cautioned from afar. The remark proved unnecessary. I had seen de Reyna leave as Veronica and I arrived. It was Littleboy I was going to.

50 &

I RECALL that night and its events with great clarity. A nearly full moon floated above Copley Square, and though shifting cirrus clouds occasionally crossed its face, the area was flooded with bright argentine light. In the east, the brown stone of Trinity Church was now pallid, while across from it, the Bella Pratt bronze ladies, their faces concealed by the shadows of their cowls, sat before the bulk of the library like monolithic sentries before a barrow. Moonlight bleached everything. The wind had grown sharp. I fastened the top button of my coat and hastened my pace. Just beyond the Square, on the corner of Blagden Street, Benjamin stood looking up at the moon. I was startled by his sudden appearance. It was preternatural. Moreover, he looked like a ghost in that etiolated glow.

"Tycho Brahe, I presume," I called to him.

He turned quickly, then seeing me, smiled. "Ah, Herr Kepler. I was just checking the moon to see if any craters have blown away in the wind. I like to look at the moon. It's great fun. Now and then I give a little howl—nothing boisterous or obstreperous, you understand. You look sad." He studied me for a moment. "You were coming to see me, eh? Something in your eyes tells me that you have heard of de Reyna's revenge or 'The Peruvian Tragedy,' a water-closet drama featuring a hecatomb in hexameter."

"Just tonight," I replied. "Did Darius buy it for him?"

"Sure, what else? He didn't buy it because he liked it." He spoke without rancor.

"That was not . . ." I began, but I got no further. A surge of anger and sorrow stopped the words in my throat.

Benjamin patted me on the shoulder. "Don't be sad. It was an unlucky picture. Danielle was right. Let's walk. This wind is too much. You don't have to reproach yourself; I'm the one who made the mistake. I'm like that other trusting soul—the one who said, 'If anyone's looking for me, Judas, I'll be down in the garden.'"

I made an effort to laugh at this sally. We walked in silence for a while, along Huntington Avenue. The flimsy clouds tore across the heavens like frightened birds.

"Was it completely ruined?" I asked at last.

"Yes, except for a few threads of canvas and a rat."

"A rat?"

"Yes, a black one in the extreme left-hand corner. He was meant to be looking out at the scene from the edge of the frame. He was the only sane figure in the thing. He was supposed to represent me." Littleboy laughed harshly. "Strange how he survived. His edges were charred and the paint near him was blistered but he was quite intact. Not for long, though. I smashed the stretcher, and it and the rat became ashes in my own fireplace. I have to give that braying ass credit, much as I hate to. He got my Althaea's brand. Ah well. Time heals all wounds, as Robespierre remarked when the blade of the guillotine caught him in the back of the neck. Let's get a cup of coffee at the Hamilton."

In the fluorescent light of the cafeteria, Benjamin's weariness was very evident. We sat near a window which rattled with every gust of wind.

"One day, when business picks up," he said as he stirred his coffee, "I'm going to make a large chryselephantine statue of a rat. There are so many statues of men, but aside from a few netsukes, none of rats. And rats and men are very similar. Have I ever mentioned that before?"

"Once or twice," I answered, trying to get into the spirit of the thing.

"It bears repeating. They are the only animals that fight wars of extermination among their own kind. Rats and men are brothers, make no mistake. Ever seen a baby rat? They're hairless and the flesh is the same color and texture as that of a Caucasian baby. What's more, rats are smart. Any farmer will tell you how hard it is to destroy them. They learn to avoid traps and to shun poisoned food. There is some evidence, too, that they can pass on what they learn to their offspring, even as we do.

"They're fine swimmers. I read somewhere that they can stay underwater for three or four minutes, if they have to. They can run as swiftly and climb as tenaciously as almost any member of the animal world, and are only caught by their foes when there is absolutely no means of escape. And then what a fight they'll put up! But usually they rely upon invisibility as a defense. They hide. A region may contain swarms of them but you'll never see a one. Only at night will they move about, and very cautiously even then. Still, they're fierce in the face of enemies and merciless to their victims." Benjamin sipped his coffee and stared out the window.

"I thought you liked rats," I said. "How can you slander them by making them human?"

"I do like them. They don't pretend to be more than they are. Rats are cruel and rapacious but they are not so without reason. Men are something else again. But why talk of men? It's the rat who will one day take over the world. Nothing can stop them. They can eat anything; they reproduce with amazing frequency and have big litters; their stamina enables them to survive in the very worst circumstances; and they are intrepid explorers. They've gone all over the world, usually aboard the ships of man and in the face of his bitter hostility. What other animal can boast such accomplishments? Do you know that even before men got there, there were rats on the Galapagos Islands? They were the only mammals there, except for bats who flew there. They must have crossed half the Pacific on broken tree limbs. Not a bad feat of navigation, eh?

"There are two kinds, the black rat and the brown or Norway rat. They think both of them came from Central Asia. That's where man came from, too, they say. The black rat got to Europe around the fourteenth century and his brown cousin a few centuries later. The brown one is bigger, stronger and more ferocious than the other and soon exterminates him when they meet. There aren't many black rats left now. I've got a good engraving of a black rat in a zootomy book but I suppose my statue will have to be of a brown one if I want to do it from life. I don't know what pose I should use. I've seen rats use their forepaws just like hands. How would something like that be?" He grinned at me.

"Formidable! You could have him winding his watch," I said.

We parted at West Newton Street near midnight. The flimsy clouds had fled the sky, leaving the moon, an eccentric unblinking eye, gazing dispassionately down upon Boston. It seemed to me that my friend was accepting his misfortunes with admirable fortitude. Nonetheless, I decided to write Darius in the morning and ask for an explanation of his behavior.

Veronica was preparing for bed when I reached home. She was angry because I had left without her, and my attempts at explanation and apology did little to assuage this anger.

IN REPLY to my letter, Victor wrote as follows: "I really had no idea that I was being used as a pawn in this game of vengeance. His wife asked me to buy the painting for her and I did. That, after all, is one of my professional functions—and by no means the least in order of importance. I do recall your telling me of the incident at the outdoor show but I'm afraid I attached no significance to it at the time. The General's action was quite Machiavellian and not to be excused but it was impossible for me to foresee. Nor do I feel that it is my responsibility to go deeply into the motives behind a client's purchase. How can I? Still, I can understand that the entire episode has been most disagreeable for Littleboy and I shall offer him an apology when next we meet. Mix-ups of this sort are forever happening in this business, but you can't allow yourself to become soppy over them." He went on to tell me of a new commission.

I was not pleased with this reply. He knew perfectly well that de Reyna hated Littleboy; it was the subject of several conversations in which he took part. I remember his once saying that de Reyna had done much for Littleboy's fame by quarreling with him. I knew, too, that Victor was eager to sell de Reyna a pair of Landseers that the General liked and that they often lunched together.

Five or six weeks later Darius came to Boston and I made it clear to him that I thought him guilty of cheap opportunism. He shrugged, made a sarcastic reply and walked away from me. We were at the opening of a pre-Columbian artifacts show at the museum. I followed him across the room to a group of dealers and repaid his mordant remark with one of my own. Obviously afraid of a scene, he offered me a few mollifying words but I was not to be appeased. Veronica tried to calm me. It was not until I had delivered myself of some loud, strong and caustic opinions, however, that I was willing to be led away.

52 &

"I DON'T think I've lost it. I've just misplaced it. I can't paint at the moment, but it will come back," Benjamin said. He was sitting on the sandstone steps of his house, his face as sallow as old ivory and his hair badly in need of a trim. There was a huge greasy gray spot on the knee of his pants and he was staring over my left shoulder with great concentration. He seemed to be avoiding my eyes. "No matter. I'm a streetcomber. You've heard of beachcombers? Well, I'm a streetcomber—which is what you become after you've served your apprenticeship as a money-looker." He laughed. "Do you know that when it is windy you will never find a dollar bill in the gutter? Under hedges or at the base of a fence is where they'll be. Snow is good, at least when it begins to thaw. People drop coins into drifts, especially around the parking meters. Their fingers are cold. Rain is a help, too. It makes coins shine. My eyes have become so sharp I can see a dime in the street from half a block away. You have to look out for chewing gum, though. When it's wet it can look like a nickel or a quarter. I guess the stuff is indestructible because you see little round bits of it all over.

"Nobody cares about money today. I think some of them

would rather leave a dime on the ground than go to the trouble of picking it up. Really. Everyone is wealthy. Who knows? The day may come when society will be glad to have streetcombers to keep the thoroughfares from becoming cluttered with derelict money. I might have to join a union. But you think I'm deranged, don't you?" His eyes slid by my face as he shifted his gaze to the space over my other shoulder.

"No more than when I first met you," I said. "Have you found that roll of bills that you've been dreaming about?"

"With the clothespin? No, not yet. You never dream, do you? I dream so much that sometimes I'm exhausted when I wake up. I dream in bright, gaudy colors like poster paints. And always of money. Crazy kinds of money. Last night I was in a room filled with shiny denarii. No kidding. I was knee-deep in them and they were clean and velvety to the touch. The heads of Caesars were all about me in glittering mounds. Another night gold Napoleons rained down on me, bouncing off my head and body. But they didn't hurt. They were like snowflakes. About a week ago I dreamt that I opened my bathroom door and found the tub full of ten-dollar bills. What a disappointment it was to awaken and find the tub empty.

"But the best dream came on Thanksgiving night. I was in a huge stone vault, seated at an enormous refectory table that was piled with sparkling coins. I was counting this treasure and calling out the amounts to somebody at the other end of the room. It was mostly gold and silver but there were pieces of brass, copper, bronze and nickel as well. Really crazy money. I'd say, 'Eighteen mohurs,' or 'Nine cruzeiros,' or 'Twenty-six obols,' or 'Five bani,' or 'Twelve chervonets.' It was so beautiful and so real. There were marks, sovereigns, florins, rupees, drachmas, zlotys, moidors, shekels, yen, satang, lire, pesos and many others that I can no longer remember. I was sorry to open my eyes that morning, too."

"Such dreams," I said, "must portend a prosperous future,

Benjamin. But you must try to paint again, no matter what difficulties you encounter."

"No," he said. "Someday, but not now."

"Then at least draw," I urged, trying to look into his eyes. "You can't surrender to a spell of bad luck."

"I have no time. I couldn't do it even if I wanted to. 'The Birth of Death' consumed me. I must go now. Will you walk down to the Square with me?"

He had little more to say after that. I crossed Dartmouth Street and he continued down toward Newbury. His good-bye was a small wave of his hand. Not once had he looked directly into my face, and this frightened me.

53 ⁊

I WALKED down to Faber's today but he wasn't home. The lady next door said that he'd gone to Vermont. He has a place near Windsor, up there. I had a sudden desire to talk to him. Sometimes I become anxious about the whole scheme. I know that it would be impossible to confide completely in Leo, but it would comfort me just to talk to him a little.

Mr. Beels invited me to his apartment. He lives only a few doors down the street. I refused. He is either a maniac or some sort of shady confidence man.

My reveries have regained their strength. The day before yesterday I was in ancient Lydia all afternoon. They were preparing to fight the Persians and everyone was excited. The sights and sounds were clear as crystal.

I think the expression on the face of the Bourg Angel is not what it was. The line of the mouth is different.

Mr. Barletty has asked me not to play the phonograph so loudly, and I told him that I rarely play the thing at all. Mrs. Chakamoulian is up to her old tricks. I can't afford to have the police coming to visit me, though, so I'd best be on my good behavior.

Barletty should stop bothering me and pay some attention to the vestibule. The tile is practically gray and this morning there was an empty cigarette packet in one of the corners.

54 ࡥ

TWO DAYS after that meeting with Benjamin a boy brought me a note from Danielle saying that he was dead. When I got to St. Botolph Street a police car was parked outside the dismal tenement and a group of subdued, whispering people moved aimlessly about the sidewalk.

Danielle rushed into my arms, sobbing convulsively. Near the front window a barrel-chested patrolman sat with a black notebook in his hands and a sad look upon his face.

"He has hanged himself," she said shrilly. "I have tried to help him, you understand. He is too heavy and he is dead now. The policeman tried but they cannot make him breathe. I couldn't hold him up. I screamed very loud but no one hears."

I patted her back and spoke soothingly to her and in time she grew calmer. Finally she sighed loudly, crossed her arms before her chest and sat down on the sofa. An elderly lady came in from the kitchen and handed her a cup of hot tea. The bedroom door was closed; I knew he was in there. When I opened it, the last rays of the cold winter sun were escaping through the window. Benjamin lay on his back on the bed, cloaked in the resulting gloom. I turned on the lamp. His eyes were closed but no one would ever think that he was only asleep. Splotches of pink, of pallor and of eggplant purple maculated his face. The rope was gone but extravasated blood had wrought a broad wale two thirds of the way around his neck, and this cruel bruise, clear as it was, was further delineated by a border of abraded flesh. His lips were blue and unnaturally thick. Between them I could see the white of one of his teeth. His hands were at his sides, the palms up and speckled with rash. I touched his cheek. It was not cold but neither did it hold the heat of life. His shirt—faded green in color—was torn; his trousers were covered with dust. His cuffs were down, his shoes off. There were holes in the toes of his black socks. I began to weep.

That evening, after Leo arrived, Danielle told the story. By then the police had taken Benjamin away. The law required an autopsy in cases of suicide, they said. The elderly neighbor had taken Charlemagne, and Danielle would go there later to sleep. The apartment was cool and filled with shadows, like a tomb. Danielle was abnormally tranquil and looked very pale. The life seemed to have gone out of her eyes, and when she spoke, it was in the voice of an old woman. Leo had called her doctor in and he had given her some sleeping pills to take later. We got food from a delicatessen but she wouldn't touch it. Neither of us asked to hear the story. Apparently she felt a compulsion to go over it all.

"If nobody else knows, you must know. You were his great friends. You must know," she said.

Early that morning Littleboy had left the house to search the streets of Brookline for money. He had been cheerfully confident and expected to find a few dollars, since Brookline was a wealthy community. He found only seventy cents, but when he returned for lunch, he did not seem dejected. He had also found a thin chain which he thought was gold. After playing with Charlemagne for a while, he left once more, saying that he was going to take the chain to a jeweler on Boylston Street and then walk around Beacon Hill.

Some time after four o'clock Danielle heard a strange scraping noise outside her apartment door. She looked into the hallway but saw nothing. The rasping sound occurred at regular intervals and came from the floor above. The apartment on that floor was vacant. The old man who lived there had been taken to City Hospital about a month before, and Danielle, though not timid, wasn't eager to investigate. Then she heard a grunt. Leaving her door wide, she crept to the staircase and looked up. The stairs doubled back upon themselves but through the balusters she saw her husband's legs and feet swinging in the air. She screamed and ran up the stairs.

Later that night Leo and I looked at this place. The feeble lighting revealed a hole in the ceiling above the staircase, and it was to a plaster-whitened rafter in this cavity that Benjamin had tied his rope. How he had done it was not clear. Leo thought that he had used an old broom that was nearby, to guide it over the beam. The other end of the rope he made into a crude noose, which he put around his neck. Then he stepped off the top step into the void. But having done this, he immediately changed his mind. The noise that attracted his wife was the sound of his fingernails seeking purchase on the wall, which came into reach at the end of each swing of his body. We could see these pathetic scratches in the dirty plaster.

When Danielle turned the bend in the stairway, she saw Benjamin looking down at her with fear-filled eyes. His head was bent forward and to one side and his face was scarlet. She took hold of his legs and tried to lift him while he took hold of the rope above him and strained to raise himself. But he weighed more than two hundred pounds and their efforts were complicated by his frantic struggling for air and her overwhelming terror. Together they succeeded in getting him up a few inches, but the loop remained tight about his throat and each time he freed a hand to loosen it, his body would drop again to the end of the rope. Try as she might, she couldn't hold him up alone. Each of these falls was accompanied by a sickening thud as the hemp tore into the flesh, muscle and bone of the neck. Whenever her exertions allowed, she screamed for help. None came. Charlemagne, who had been sleeping, wandered out into the hall to see what was happening, but the sight of his father hanging from the ceiling and his mother shrieking at the top of her lungs soon sent him scurrying back into the apartment.

From time to time Benjamin forced an agonized groan from his constricted throat. His wife at last abandoned her efforts to lift him and sought to push him back to where he could get his feet on the top step. On the first attempt, she almost succeeded. He was able to place the soles of his feet firmly on the landing, and Danielle below him pushed with all her strength to raise him to a perpendicular position. The rope became slack and Benjamin's fingers worked desperately to get it off. But even as he tugged at the noose, the leather of his shoes slid smoothly from the wood of the landing. Danielle clung to his shirt but the cloth ripped; his heavy form brushed her aside and swung out once again over the staircase. After that she was never able to get his feet back on the step. The strength had gone out of his legs.

By this time she was no longer sane. Her shrieks had brought no one. The red in Benjamin's face was rapidly darkening. She ran down the stairs to the apartment and ran back up with a kitchen chair. It proved useless. Set on the stairs, the seat was too low, and when she put it on the landing, she couldn't get his feet to stay on it. She saw then that his eyes had closed. When she tried once more to raise him, she discovered that his legs were limp and lifeless.

Tearing her hair and screeching, she fled down the stairs to the street. Wildly she banged on the door of the barber shop on the ground floor, but it was Wednesday and the place was closed. A man driving by, however, heard her cries and got out and went to her. Unable to speak coherently, she led him up the stairs, but lacking a ladder, they were still powerless to get him down. It was only after the arrival of the police several minutes later that the rope was cut and the noose taken from his neck. It was too late. A respirator and a tank of oxygen were unable to revive him.

Faber thought that the final fall had pushed the knot of the rope into a position that closed the windpipe totally, and that once that happened, death by suffocation followed in a few minutes.

"A beautiful man," Danielle said, sighing, "but very, very crazy."

55 ঌ

NOT MUCH went right after that.

56 ঌ

FOR A long time after Benjamin's death I didn't want to see people. I couldn't bear to look at them—anyone, people I knew, strangers, my wife, Leo. I rushed to my studio early each morning and did not return until dark. I worked all day long, with few moments of rest. I did not even like to go to the restaurant for lunch because of the people I would see there. I skirted the Public Garden to avoid the mothers and the children and walked the street with eyes averted. When for unavoidable reasons I had to speak to people, I found my tongue oddly awkward. My brain deserted my vocal cords; I became asphasiac.

The thought of God took possession of my brain. One day I flew into a rage when Veronica came into my room and interrupted my meditations.

But this terrible period lasted only five or six weeks. Gradually I returned to normal. I thought less of Him and no longer fell into trances. My repugnance for people lessened greatly, too, and I went occasionally to Leo's.

Though I had refused to accept any new commissions from Darius, I finished some things that I had agreed to do before the de Reyna betrayal. My wife sought to bring about a reconciliation but I would have none of it. Before the rupture in our relations Victor had obtained a fine piece of white marble from Penteicus, and since I had paid him for it, I kept it. From it, I fashioned a flagellated Jesus that was very strong. Unfortunately, the face of this Christ—much against my wishes —wore a very crafty expression.

One day I tipped over a jar of varnish and ruined a chalk drawing that I had done years before. It was a rather charming head of a middle-aged woman and I was saddened by its loss. The annihilation of Littleboy's picture sprang into my mind and gave me a sudden insight into the true nature of art and the futility of the artist's quest. Just how long, thought I, can a painting hope to survive? Or a piece of bronze or stone, for that matter? Modern science might preserve the "Night Watch" for two or three thousand years, and the Hypostyle of Karnak might endure ten times this period, but where will they both be a million years from now? Where will Ghiberti's doors be? Where will Michelangelo's Moses sit? On whose wall will the "Concert Champêtre" hang? And if by chance an artist could devise some work that might last a million years, could he make one that would live a billion years? And in our universe a billion years is no more than the twinkling of an eye. What then, I asked myself, is the point of it all? One might as well make sand pictures, as the Japanese do, pictures that can be dispelled by a breath of wind. What did anything matter?

In the weeks that followed this incident I found it increasingly difficult to concentrate on my labors as their utter futility became increasingly apparent. Each man seeks to be immortal. Most satisfy this desire by fathering children. Some—the soldiers and politicians—strive to live on in legend. Others—the men of business—find their hope of eternal life in the perpetuity of houses of commerce and great fortunes. Of all, however, it is the artist who is most greedy in this respect. He it is who is most conscious of eternity and most eager for everlasting fame. Only he attempts to challenge God by creating that which has never existed before and may, if his work perishes, never exist again. Only he and God can produce beauty. Only he and God can make a world. Only he can compete with the Deity in matters of intellect and sensibility.

But the artist cannot win, for the works of man, unlike those of God, eventually disappear and the universe retains nothing of his often incredibly arduous and brilliant endeavors. Somehow, in the course of my life, I had never paused to consider this simple truth. Maybe I accepted the fantasies of those who claim that nothing good is ever lost, that a heaven lies ready to receive the bounty of the earth and that the pictures of Cranach and Goya are there alongside those of Polygnotus and Zeuxis. I could not accept these fables now. A horror slowly came over me. The realization that all the masterpieces of the world were pitilessly doomed was a shrew in my breast that fed upon my heart.

Again all my thinking commenced to revolve around God and His justice. There were times when I longed to speak to

Him—to explain the folly and criminality of destroying beauty.
I prayed—a thing I had never done before—at home and even
at the Arlington Street Church. But I gave it up. It was nonsense, I decided. God knew perfectly well the results of His
actions. He ordained the whole miserable system, and my
modest prayers would never cause Him to alter it. I began to
wonder if He thought beauty His own special preserve and
that for this reason He would tolerate no encroachment by
man. If that were so, what iniquity it was! My mind turned to
other injustices. I brooded. I began to think of God as evil, as
an ominous Dominus Whose role was to enslave, torment and
ultimately destroy humanity. Man was the dupe of God. One
afternoon this thought penetrated my mind to such a depth that
I fell to beating myself on the face and head. My rage was
like a holocaust. "Vengeance!" I screamed to my empty studio.

I tried to discuss these enormities with Faber but he seemed
to miss the point. Being an atheist, his arguments were mere
word play. Littleboy would have understood it at once. Indeed,
his "Birth of Death," with the light of God forming a halo
about the monster of destruction, was a clear exposition of his
understanding. But Benjamin was dead, completely and utterly
so and for eternity. Heaven, hell and the immortality of the
soul meant nothing to me, and having rejected these theological
conceits, I was left with only death—real death, total death,
forever.

"What tyranny is this? I must speak with God," I would
whisper to myself. Yes, I would speak to Him and He to me.
And I would not come away without some solid answers. Not
for me the arrogant drivel that He gave to Job. Real explana-
tions—that is what I would have. No longer could I tolerate the
abasement and nullification of man.

On my easel, at this time, was a half-finished "Prometheus
Bound." I resolved to complete this one picture and never
again lay my hand to another work of art. I painted in a frenzy.

While I worked I seemed to lose consciousness. I would come to the studio in the morning and return home when it was dark, but aside from the evident progress of the painting, I knew not how my day was spent. In a week the work was done and I was startled by the figure I had wrought. It was more real than reality, more alive than life. It throbbed before my eyes. It was incandescent. Nothing I had ever done before possessed its power. A faintness came over me when I gazed at it. But it wasn't Prometheus that I had chained to the rock; it was God.

The following day I conceived the idea of a divine coup d'état. What if I wrested the scepter from this Despot's hands? What if I could snatch the throne of the Almighty and trade my blood for ichor? Mad? Possibly. But with annihilation certain in any event, what had I to lose?

57 ❧

I FINALLY caught Faber at home. I called him this morning and he had just arrived. He drove back from Vermont with one of his models and they did not arrive until one o'clock in the morning, but he seemed fresh enough when I spoke to him, so I went to his place about eleven. Many things have been bothering me lately, not the least of which is the persistence of those odious birds at my window. The noise they make is insufferable. It's termed a "coo" but I find it more like the death rattle of a drowning man. And they will not eat the poison. Moreover, I have reason to believe that they are gathering on the ledge at night. A few nights ago I was awakened by some very low, muffled sounds. It was eerie. I even imagined—and I fervently hope that it was no more than imagination—that someone or something was trying to raise the window! It was locked, of course, but what was out there? After a while I got up and looked, but there was nothing to be seen. I remained awake until morning.

Beels is another source of irritation, for he is in the Garden more and more frequently and never leaves off watching me. On one occasion I thought to reverse our roles and sat at a bench directly behind him, but my essay at espionage was swiftly foiled when the swaddled buzzard, almost as if he sensed my presence, turned his head and discovered me. A moment later Johann had wheeled him up to me and I was forced to flee those glittering green eyes, that acrid cigar smoke and that cackling voice offering me the key to affluence. And in my hurry to get away, I nearly collided with the ridiculous April Dandelion. Ah, the look she gave me! Such malevolence! These curious episodes, added to my fears of the police and the absolute evaporation of all sugar bowls in this region, have unnerved me. An hour or two with a friend, I hoped, would to some extent restore my peace of mind.

When I arrived, Leo was drinking coffee and pasting some newspaper clippings into a large scrapbook.

"That's an interesting collage," I said. "What do you call it?"

He laughed. "I call it 'Butt for an Idiot's Humor.' Do you like it?"

"But for an idiot's humor, you'd be a full butt of the wine of wit. What do you eventually do with all those bits of paper?"

"I've got trunks of the lovely things," he said, bending his tall frame over the table to pour me a cup of coffee. "Your mind is quick but you look tired. Sit down. Have you resumed working?"

"If by working you mean daubery, no. A juvenile pastime, Faber. A game, a toy—you will discover it yourself one day. Get yourself an honest job, my good fellow, and abandon your canvas-dappling ways. Farming, I am told, is an excellent profession or, perhaps, driving a taxi."

"Ha, ha. No more Mona Lisas, then? No more Leonardo portraits?" His eyes held a twinkle of sly merriment, as if we shared some droll secret.

"Not for me. The 'Mona Lisa'? What is it, after all, but a rotting plank smeared with colored dirt. And the rest are no better. All those revered masterpieces of Rembrandt, Vermeer, Raphael Sanzio, El Greco and the others—what are they really? A collection of greasy rags hung out to dry!"

"Then you are not secretly at work on a 'School of Athens' or a Sistine Chapel? You are not attempting any 'Laocoöns' or 'Borghese Warriors'? What are you up to, I wonder? You must be attacking the connoisseurs in some way."

"They are nothing to me. Less than that. My assault is on the ramparts of heaven, and if I carry them, I will do something worthwhile for you, old friend. How does being a demigod sound to you?"

"It sounds like a halfway measure. You're still working at the cryptic lore, then. The great solution still eludes you."

"For the moment, but do not scoff. It is always darkest before rosy-fingered Aurora makes her appearance."

We bantered each other in this fashion for a while and then he showed me a picture that he had done in Vermont. It was quite charming but I found it difficult to speak seriously of painting to him. I longed to talk about God, but just as I turned aside his remarks on art with raillery, he repulsed mine on religion with mockery. I had no intention of revealing everything but I did want to get his opinion on theodicy.

"Have you seen Darius lately?" he asked at one point, to my surprise.

"No," I said. "He's not likely to come near me."

"I saw him at Harrington-Worth's about a week ago. He was talking to the Governor of New Jersey."

"Was my wife there?" I asked in spite of myself.

"No, but someone did mention that she, too, was in New York. They saw her at a charity luncheon. Do you never hear from her?" His soft voice was apologetic, yet he watched me closely.

"No, nor do I want to." It was annoying to be reminded of their existence. Still, I wondered if they would come to Boston. I did not like that thought at all. At this juncture I wanted no disturbances. There seemed little chance that they would visit me, though.

We exchanged a few more remarks and then I left. As I was going out the door, Leo seemed on the point of saying something more but then appeared to change his mind. It occurred to me that some of his conversation was a little strange. He looked at me in a peculiar manner, too, but of late everyone was casting bizarre glances my way. It was nice to see him again but I derived little solace from the visit.

58 ॐ

I HAVE spent the entire day wandering in and out of restaurants in Dorchester. Before I knew it, it was growing dark and I rushed home, my stomach filled with coffee, tea and brownies. No success. I will wait a day or two and then go over to Charlestown.

The Bourg Angel seemed very shiny this morning. I'm sure I haven't polished it lately.

59 ও

AFTER BENJAMIN's death Danielle and the child went to live with her sister in New Britain, Connecticut. The sensational nature of his end soon attracted the attentions of the very dealers who rejected my friend when he was alive. One vulture, a chum of Veronica's, offered a flat sum for his entire output, but Leo, who handled the things for Danielle, declined the offer. Instead, we placed his work in the hands of Helmut Hetzel, a dealer of character and intelligence, and this proved a wise move. A great demand immediately developed. The income from only a part of these drawings and paintings has far exceeded the offer of my wife's greedy acquaintance. All Benjamin ever needed was a place to exhibit.

As for de Reyna—he outlived his victim by a scant six weeks. In the course of a burglary at his opulent residence, he was beaten to death by an eighteen-year-old Winthrop youth. He tried to destroy death but death destroyed him.

60 ও

HAVING DETERMINED to confer with God, I made a list of all the literary works that might assist me in this enterprise and then set about reading them, one after the other. An alarm clock would summon me at six in the morning, and after a hard-

boiled egg and coffee I would tear across the Garden, fearful of
losing even a moment. Before most people had left their beds,
my nose was thrust between the pages of the Old Testament or
the Zend-Avesta and it would remain there for the next five
hours. Just before noon I would rush to a nearby diner and
gobble a meager lunch. Then, after a five- or ten-minute walk,
I returned to the studio and the words of those who I hoped
would guide me into the divine presence. Rarely did I return
home before seven in the evening.

During this period I ate sparingly, as I was convinced that a
full stomach dulled the senses and slowed the mind. I lost
weight rapidly, and while never stout, I was soon as slender as
the young man from El Dorado, who "had to stand in one place
twice, to cast a shadow." Veronica called me insane. I had
discarded all social amenities. I refused to attend teas, dinners,
receptions, parties, openings, balls and the opera. I refused to
apologize to Victor Darius. I refused to go with her to her
sister's. I refused to resume painting and I refused to see a
psychiatrist. I had heard a rumor that my wife and Darius were
now more than friends and this did little to mitigate my ob-
duracy. Our quarrels were frequent; our periods of reconciliation were seldom and brief.

But all that was peripheral to my studies. I consumed books
like a raging fire in a library—the one, perchance, that Caesar
set in Alexandria. I chewed on words, swallowed sentences and
digested dicta. I engorged the wisdom of the ages, feeding on
the brains of sages. Isaiah, Guatama, Aquinas and Albertus
Magnus underwent my hungry scrutiny. St. Augustine, Pierre
Abélard and Spinoza had their turn as did Lao-tse, Kung Fu-
tse, Plato, Lucretius and Mary Baker Eddy. About me, like a
Vauban bulwark, great piles of books of varied hue and size
rose neatly from the floor. On and on I read, my mind ampli-
fied by each new thought it ingested, but my appetite unap-
peased. In the evening I haunted the public library and the
book shops on Huntington Avenue, ever in quest of new

fodder. Greeks, Jews, Chinese, Italians, Hindus, Frenchmen, Arabs and Germans were my only companions and my stern instructors in my lonely garret. Sometimes my head reeled, my mind shuddered and my overburdened brain felt as if it would crack like a porcelain cup if I filled it with any more of this boiling erudition. But I persevered pertinaciously.

Yet in spite of these titanic exertions, I could not find the clues I sought. Amongst all these words on all these pages, no tangible route to the Master of Creation could I find. There were instructions enough, to be sure, but none that gave promise of a physical confrontation. Most of the rascals could offer such an audience only after death, but like the young man from Skye, I "wanted to go to heaven, but I didn't want to die."

How I hunted! Sundays found me in churches, and Saturdays in mosques and temples. I joined societies, attended lectures, subscribed to periodicals. I argued theophany with doddering old ladies, Sivaism with intense young students from Bombay, and Shinto with perfumed gentlemen from Nippon. I prayed, I confessed, I fasted. I even had a whack at flagellation and the mortification of the flesh, but to no avail. No sign did I receive, no divine tokens, no evidence of godly notice. My hopes soared with Swedenborg—and then plummeted. Jakob Bohme followed him and was in turn followed by Madam Blavatsky as I struggled with those seductive doctrines of Theosophy, vainly hoping to be set aflame by a spark of revelation.

Where did I not search? I had my horoscope cast, went to mediums, fiddled with ouija boards and Tarot cards, bought a crystal ball and spent half a day talking to a bearded man with a Yiddish accent who claimed to be Abraham reincarnated. I pored over Fraser and other accounts of ancient beliefs. White magic, black magic, shamanism and obeah fell beneath my anxious scrutiny. I was going ga-ga over voodoo, hoodoo, juju, mumbo jumbo and similar hocus-pocus. I delved into Rosicrucianism, cabalism and vegetarianism. I tackled chiromancy, dactyliomancy and omphaloskepsis. I read Celsus with amuse-

ment and Paracelsus with amazement. I even read some
nineteenth-century Anglican sermons.

Word soon got about that I was willing to pay hard cash for
a conversation with God. Bogus proposals deluged me. I did
witness one delightful trance and a couple of genuine fits, but
God always failed to appear. This, I was told, was due to
"interference," or the fact that I was not in a "state of grace."
Of course, everything could be arranged eventually, they declared blandly, but it required time—at so much a visit. One
baldheaded old lunatic, in the course of his efforts, actually
sacrificed a live, bleating lamb on a gray marble altar in a
house on Stuart Street, and then very professionally read the
gory entrails and prayed for a divine manifestation. God didn't
come, however, and it cost me two hundred dollars and my
nearly new topcoat, which was splattered with gore. I de-
spaired. In the studio ceiling was a skylight that opened and
closed by means of a stout rope, some pulleys and a ratchet. I
fell to contemplating this length of hemp and wondering if it
would bear my weight. It was about this time, too, that I
slapped Veronica across the mouth after a particularly tem-
pestuous argument and we ceased to speak to one another
from that moment forward. But a ray of light at last pierced
the gloom.

I was reading a book on Cagliostro in my room one night.
My wife was out and the place was as silent as the moon. I
remember thinking that my eyes were tired—they often were in
those days—and that I had better put the book aside and prepare for bed. My glance became mired in a sentence that began, "The Queen disclaimed any knowledge . . ." and I read
it and reread it a number of times without deducing its sense.
Then, without any warning, I was suddenly aboard a ship.

One moment I was in my room, stretched out on my bed
with the little lamp shining over my shoulder, and the next I
was standing on a rolling deck, beneath an inconceivably purple
sky, staring out across white-flecked green water at a walled

city on the tip of a headland. The creaking of the ship's timbers
and the rhythmic chant of the rowers who, though I saw them
not, I knew to be below me, mingled with the rush of the breeze
and the cry of a sea bird to astound my ears. Salt spray fell
upon my face and the smell of the sea filled my nostrils. Of
the ship itself, I could discern little. I appeared to be standing
near the starboard beam but my vision forward was limited by
a young thick-bearded man in a blue cloak who stood smiling
just to my left. This man had only that moment asked if I had
eaten, in a language that while not English was nonetheless
comprehensible to my ears. An ornate copper fibula fastened
his cloak about his chest. White sea-salt and drops of moisture
speckled his brown beard. Behind him rose the town. Sunlight
reflected from the roof of a kind of minaret that seemed almost
to hang above the terra-cotta walls and a lonely figure looked
out at us from its balcony. All this I experienced in an instant.
Then I was back in my room.

It was my first reverie, and its effect on me was devastating.
I would have been less startled if God had appeared before
me, I really do think, since His arrival would to some extent
have been expected. But this sudden vivid, brilliant scene was
totally unanticipated. The perfect reality of it left me breathless.
I grew afraid. What forces had I unleashed? I leaped from the
bed, suddenly fearful that I'd be whisked away a second time.
I went into the kitchen, heated some coffee, drank it down and
then sat for an hour looking out my window. I wanted to go out
and walk the streets, pondering this strange new experience,
but even then I was loath to be abroad at night. At last I returned to bed. I went to sleep at once.

With daylight, my curious transmigration seemed much less
credible. My head became heavy with unwelcome speculations.
Was I mad? Veronica seemed convinced of it and perhaps she
was right. Minds have been known to crumble beneath lesser
burdens than that which oppressed mine. Was all my thinking
merely the symptom of some raging cerebritus? Was my search

for God inspired by nothing more noble than a malfunctioning blood vessel in my brain or a blob of broken-down tissue in one of its convolutions? Perhaps a little oxygen shortage somewhere had produced that violet sky and pitching deck.

I ate my breakfast and went out. My heart felt hollow. After an hour's walk I sat in the Public Garden, idly watching a scrawny-looking man feed peanuts to the squirrels. An airplane hummed overhead and a little girl bounced a large ball while chanting a monotonous rhyme. All at once I was riding a small shaggy pony across an Asian steppe in the company of half a dozen Mongols. I could smell the beast under me as well as the odor of myself. The sky was gray and black and it was bitter cold. The air that entered my nostrils was as sharp as a knife and my nose tingled. I could see my rough brown hands holding the leather rein and feel my legs clinging to the pony's warm ribs.

That was all. It was a shorter journey than the first but it proved that I was not ill. Far from suffering from disease, I realized that I was abnormally healthy and that these transportations were the result of an extraordinary heightening of all my perceptions.

From then on, few days passed without a reverie of some sort.

61 ☙

MY YOUNG friend Randolph was eating popcorn. His friend, Sebastian, watched him from a shirt pocket.

"Don't you like popcorn?" my friend asked me.

"I like it," I replied, "but I don't like to eat it."

"Yes. I suppose if you really liked something, you wouldn't eat it. You'd let it live forever, right?"

"Precisely."

"But popcorn isn't alive, anyhow. Besides, if I brought it home, my sister would eat it. She's greedy. Do you know any Italian jokes?"

"Yes," I admitted.

"Tell me some, okay?"

"Some? I'll tell you one and no more. What's the difference between sixteen ounces of spaghetti and an Italian piano player?"

Randolph thought. He even stopped chewing to give the problem his full attention. But in the end he capitulated. "I give up," he said.

"The spaghetti weighs a pound"—I leered triumphantly—"and the piano player pounds away. Get it?"

He laughed, his eyes sparkling. "Tell me another."

"No more today."

"Can you do a somersault?"

"Not now."

"Do you know why they call it a somersault?"

"No," I answered diffidently. "Why do they call a somersault a somersault?"

"Because it starts with a spring," said the boy, licking his oily fingers. "You never heard that one before because I made it up."

"But it often ends with a fall," I reminded him. "Besides, you know you didn't really make it up. Don't tell lies. And don't keep asking me for jokes. Try to be serious once in a while. Don't you know any serious questions?"

"Sure."

"Well, ask one for a change."

"How did God make Himself?" he said, knitting his brows and wiping his lips and chin with the empty paper bag.

"How did what?" I asked in some surprise.

"God was the first person, wasn't He? How did He make Himself? That's a serious question, isn't it?"

"I should say!"

"What's the answer, then?"

"Ah, yes," I said, playing for time. "Well, my boy, He was very clever about it. First He got a hammer and some nails . . ."

"That's not a serious answer!" Randolph exclaimed, his small face glowing with indignation. "You shouldn't tell lies, you know. You always say you know everything but you don't, really. I caught you. You don't know how God made Himself." He was quite excited. Even his frog nodded his head up and down to express his approval of this indictment.

I beckoned to the boy to come closer. "Do you?" I asked in my most confidential manner.

"No, but it wasn't with nails and a hammer."

"I see. Well, you're right. I don't know how God made Himself. I had to go to the store for my mother that day and I missed it. But it's just one small thing. I know everything else."

After a few strident cries of mocking protest he departed for the frog pond on the Common across Charles Street. Recently I told him about the witches, thieves, Indians, pirates and Quakers that the early Bostonians used to hang there and he's become very fond of the place.

His remark about God, however, set me thinking. Is there more to the child than meets the eye? His precocity is almost weird.

THOSE FIRST two reveries were quickly followed by others of greater duration. My eyes were dazzled, my senses stunned by the marvels that I witnessed. I walked the streets of Tyre and Timaru. I watched the sun glance off the shimmering waters of the Xingu and the Yantra. I fought at Poltava, saw James Wolfe die, was wounded at Paardeberg and captured at Sumter. One day I dined with Aristides or with Vespasian, the next I ate with the Yorubas or gnawed a reindeer bone in the Dordogne. In swift succession I looked upon the glory of Cyrus the Great, the savagery of Chaka, the courage of Cortez, the splendor of Sheng-tsu, the folly of Nero, the fury of Timour and the cunning of the Medici. I heard Mozart play and Dr. Johnson talk. Thus did I pass my days and nights for several months, my mind vagrant and viatic.

It became my habit to reverie on a bench in the Public Garden. For some inexplicable reason the transposition was easier there. Perhaps the walls of the apartment hindered the flow of imagery, I do not know. In bad weather I was obliged to dress like an Eskimo and huddle beneath an umbrella upon my soggy bench, but I did it willingly, knowing that in a few moments I might be basking in the sun of Ponta Delgada or Medina. Only snow, violent rain or the most frigid temperatures could drive me from my perch. Then I would retreat to my room to make another attempt beneath my bed. But indoor journeys were poor. Brief, plagued by distortions and vibrations, too often concerned with meaningless matter and seldom in color, they were hardly worth the effort. In the end I abandoned them. If the weather was bad, I sat in idle contemplation in the library or at a restaurant table.

ONE DAY I came home and discovered that Veronica had been poking about my room. That evening I broke my resolve and spoke to her.

"Why did you sneak into my bedroom and go through these sketches," I said, waving a sheaf of drawings in her face. They were things that I had neatly stacked, thinking to remove them to my studio. It was obvious that someone had disturbed them. The edges were well out of line.

She looked at me coldly, considering whether she should deign to answer. "I didn't," she said finally.

I restrained my anger as best I could. "You're a liar. Stay out of my room. I'm warning you. Keep your paws off my things."

Her cheeks tinged with pink. Her lips, meticulously coated with crimson, curled in a sneer. "Dementia praecox," she murmured.

"Ah, Veronica, go softly. You will make me lose my temper."

"You need help—you really do, and soon." Her eyes, so full of blue, watched me intently. "How long do you think you can go on this way? Agnes Madden says she saw you in a cafeteria whispering to yourself. Victor thinks that you should be committed while there's a chance to save your mind." There was no ignoring the sharp edge of the threat in this final remark.

"Victor, eh? Your little English muffin. I'm told by one of your very good friends that you and Victor have become great pals." Her eyes flickered but remained on my face. Once so powerful that they could cause me to tremble, those shiny aquamarine orbs meant nothing to me now. "I hear that your weekends with sister are spent frisking in New York with that lovely Lovelace. No need for him to whisper to himself, eh?

There are two welcoming ears agape to catch his susurrations, aren't there? Your good friend says that you can't tear yourself from his side, that you follow him about like a stray bitch. How easy you've become, Veronica!" I threw the drawings on the table.

The pinkness in her face increased. She seemed about to protest, but thinking better of it, she held her tongue long enough to regain her composure. One white hand gently touched her carefully groomed hair in a characteristic gesture. At last she shrugged and said, "And if I have, who would blame me?"

At this, my equanimity fled. I took a book from the table and hurled it at her. It was an interesting thing on the space-time continuum and rather heavy. One flat side of it caught her on the ear. I'm sure that it didn't do her any real damage but it did knock her down and caused a surprising change in her demeanor. She began to weep hysterically. Suddenly she was utterly terrified. The expression on my face must have been ferocious. Maybe it was as well that she did cry, for I might have struck her a second time if she hadn't. I ran out of the apartment. There was Barletty, two steps from our door, his mouth fixed in a sheepish grin. Unfortunately, I had nothing to throw at him.

That was the last I saw of Veronica. How frightened she looked! The next day there was a note on the floor before my door saying that she was going to travel in Europe and that I should hear from Mr. Dean, her lawyer. I was relieved. The Maestro was fond of saying that the two happiest days of a man's life are the day he gets married and the day his wife dies. I could now appreciate the wisdom of this apothegm.

I looked in her room and saw that she had left much of her clothing. I was touched to see that she had taken one of my paintings, however—a small gouache "Ganymede" that had hung beside her dresser.

There were six or seven thousand dollars in my savings account and pondering the distant future was foreign to my nature. I felt marvelously free.

My reveries were soon occupying most of my time, even though I had abandoned my night voyages out of fear of the darkness. I read less but I had by no means forsaken my hunt for God. I was convinced, on the contrary, that the reveries were in some way connected with my mission and that they would soon lead to other phenomena even more remarkable.

64 ?~

NOT LONG after Veronica departed I became sick. An icy rain had soaked me to the skin when I thought to brave it out in the Garden, and when I reached home, I felt distinctly ill. Oddly enough, there were none of the usual symptoms of a cold—no sneezing, no runny nose, no cough or sore throat. There was a little nausea and a pain in my back. My head ached and there was a sensation of weakness in my limbs. I went to bed. In the morning the pain in my back had moved on to my right side, but other than that, I was much improved though I had little appetite. I remained at home all that day and went to bed early.

In the dead of night I was awakened by violent pangs in my stomach, and for what seemed an hour I writhed in agony. When these pains at last subsided, I was immediately overcome by a severe chill. I shivered beneath my blankets until daylight, then crawled to the telephone and called a physician who lived in the next building. My body felt as if it were encased in ice while my head felt filled with live steam.

The doctor came, explored me conscientiously, asked me

many questions and gave me some pills. He went to great dialectical lengths to persuade me that my throat was sore and that I had a streptococcic infection. The good fellow was appalled to learn that my wife had left me and that there was no one to take care of me. He promised to return that evening. These earnest ministrations, however, did little if anything to relieve my torment. I was a battlefield for the contending armies of fever and chill.

A few days before, I was with Hannibal in the Pontine Marshes and this led me to suspect that I had malaria. But when I broached the subject of tropical diseases to my Aesculapius (omitting mention of the reverie, of course) he laughed quite heartily and assured me that there were few mosquitoes in Boston in January. He then stuffed me with powders and pills, prodded me here and jabbed me there, painted my throat, listened to my heart and lungs and then gave me an injection. I found it hard to tell whether my discomfort was due more to the disease or to the cure. None of this helped. The ague held fast. I remained in this wretched state for a week. I ate nothing and was certain that I was going to die. Then one morning the fever was gone. I was weak but the fire and cold had left me.

The doctor, who by this time was scrabbling the bottom of his barrel of confidence, was obviously relieved when he read his thermometer that day, but he was brazen enough to tell me that even the worst streptococci are bound to succumb to intelligent medication. I did not have the heart to tell him that my germ—whatever it might have been—had died of old age. He fed me some bouillon and left. I gazed out my window at a rain-swept Boston and dozed on and off. Toward noon the driving rain became a silent fall of snow. In moments the elms in the Garden were decked with white. I had some more bouillon and a little cream cheese and then fell into a deep sleep.

I was awakened by a knock at my door. Struggling into my robe, I tottered out to see who it might be. A man in a misshapen felt hat, a second-hand overcoat and buckled boots greeted me with a mournful smile. His face was long and narrow. It was a face that I knew I had seen somewhere before. In one hand he carried a paper shopping bag, but its contents were concealed from view by a folded newspaper that had been placed on top to keep out the snow. This sorry figure was so splattered with snow that he might well have been the victim of an avalanche. He stood uncertainly amidst the contiguous puddles that formed from his dripping hat, cuffs, coat tails and sodden paper sack.

"I got some books," he said in a voice that was both confidential and apologetic.

"Books?" I asked in bewilderment.

"Yeah, occult science books. You remember me—Fritzie's Second-Hand Books on Columbus Avenue. These just came in this afternoon and knew you'd want to see them first." He wiped his face with a handkerchief that was already wringing wet.

I placed him now. A grimy shop, chaotically filled with dusty volumes. Complete sets of Balzac or Dickens, less a few numbers; a tooled leather edition of Cowper, with a broken spine; Petrarch with stained woodcuts and the cover nearly eaten away by voracious mice. It was a literary graveyard that would lure only the hardiest of browsers.

I said, "Yes. I've been ill. I've rather left off reading."

"They're not expensive. I got them from a German lady— from her estate. She died last week." The book dealer's long face grew still longer and assumed an expression of profound injury. "They're collector's items, twenty-five of them. You told me to bring you any I could find, so I rushed all the way over here. You can have the lot for a double sawbuck."

I hesitated. The fellow was evidently in dire need of money.

"A lot of people want occult stuff these days," he whined. "Twenty bucks is coffee-and-doughnuts money for what's in here."

I found my wallet and paid him. "Don't bring any more," I said.

He tipped his grotesque hat. "You got a buy," he said wistfully.

Not until the next day did I inspect my soggy bundle of lore, but when I did, all sympathy for Fritzie vanished. There were twenty-two and not twenty-five books. Nine of them were in German, two in Cyrillic, two in Italian and one—on Urbain Grandier—in French. Of the remainder, only a few were at all promising. One, *The Magic of Jehan Tritheme, Abbé of Spanheim and Wurzberg, 1462 to 1516,* was rather a gem. I set it aside. Another, a treatise on the paraphysical properties of perfumes, potions and lotions, provided me with an hour's amusement. I then turned to a ragged, oversized pamphlet that looked to be at least a century old, though it bore no date of publication. Its cover had been green originally but was now mottled with brown and leprous white. Mildew adorned its brittle yellow pages. The frontispiece bore the likeness of a man with a pointed beard and oriental eyes. On his head was a tall conical cap tipped with a striped ball. A great deal of hair flowed from beneath this hat and over his shoulders. He wore a buttoned jacket with a triskelion of wings on the left breast, and looked a formidable old bird indeed.

Opposite this steel engraving, the title page proclaimed: *The Life and Precepts of Jozef Casimir, The Wizard of Podolia, as Written by Himself.* Beneath this was the information that Sir Norbert Anson-Deal had translated the book from the Polish and that it had been printed by Millot et Fils, 116 Rue Caumartin, Paris. I began to read it and was soon engrossed.

It was immediately apparent that the writer was a man of extensive intellect and singularly forceful views. Every phrase, every word bespoke a powerful conviction. The translation, aside from the printer's mistakes in spelling, was good. The ideas, unusual as they often were, were presented in concise, vigorous sentences that were easily read and readily assimilated. It was the work of a deep, broad and agile mind. True, it contained some questionable science and some hard-to-believe events, but these were more than compensated for by the author's sense of humor and his keen understanding of men. I read the book at a sitting and was enormously impressed. Perhaps being convalescent had something to do with it.

Jozef Casimir, the Wizard, was born at Jaroslaw in the Kingdom of Poland, the only child of a baker and his Lithuanian wife. No date was given but the first quarter of the seventeenth century seemed to be indicated. His mother taught him some Latin (she had lived for a while in a convent) but he received no formal education. At the age of fifteen he ran away from home and went to Krakow, where he "subsisted by petty thievery and knavery" until he was nineteen years, nine months and nine days of age. Then an event occurred which transformed him. This part of his tale was of great interest to me. It was in the nature of a revelation.

Having heard that a certain farmer was easily gulled by a nimble tongue, Casimir went to him and with little effort sold him a sliver of fish bone as a piece of unicorn horn. Returning from this profitable expedition, he stopped at an inn on the outskirts of the city and ordered kvass and sausage. He sat at a deal table in a long, ill-lit room. The innkeeper's face was like a potato that had been too long in the ground; his wife was wall-eyed and had a nose no bigger than a raspberry and much the same color. The *kielbasy* was very fatty but the kvass was not bad, and when he had finished one cup, he called loudly for a second.

Across the room from him, the only other guest was busily eating black bread and cabbage soup. This man was clean-shaven, exceedingly tall and had a merry glint in his eyes, and when Jozef had finished his second cup he addressed a few friendly words to him. The stranger replied in kind and

before long they sat at the same table and drank each other's
health. The narrative continued:

"What is your name?" I asked him.

"God," said he.

"God?" I repeated, raising my eyebrows.

"Yes," he affirmed. "A short name but a good one."

*I thought about this for a while and then, thinking to
ensnare him in his own words, asked, "And was it your
father's name as well?"*

*He laughed and replied, "Do you take me for a bastard,
young man?"*

*I joined him in his merriment, relieved by this answer.
"Then you are not the God Who is almighty and Who
art in heaven?"*

*"But I am," he said, popping a piece of bread into his
mouth and looking rather pleased.*

*"How can your father's name be God? Almighty God
has no father."*

*He finished the bread and took a sip of beer. "My
father's name is God because I am my own father and
my name is God. Let us not argue theology; it would
bore me and be bootless for you. What is your name?"*

*"Ah!" I exclaimed in triumph. "Surely my name is
known to you if you are really the One you claim to be."*

*"It's Jozef Casimir," he declared calmly. "Surely you
must see that, unless I speak to you as though I were
ignorant of your replies, our conversation must come to
an end."*

*On hearing him pronounce my name, my mouth fell
open. My mind searched my skull for an explanation.*

"You know me from Krakow," I managed at last.

*He licked his lips and studied me for a few moments.
Then, extending his long right arm and pointing his long
index finger at the far end of the room, he said, "Watch."*

*I looked in that direction and soon detected some vague
movement, but the darkness and the shadows prevented
me from seeing the cause. An instant later, however, my*

eyes gaped in amazement, for from this gloom came a chair—a rough-finished black oak chair—dancing in the air like a fairy maid. Down it came, gliding and swaying. As it passed us it increased its gyrations till it was cavorting like a drunken Tatar. When it reached the other end of the room, it came down with a clatter, landing squarely on its four legs, and lost its animation.

The stranger looked at me and I at him and neither of us spoke a word. We remained thus for something less than a minute, whereupon a large yellow cat appeared on his shoulder. Where it came from I could not tell, but its appearance was less cause for wonder than its subsequent actions, for after leaping to the floor, it bounded across the room, ran up the far wall, raced upside down across the ceiling and returned to my companion's shoulder by way of the wall behind him. There it rested only long enough to lick its whiskers before it vanished before my eyes. I raised my cup in a none too steady hand and drank deeply.

"Well?" he asked softly.

I was young and brash. "Trickery," I said with more confidence than I felt. "Black strings and pulleys. A traveling magician is what you are. But I'm no country boy." I restrained an urge to leap over the table and look behind his back for the cat.

"You are difficult to persuade," he said, his eyes twinkling like two stars.

"It is a dark room. You might have all manner of machines hidden away in the corners. Why, at Lublin I saw a German sorcerer make a twelve-year-old boy dissolve into thin air and reappear at the other end of the fair. Even here in Krakow, right in the marketplace, there is old Mother Tulitski who can produce a hen from an empty basket or an egg from behind your ear. If," I went on, emboldened by my own words, "you are who you say you are, perform some miracle less easily explained. Make me empty that upon my head," I said, pointing to the earthenware jug on the table between us, which was more

*than half filled with kvass. "You might well find that
a prank beyond your skill."*

*The stranger smiled. Suddenly I felt that I had spoken
recklessly.*

*"But," he said gently, "it is so dark in here. How would
you know that it really happened? First we will have
light, and then we will have the miracle."*

*No sooner had these words left his mouth than my nose
burst into flame.*

*"Mother of God, I believe You!" I shrieked as I bolted
from my seat and hopped about in the grandest torment
imaginable. With fire and smoke blinding my eyes and the
pain robbing me of my wits, I whirled about the room
like a leaf in a cyclone, my reluctant hands making futile efforts to extinguish the blaze. After what seemed
hardly less than a hundred years, my frenzied polka
brought me again to the table, and feeling the cool surface of the pitcher on my fingers, I wasted no time in
pouring its contents over my head. At once my anguish
ceased.*

*I dropped in my chair, the sweat pouring from me as
freely as if I had run up the steps to the belfry of the
cathedral, while God laughed so loudly that the innkeeper
thrust his lumpy face through the kitchen doorway.*

*"More drink!" He commanded, in the voice of a lion.
"More drink and quickly. My friend has anointed himself
with the last jugful, so excellent does he judge it." Then,
transfixing me with His sparkling eyes, He said, "Your
movements are graceful and not without originality but
much too fast for a mazurka. You would finish long before the music."*

*I felt my nose and found it to be no different from
what it had been before it had been set alight. The pain
had left me and been replaced by a fear that was nearly
as bad. "Is it really God?" I wondered. "Or is it the Other
One?"*

*But the thought had barely formed in my mind before
He spoke again, saying, "No, no, my boy. The Devil would*

never have handed you the pitcher, and you might have danced forever before finding it yourself. Oh, I am God, all right, and much as I like laughter I am neither fond nor feeble." His face suddenly took on the appearance of a mask of iron and I wondered what next would befall me.

I had no reason to fear Him, as events were to prove. He treated me with courtesy and calmed my apprehensions. We drank and talked well into the night. All of the magic that I own was bestowed on me during this memorable conversation. I was given the language of the Muscovites, the Ukrainians, the Roumanians, the Germans and the Romany Gypsies, as well as the two great tongues of the ancients. Placing His finger upon my brow, He filled my head with the past and with the future, the knowledge of curing all but the dead, the secrets of natural philosophy, the three rites of exorcism and the signs and incantations needed to raise a devil or fetch an angel. He told me, further, that I could summon Him if I chose to, but that I must have good reason. And He instructed me in that procedure.

At last He drained his cup and stood up. His head nearly touched the black beams of the ceiling. I left some money on the table and followed Him at a respectful distance out of the place. The night had neither moon nor stars.

"Go to Kamenets," He said. "Fame and fortune and a good long life await you there. But remember one thing, if you forget all else: God can do anything—and will, if He so desires."

With these words, which cleaved the stillness of the night like the clangor of a great bell, He nodded His head in the direction of the inn and it, too, burst into fire, even as my nose had done earlier. I turned from this terrible sight to look at Him. He was gone. On the trunk of a linden tree, near where he had stood, was a white spiral pommée, drawn as if in lime but with great precision. As I looked on it in the palpitating light of the inferno behind

*me, it slowly disappeared. From the interior of the inn
came a series of sharp screeches. I ran down the road in
an easterly direction, toward the Ukraine and Kamenets.
God can do anything and will, if He so desires. I would
remember.*

After this extraordinary anecdote, Casimir goes on to tell of
his encounters with the Devil, whom he describes as "an awful
liar—worse than a Magyar—and very miserly. In conversation,
though, he can be most witty and comical, particularly when
telling stories of the Hun, Attila." There are accounts of
dialogues with lesser demons, angels, archangels and people
long since dead, but he never again spoke with God, "for the
need was never enough to overcome the fear." There is a chap-
ter containing various formulas for communicating with the
other world. The one for summoning God requires the murder of "seven innocents, without regard to sex or age so long
as they be completely human," after which you draw a spiral,
mutter a few words and the Supreme Being makes His appearance. Nothing to it, once you're past the slaughter. Angels
are a simpler matter. Here, one must kill a bird, draw two
triangles—which represent the wings of both bird and angel—
on a piece of goatskin and sleep with the skin beneath your
head and the bird at your feet. The angel will be there when
you open your eyes in the morning.

But the most readily available of all is the Devil, who "often
as not comes without invitation." He is bound to materialize if
you place a sketch of a trapezium (this figure represents dis-
cord) beneath your pillow and burn a red candle at each corner
of your bed. Minor fiends, spirits and apparitions can be had
for two or even one red candle and a short incantation.

Along with this information, there are instructions in
alchemy and medicine and some accounts of Casimir's life in
Podolia. The remainder of the book is devoted to philosophic
discourse and is both pleasant to read and oddly instructive,

being a blend of Christianity, Judaism, Paganism and the mathematical doctrines of Pythagoras. A footnote by the translator tells that Casimir was stoned to death by a mob and that his house was burned to the ground. The Wizard was 119 years old at the time of his death.

I put the thin tome down on the counterpane and went to the window. The garden was deep in snow. I thought of God burning the inn and incinerating the innkeeper and his wall-eyed wife. Could it be true? The writer, for all his extravagances, did not sound crazy.

I sneezed and returned to my bed. My strength was returning to me. I would reverie soon, I decided.

65 ᏘᎦ

THERE IS a new antique shop on Charles Street, run by two young ladies. I bought a scimitar there—one almost two feet long—though why I could not say. When I looked in the window, my eyes immediately discerned a wonderful bronze of a leopard attacking a bullock, and I went in at once. I was not surprised to see that this sublime sculpture was from the hands of Barye, that incomparable portrayer of wild beasts. The price of it was very low, but of course I have no reason to buy such things now.

Before I could depart, however, one of the young ladies took possession of me and gave me a tour of the place. It was all quite charming. There were china closets of bisque figurines and Parian ware busts. There were Waterford goblets, Delft tiles, Japanese fans, Roman tear bottles, Quimper plates, Meissen cups, lyre-backed chairs, piecrust tables, a Victorian doll house and other oddments of a similar nature—all arranged with admirable regard for good taste and sensible proportion. Despite the quantity and variety of these objects, the total effect was one of peace and felicity. The girl, too, was charming. When the time came for me to depart, I felt that I should not do so empty-handed. That is how I came to own a scimitar.

The handle is made of brass but is inlaid with silver and copper—Damascene, this is called—forming Arabic letters which, doubtlessly, make up a pithy verse from the Koran. This technique is one that I myself have used. You must etch a groove in the brass and then heat it. The silver or copper wire is pressed into this now-expanded cut. When the brass cools and the groove contracts, the inlay is firmly fixed in place. The blade has the wavy, watery lines that steel from Damascus is supposed to have but its surface is somewhat pitted. Still the edge is surprisingly sharp. Even the small convexity at the top, running back from the point, is well honed. A pretty instrument but deadly as well. Perhaps I can find a use for it.

There was no scabbard for it but the young lady was kind enough to wrap it in brown paper for me. It cost twenty-seven dollars.

66 ह्ल

I THOUGHT I saw Darius today on Commonwealth Avenue but when I caught up with the fellow, he proved to be a much older man.

April, that mad investigator of the Homicide Club, is rapidly getting worse. Yesterday she accused me of kicking one of her pigeons. Since there were other people within earshot, the incident caused me considerable embarrassment. Of course I didn't do it, but I made no attempt to defend myself. How can one debate with a lunatic?

There is a crackbrain on the other side of the Garden now. I saw him only this afternoon. This one is bald and in his seventies and fancies himself an entertainer, for he dances about while accompanying himself on a small harmonica and one of those clappered frying-pan sistrum things. The people gather and gawk. The poor deranged clown produces no music—neither melodies nor even rhythms—from his instruments. A disagreeable series of squeaks and rattles is the best he can provide. A pitiful spectacle. The authorities should do something about this plague of madness.

67 ?~

I RECOVERED from my illness rapidly but it was still several days before I felt strong enough to try a reverie. It proved only mildly successful—a trip to Lindos on the island of Rhodes in the fifteenth century.

I listened to my records, looked out the window, ate frequently and read the book on potions, part of the one on Tritheme and some stories by von Kleist. Faber came to visit me and brought me some chocolates and a copy of an article he had published in a magazine. He suggested that I go to the country for a few weeks and offered me the use of his place in Vermont, but I did not want to leave Boston. My mind kept returning to Jozef Casimir.

One morning I left the apartment and walked to the restaurant on Charles Street. The next day I walked to the library and spent an hour hunting vainly for references to anyone named Jozef Casimir or Joseph Casmir, Josip Cazimir, Kasimir, Kazmir, et cetera. I was toying with the idea of raising a demon but I was nervous about going to sleep with candles burning near my bed. I had less fear of hell and its denizens than I did of being burned alive. The weather was very cold and I dared not attempt an outdoor reverie.

One afternoon I bought a goatskin wine bottle at Newcastle's and a finch at a pet shop on West Cedar Street. The bird came in a little white cardboard box. When I came home I made some coffee and filled a basin with water. Then I put the box into the water and held it beneath the surface until the bird's fluttering ceased. After drinking a cup of coffee I removed the dead finch from the box, put him in a saucer and set him on the radiator to dry. With its feathers wet and depressed, it looked only half its original size.

Before going to bed that night I drew two triangles on a piece of the goatskin in India ink and in the manner prescribed by the Wizard. I placed this beneath my pillow and the dead bird at the foot of the bed. Then I retired. I was confident that nothing would happen. I was mistaken.

68 ❧

IN THE morning I did not at first remember my preparations of the night before. There was snow piled high about the glass of my window and it was on this that my drowsy gaze rested. Then I heard a slithering sound and the dead finch leaped into my mind. I propped myself up on my elbows and looked to the foot of the bed. The bird lay there just as I had left it. The slithering sound occurred again, from the direction of the mantelpiece, and I spun my head about. There, in the center of the marble shelf, the Bourg Angel was coming out of her panel. The head and shoulders had already cleared the frame and the upper torso was following rapidly. She rose smoothly, like smoke from a chimney, accompanied only by that soft rustling sound that had puzzled my ear.

I gasped for air and fell back on my pillow. The urge to duck beneath the covers was repressed with difficulty but I did close my eyes. My head felt very light. I rubbed my temples with trembling fingertips and looked once more. A moment later she floated easily to the floor not six feet from where I lay in stupefied wonder.

She was still wood, at least as far as eye could tell, but it was a supple wood that never had its origins here on earth. The tight curls of her hair and the feathers of her now fully revealed wings, for all their graininess, looked as soft and natural as real hair and true feathers, while the eyes, the pupils of which I knew to be no more than dimples in the mahogany, surveyed me with as lifelike an expression as my own. She was small, scarcely more than forty inches high, but she had great dignity.

We looked at one another in silence. I had trouble breathing.

"What is it you want?" she said at last, her fiber lips moving as flexibly as flesh. The voice was melodious—like the tinkling of small silver bells.

I was unable to reply. My brain had not caught up with events. I wanted to reach out and touch her, to verify the report of my eyes and ears, but my backbone felt like a length of old wet rope and I continued prone.

"It was you who brought me here, was it not?" she went on sweetly.

But still I could not respond. My fingers gripped the sheets under me as I tried to raise my body. The room seemed suddenly very small, as if the walls had contracted about us.

"Why are you so frightened?" the Angel asked. "You summoned me and I have come. Wasn't that what you desired? Why do you not speak? It isn't possible that there could be a mistake. One could not perform the rite by accident. You did call me, didn't you? Why are you dumb?"

"Yes, I . . ." I stuttered finally. "It was I. I called, yes."

The silence fell again while she waited for me to continue, but I could not manage another word. Her polished forehead, waxed so often by me, formed the beginning of a frown. Even parallel creases etched the wood. "Well? What is it you wanted? Have you forgotten already? Was it an explanation of something?" She fired the questions at me swiftly and with a trace of exasperation. "A favor of some sort, was it not? Has it to do with wealth?"

I shook my head and whispered, "No."

"Love? Do you desire someone? Or is it a special knowledge or particular skill that you seek? No? What then? A matter of health, maybe? For you or a member of your family? Or do you wish to know the future? Or to speak with one who has left life?" The lovely face appealed to me, the eyes searching my own.

"I want to see . . ." I began and then my voice cracked and stopped.

"Yes? Who? Who or what do you want to see? What do you wish to look upon? Speak out. Do not be afraid." Her voice had assumed its original gentle tintinnabulary tones.

"God," I said in a husky gasp.

"What did you say?"

"God."

"Who?"

"I want to see God," I said more loudly and struggling once more to a sitting position.

She raised a small hand to her throat; the other was at her side but the palm turned slowly upward in a supplicatory gesture. "You cannot," she said firmly.

"I must." My timidity was leaving me.

"You cannot see the Lord God," she said, wonder filling her varnished eyes.

"Why not?"

"It is impossible."

"Why?"

"It is forbidden. I have not the power."

I sensed that our positions had reversed, that it was she who was now afraid while my courage was growing. I leaned toward her. "Who has the power?"

"Not I." Her feet were no longer touching the floor. She was floating.

"Who has the power?" I asked again, my voice rising.

"It is beyond my authority." The ring had gone from her speech. A definite tremor of fear had taken its place. The lovely face bore unmistakable signs of anxiety.

"Why can't God come here, just as you have done?"

"No."

"But why not? He can do anything, can't he?"

"He could if He so wished," she agreed, drifting upward.

"Well, He must. I must see Him. I have to see Him."

"I can do nothing. I have not the power," the Angel murmured as she glided toward the mantel.

"Tell Him I must see Him, do you hear? Tell Him that I must see Him at once. He knows why." My voice had become quite loud. "He knows the reason why. I have to kill Him. I have to destroy Him."

"Never! Never!" she cried, her brown face stricken with horror.

"Yes. He is evil and must be annihilated. And I will do it."

She had begun a swift descent into the frame, the slithering sound once more making itself heard. "What are you saying? How can you speak so?" She was incredulous but filled with alarm. "The consequences! Think of the penalties! Who has told you to say this? How can you afford such folly? Eternity. The consequences. Infinity. The Lord God!"

"I must see Him," I shouted. "Don't go! Tell me what will bring Him here. Stay!" She was going into the frame now, like liquid into a wooden bowl.

"Nothing. I can do nothing. Think of the penalties. Endless."

The voice was growing faint. Only the upper part of her body was still in view.

"Then take me with you!" I yelled, throwing back the covers and leaping from the bed. But as I strove to reach the mantelpiece, my feet tangled in the sheet and I fell to my knees. I freed myself and sprang to my feet. The Angel raised her small hand to ward me off, but even as I watched, this too vanished into the molding. I lunged. My fingers clutched at her hair and I could feel the softness of her ear beneath my palm—but the sensation was momentary. The panel toppled from the shelf, eluded my nervous grasp and fell to the hearthstone with an explosive *thwack*.

I picked it up. It split in two in my quivering hands. Stunned, I sat on my bed and looked at the two halves. They were now no more than fragments of old stained wood. I could see the depth to which the color had penetrated the yellow fiber as I examined the raw surface of the break. My little visitant had returned to her native sphere.

"Tell Him," I said to the broken face, "that sooner or later He will have to see me. His universe isn't capacious enough to conceal Him from my eyes. I will find Him. Tell Him that, Angel."

I became suddenly aware of the odor of my sweat.

69 ❧

THE PIECE of goatskin was still beneath my pillow but the dead bird was gone. That same day I borrowed some large C-clamps from Sharkey, the framer on Charles Street, and glued the Angel together. Two days later I bought another finch and repeated the ritual. Nothing happened. Another try and another were equally fruitless. I turned, then, to the burning of red candles in hopes of calling up the Devil or one of his minions. To prevent my going up in smoke, I took elaborate precautions. Even so, I found it very difficult to fall asleep. The flames cast weird sinuous shadows up and down the walls and the fumes from the burning wax assailed my nostrils. It was well into the morning before I relaxed enough to sleep.

I had the apprehension for nothing. The demons turned me down, too.

70 ह∾

WAS IT a dream? Definitely not. Aside from the fact that I have had only one dream since childhood, it had nothing of the vagueness and obscurity of dreams. I was fully awake throughout the episode and stayed awake for the rest of the day.

Was it then a reverie? Since this occurred to me even while I spoke to her, it seems most unlikely. I might have drifted off into a reverie without noticing it—that's happened a few times —but the return to the present always produces a clear feeling of transition. There was no such sensation that morning. What's more, it was not a reverie-type experience. I have never reveried in Boston. I have never reveried in my own era. To be in my own room in both reality and reverie is beyond belief. It would be an unbelievable coincidence.

And what of the physical changes that took place? The panel was actually broken and the dead finch gone. How is that to be explained?

No, it was real, and no mistake! The Angel did come, did

speak, did refuse my request and did flee in fear. No aberration could induce so substantial a being. I believe my eyes and ears then and I believe them now.

What did puzzle me were some of the Angel's words. What were the consequences and penalties of which she spoke? Above all, what did she mean by the question, "Who has told you to say this?" Has God another antagonist? Surely she was not referring to Old Scratch, the Prince of Darkness, the Adversary, His Satanic Majesty, the Devil? All that would be much too like a Gothic romance. I suspect a deeper and far more interesting meaning.

71 ᶘᵛ

MY REVERIES, interesting as they were, contained too much death. The history of man, I found, is the story of butchery and murder. In Russia, I saw people pushed beneath the ice of the Moskva River at the behest of Ivan the Terrible. In France, I saw the Calvinists beheaded and their bodies dragged through the streets by children. Atop a *teocalli* in Tenochtitlan, I watched an Aztec priest deftly open a man's chest with an obsidian blade and wrench from it a pulsing heart. I have been with the dying Athenians in the quarries of Syracuse, seen Bannockburn, Poltava and the siege of the Alamo. I have witnessed a crucifixion in Tyre and seen men thrown from the Palatine Hill. I have observed the Ghurkas cut a Kumaon village to pieces and the Iroquois spear a Dutchman to death.

These scenes had a dual effect on me. I became, to some extent, inured to suffering. It shocked me less and less. The other result was that my hatred of death as a principle increased enormously. I could not accept that all men were doomed. If nothing could live forever, then life was without meaning.

These two almost ambivalent reactions made it easier for me to seriously consider the instructions of Casimir. If by the murder of "seven innocents" I could abolish death once and for all, there could be no question but that they had to perish. Anything is better than nothing. Then, too, when once I had the reins of heaven in my hands, I could repair these wrongs and give them back their lives. It was an intoxicating idea. Exactly how I could wrest the universe from God was not clear in my mind, but I never doubted that a solution would present itself. Seven lives for the whole of creation seemed a small, almost insignificant, price.

I did not come to a decision quickly; I leaned on my window sill or lay beneath my bed in the darkness, pondering this cruel answer to my great problem. The fear that loomed largest was the fear of failure. To execute seven human beings and not achieve my end—what a horror that would be! But the Angel had definitely appeared. I had seen her and spoken to her.

I reread the *The Life and Precepts* once more.

72 ◈

TOWARD THE very end of last winter I went to the Braden Cafeteria on Boylston Street opposite the Public Garden, and in my pocket I carried some strychnine in a fold of wax paper. I had not been in this restaurant for several years, for I had found the food and service both poor. Thus, I ran no risk of recognition. There were a few office workers there, having their mid-morning coffee—enough to prevent me from being conspicuous but not enough to constitute a hazard. I bought coffee and took my tray to a table against the wall.

Walking across the Garden, I had been distinctly uneasy. But now an abnormal tranquillity came over me. My mind appeared to have detached itself from my body and its weaknesses. I felt almost omnipotent.

The table I chose was the best possible for my purpose. My only neighbor was a youth with a singularly vacuous expression on his face, and even he could watch me only by turning half about in his chair. Nevertheless, to forestall even that remote possibility, I draped my overcoat on the back of a chair between us, shutting him out completely.

At any moment, however, a new arrival might intrude. I was constrained to act without delay. I put sugar in my coffee. Then, in a single smooth maneuver, I emptied the strychnine into the sugar bowl and closed the lid. I returned the wax paper to my pocket and suppressed the temptation to look over my shoulder. I drank my coffee as leisurely as any other patron, feeling all the while as dispassionate as a machine. Through the glass of the bowl I could see the small mound of poison rising slightly above the level of the sugar. There was no difference in their colors. When I finished, I put on my coat and left.

It took hardly more time than it takes to describe it. I was back out on the street before I knew it.

I should have gone home or at least to the library, but I did neither. So effortlessly had the thing been accomplished, and so curious was I to learn its issue, that I determined to flout danger and linger in the neighborhood. I walked around the block. When I got back to the cafeteria, I glanced through the window and saw that the table was unoccupied. Crossing the street, I wandered about the Garden, my eyes fixed on Boylston Street and the restaurant. A while later I had another cup of coffee but in a diner at Park Square, and though I was hopeful when I went back, the table at the Braden's was still empty. I began to lose my detachment.

It was a chilly, damp day. There was slush in the gutters and the sky looked heavy with rain. I pulled my coat about me and sat upon a bench in the Garden, directly across from the cafeteria. From there I could not see the table, but the arrival of an ambulance or a police car would signal the success of my scheme. A half hour later I was very cold and very worried. My Olympian objectivity had given way to Chthonian dismay.

Criminals, I imagine, are fretful creatures, for their work is carried out in an atmosphere not merely inimical but appallingly unstable as well. The meek bank clerk may press the alarm. The little old lady might have a voice like Stentor. The massive safe may yield only a petty-cash box. The hijacked shipment of footwear is found to contain only left shoes. The getaway car may choose the crucial moment to blow a headgasket or throw a rod. Crime is a business filled with variables. As I sat on the bench I considered all of the uncertainties of my own venture into the field. It suddenly became clear to me that the whole day could pass without a victim. It was entirely possible that no one would sit at that particular table, or if they did, would not use the sugar. It was also possible that a busboy would refill the bowl and the strychnine would be buried for days. Indeed, the granules of poison and those of sugar could become so evenly mixed that a teaspoonful of the stuff would achieve nothing more than a headache. And if the consumer became sick but didn't die—what then? The stuff might be too old; it may have lost more of its potency. A man is, after all, something more than a cat.

I began to wish that I had never heard of Casimir. I thought of calling the place anonymously and telling them to get rid of the bowl of sugar, but I didn't think they'd believe me.

And, doubtlessly, some fool would be sure to taste it on his tongue, and when he died, my phone call would provide a fine clue. My simple plot was suddenly a tangled mat of peril.

It began to rain. The sky seemed just above the treetops. People hurried along the street to find shelter, and the windshield wipers of the cars began to click like metronomes. The raindrops were ice water. I put up my collar and left my bench. A man in a near-white raincoat, holding a briefcase under his arm, nudged me as he raced by. Two girls, dressed identically and quite evidently twins, trotted by on tapping heels. I followed them, making for the subway entrance. I would take the train to Copley and seek solace in the library reading room. I cast one last look in the direction of Braden's but nothing unusual was happening at its front door. The rain increased its tempo and I my pace.

In front of me, the twins had stopped. One put her hand to her neck and said something to the other, who shrugged and looked puzzled. They resumed walking. As I drew near, the girl with her hand to her neck spoke again and I could distinguish the words "funny" and "stiff" and I looked at them curiously. Just then a gust of wind lashed us with the freezing rain, and as I turned my head to avoid its fury, I heard a sharp cry. I looked again and saw the girl on the sidewalk on her back.

The sister leaned over her, uttering frightened little cries. "What's the matter, Janice? What's wrong? What's the matter?" she asked anxiously, in a voice that was shrill as a whistle. The stricken figure on the ground stiffened. "Something's happened to my sister. She can't get up. She can't talk. She just fell down all of a sudden. It must be a fit," she said to me, almost apologetically, as she crouched beside the sick girl and tried to lift her head. Her own face was draining of color and her wide eyes presaged panic. "Can you help me?"

She's fainted, I thought. I knelt down. She looked oddly

tense for someone who had swooned, however. Her face was round and full-cheeked and there were freckles beneath the closed eyes. Her mouth was small and she had a pointed chin. I put my hand beneath her shoulders and tried to get her to sit up, but her body was inflexible. All at once the lips began to tremble, then to part. The teeth became visible; they were clenched. I knew. As I watched in grim fascination, the lips curled back, revealing the pinkness of her gums. It was Mitya's grin. Here was my victim. Beside me, the other twin began to weep. I was suddenly seized with horror.

Two middle-aged men had drawn near. I turned to them and shouted, "Get an ambulance! Get one quickly. This girl is very sick. Hurry!"

"I'll phone," one of them said and started across the street.

A lady with an umbrella came and held it over the girl's head. The sobbing sister wiped the face with a handkerchief, and as she did, a tremor shook the tortured form and it grew instantly rigid. The head jerked back violently until the sharp little chin was pointed at the tenebrous sky; the back arched fantastically. The onlookers gasped. At the same time the eyes opened above this hideous grin and the face took on an impression of boundless terror.

"A convulsion," a man's voice pronounced.

"Is anyone a doctor?" I asked the crowd that had gathered about us. No one answered. "Get the police, then," I demanded. "She needs help at once."

"Hold her tongue or she'll choke," the lady with the umbrella advised.

"Can't you get her out of the rain?" a voice asked.

"Better not to move her," another cautioned.

I said to the umbrella lady, "A man went for an ambulance."

Gradually the body of the girl on the sidewalk began to lose its frightful tension. The smile lessened; the back lost its awful curve.

The man came with a car blanket and placed it over her. We waited, and the crowd increased while the sister strove to comfort her twin. Rain pelted the umbrella.

"Give her a little air," said a man behind me.

"A heart attack?" another asked.

"Such a pretty girl," a woman said.

Then the grin returned. The lips receded, distending the mouth. The teeth sparkled.

"Where is the ambulance?" I muttered. At that moment I believe I would have given my life to save that of my victim.

Again the body became convex. Incredibly, it rested on head and heels alone.

There was a shuffling of feet in the crowd. A voice said, "I'm a physician. Let me through, please." A youngish fellow in a trench coat came to my side. I got up to make room.

"How long has she been in this tetanic condition—stiff this way?" he asked.

The woman with the umbrella began to describe what had happened. I made my way out of the crowd. I knew that nothing would save the girl now. It was too late. I crossed the deserted Public Garden, went home and crawled under my bed.

73 ❧

I REALLY am a little disturbed by objects. If I put a book on a table, it invariably tumbles to the floor. If I try to stand the broom up in a corner, it unfailingly falls. Yesterday I knocked over a cup of coffee. The cloisonné lamp in the dining room works or doesn't, depending on its mood. And the bedroom window sticks so badly that I nearly broke the frame today, trying to get it up to chase those birds. The wood is probably swollen from the summer heat and moisture—or so I hope. How I hate petty annoyances!

74 &

I CONFESS that I was rattled by the events of that terrible day. I did not anticipate so youthful a sacrifice. The newspapers said that the girl, Janice Mahoney, was seventeen and that she lived in Belmont. The police surgeons had no difficulty in identifying the cause of death as strychnine, and once they had questioned the surviving twin, they were quick to discover the poisoned sugar in the Braden Cafeteria. There was a good deal of speculation as to how it got there, but the following day's newspapers carried only small stories about the death and by the next day all mention of it had disappeared.

I considered abandoning the entire business. Nothing, I thought, could justify such agony. But if I gave it up, she would have died for nothing and lost all chance of eventual resurrection. I struggled for days with this dilemma. The pain of her death preyed upon my mind; the hideous smile haunted me. I got out the apothecary chest and looked through it for cyanide or any poison that might kill more humanely than strychnine, but there wasn't any. There was a belladonna vial but it contained only a little dust. The morphine jar held not so much as a crystal.

For the next week I could think of nothing but the murder, but then the weather became warm and springlike and my spirit brightened. Reveries of great clarity and length came to me. One, a four-hour visit to the court of Zenobia at Palmyra, was the longest I have ever undergone—and one of the most delightful.

About this time, too, I met Randolph and he did much to improve my mood.

"What's your name?" he would ask, his mouth crammed with candy and the air about him perfumed with peppermint.

"Garrou," I remember replying the first time. "My name is Lou Garrou. I'm one of the crew at the zoo. Really, it's true. Who are you and what do you do?"

Each day the sun grew stronger. My resolution returned. I would go on, I decided one morning.

About a week later I dropped another dose of *nux vomica* in a sugar bowl on Massachusetts Avenue. This time, however, I did not hang about to see the results. It was just as well. Three automobile mechanics died after being rushed to Peter Bent. I was much less affected by these deaths, not having witnessed them. Indeed, I was very pleased to have killed so many at one time. Now I needed only three more to complete my task.

The newspapers produced a hue and cry of alarming proportions, however, and I found myself instinctively shying away from passing policemen. Moreover, sugar bowls began to disappear from restaurant tables and packaged cubes were given out by countermen instead. To meet this threat, I was compelled to act quickly. I poisoned a bowl in the South End and another on Cambridge Street, both on the same afternoon. A fifty-two-year-old bookkeeper, a woman named Isabel Bailey, died in the South End, but at the other place, a twenty-year-old youth escaped death because they were able to get him into Mass. General in a matter of minutes. That left me with two to go.

A reward was offered for my apprehension, and the papers—displaying their usual fertility of imagination—bestowed on me the epithet of "The Boston Borgia." Mysterious leads were mentioned and promising suspects taken into custody. Now and then an honest citizen would be picked up for unscrewing a clogged salt celler or stirring a pot of mustard or probing a recalcitrant catsup bottle. Sugar bowls had become extinct. Even the greasiest little eateries had removed them from their tables.

75 &

SOMETHING HAS happened. Today I went to my studio to fetch Swedenborg's "Heaven and Hell" and found the loft completely empty! There was nothing there. It was bare. Every canvas was gone, and all the figures and drawings. Even the paints, brushes, easels and all the rest of the paraphernalia had vanished. No books, no furniture—not so much as a coat hanger! At first I thought I had entered the wrong room, but the number on the door soon dispelled that hope. I staggered out.

The elevator operator knew nothing, but he took me to the basement, where I found Olsen, the superintendent, reading his paper in a cubbyhole.

"Where are my paintings?" I shouted while I was yet five yards distant from him. "What have you done with my work?"

He is an old man, nearly bald and rather red in the face. He stood up at once, obviously flustered by my words.

"What? The paintings? Why, your missus came and took the lot," he said. "They went out of here last week—Friday night, as a matter of fact. I was here myself. Everything was loaded into a New York moving van."

"My wife? My wife took them? To New York, you say? Why would she do that?" I felt light-headed; I wanted to sit but there was no chair.

"She never said. I figured you were moving out of Boston," he said, his forehead wrinkled with worry.

"Why did you let her take them, Olsen?" I asked in bewilderment. "They were mine. They belonged to me. Nothing there was hers."

"Well, her name was on the lease, you see. It was made out to her. The boss told me to go ahead. Is there some kind of trouble?"

"My wife and I are separated," I said, remembering now that Veronica had handled the renting of the place.

"Ah-h, I'm sorry to hear it. Very sorry." The old man shuffled his feet in embarrassment. "I didn't know that. The boss said it would be all right. I stayed on after supper, you see, to run the elevator for them. She gave me ten dollars and then left in a cab with the English young man."

"The English young man?"

"He was either that or one of those Harvard fellows, judging from the way he talked."

I clutched my head and tried to think. "Where in New York? Do you know where in New York it was going?"

"One of the movers said something about going straight to the docks," Olsen said, as I shivered with fear.

I ran out of the building as if it were on fire, but when I reached the street, I did not know where to go. I started across the Garden and then came back. I started across a second time but again changed my mind and my direction. This time I hurried toward Arlington Street. I wanted to pick up my heels and run, but I had no goal. The need for speed was evident, but to where?

From a drugstore, I called Leo Faber, but there was no answer. With trembling fingers I dialed the Chester House,

where Darius usually stayed when in Boston, but they denied
that he was there and refused to say if he had been. I tried
the Crillon and a few other fancy hotels, but with no more
success. My agitation was extreme. I sat at a counter and ordered some coffee.

Why had they taken my paintings? What were they going to
do with them? They were crazy if they thought that they could
steal them. To whom could they sell them? Have they gone
mad? Is it some sort of vengeance that they are after—like
that snake de Reyna? The work represents years of my life.
Why, the "Shackling of God" is among those things. And the
bronze of Littleboy. They've got everything. The marble Jesus,
the bas-reliefs, the Tantalus—even the few things I had from
the hands of Serafino Loupa. They've taken it all.

And Darius with her! All the rumors, then, were true and
the rascal was as lecherous as he was treacherous. But they'll
not get away with anything. I'll see to that. I'll find them. To
the docks, he said. Friday, he said.

"What day is this?" I asked the girl behind the counter.

"The second of August," she replied.

"No, no," I said impatiently. "What day of the week?"

She looked me over quizzically, shifting her chewing gum
from one side of her mouth to the other. "Wednesday, mister.
Where've you been?"

Four full days—almost five. On board ship by now, I decided,
and the two brigands traveling with the plunder. My heart shriv-
eled up inside me. I had to see Faber.

HALF A dozen phone calls later, I reached Leo. I told him briefly what had happened and then took a taxi to Kenmore Square. I must have looked like a wild man, because he ordered me to sit down and poured me a glass of whiskey. I drank it and related my story. Faber was as puzzled as I was but he was certain that they'd never be able to sell the things, if that was their intention.

"Even in Europe?" I asked.

"Yes," he said reassuringly. "There are international laws. It is more likely some spiteful plot. I'm amazed that a man like Darius would lend himself to such a piece of childishness."

He telephoned several people, but none could (or would) tell if Veronica or Victor were in Boston. Old Lord had seen them Saturday but he believed that they had returned to New York the next day. Leo then called Harbarin and a couple of other people in New York but learned nothing.

"Perhaps she is finally opening her gallery," he suggested, handing me a second drink.

"That occurred to me. But why would she take every single piece? They didn't leave a scrap. What would she want with work books and plaster fragments? I tell you, there's something extremely sinister about it all. They're an evil pair, Leo."

"Well, try to pull yourself together. We'll find them tomorrow, I'm sure. It's only a matter of making enough phone calls. They might still be in town, in which case the whole matter could be settled by this time tomorrow. Tonight I'll make up a list of people to call. I'll call my lawyer, too, and see what he has to say. Go home and try to relax. You're as coiled as a bed-spring." His lean face parted in a kindly, confident smile.

I left feeling a little better. Faber was a very shrewd and competent fellow when it came to business and he knew many people.

It was growing dark. I hurried back to my room.

77 ॐ

THE NEXT morning, when I left the house, I saw a dead pigeon on the sidewalk almost directly below my window. It was a light caramel color, with flashes of white on its wings and tail, and the sight of it cheered me. "A favorable auspice," I said to myself.

I went to Faber's directly and spent the whole morning and part of the afternoon making phone calls. I had found an address book in Veronica's escritoire and we worked from this and the list that Leo had prepared. We began in high spirits, but as the day wore on and we could discover nothing, our hopes shrank. Even Veronica's sister could cast no light on her whereabouts. Her last letter had come from Washington, D. C., but that was three weeks before. Todhurst said that Victor had gone back to New York four days ago and that he was going from there to Salt Lake City. Gault, on the other hand, was sure that he was going to England. But no one knew where they were at the moment.

"They've got to show up sooner or later," Leo declared.

"Yes, they do," I said. "But in the meantime my pictures may disappear forever."

"Let's wait another day, at least. I don't think that we should call the police except as a last resort."

His words upset me. The police? I wanted nothing to do with them at this time. But I made no contradictive reply.

Dejected by everything, I walked home. On the way I stopped at my doctor's and got some sleeping pills, as my nerves were still tingling. I sometimes feel a twitching sensation at the corner of my mouth and I suppose it's a tic, but when I look in a mirror, the pulsating stops and I can't be sure. Perhaps I imagine it. My thought processes are a jumble. I have too much on my mind.

If the police come into it, anything might happen.

I knew it would be impossible but I attempted a reverie in my bed. Absolutely nothing.

78 ह⹀

I TOOK one of the pills and slept soundly until five in the morning. As I was afraid a second one would render me unconscious until noon, I got up instead, made some coffee and sat in the kitchen until seven, reading Kerner's *Seeress of Provost.* I do not like medicines. They make me feel quite odd, as if I were inhabiting someone else's unhealthy body.

I must settle down. I must forget my troubles of the moment. I will put them aside and consider those actions of the past that will, I trust, eventually repair everything.

So I had assassinated five people. With the police, the public, the newspapers and the radio all promulgating the most gruesome accounts of the poisonings, and with every restaurant, from the elegant Luxembourg to the meanest hash house, on the alert, I thought it best to remain quiescent for a few weeks. In that time things did grow quiet. I reveried in the Garden and the weather was lovely. Then I went looking for my sixth victim.

My previous campaigns had been easy compared to the grueling operation that confronted me now. There were no more sugar bowls anywhere. And as for fiddling with salt cellers or any of the other condiments on a restaurant table—that was tantamount to giving myself up, since every diner spied upon every other diner with open suspicion. I toured the city. I prowled through Cambridge, Arlington, Chelsea, Brookline and Newton. I consumed vats of coffee in innumerable cafeterias, but always with cubed sugar dispensed by a waiter. The prospect of stabbing someone with a knife or perhaps an ice pick arose in my mind, but I felt I'd never be able to carry it out. Fortunately, I was spared this horrible possibility—at least for the moment. I found a sugar bowl, at last.

It was in Watertown, not far from the Square. The place was large and half filled with eaters when I arrived, but I was so happy to see the little round glass bowls with their nickel-silver covers that I acted at once. A corner table near the window was empty, and since the window was crowded with placards, cactus and rubber plants, I did not hesitate to sit there. One side of me was partially concealed by a water cooler. A couple of middle-aged women sat nearest to me but their backs were turned. I drank my coffee, dumped the poison in the bowl and then left.

So eager was I to make certain of my success, I stayed about the neighborhood, looking in shop windows. My wait was a short one. A shipping clerk named Belisle, thirty-six years old, sat at the table shortly after me. There he was, on the ground in front of the place, the center of a small group. His grin was enormous—a *rissus sardonicus* that revealed pale, toothless gums. His body arched in the same preposterous fashion as that of the Mahoney girl. The face bore the same impression of impending calamity but the eyes bulged far more. They seemed ready to burst from the sockets and roll down his cheeks. Beside him, a younger man knelt, holding in a handkerchief in his hand a pair of false teeth.

Moments later I was on the Boston bus. I felt very little compassion, I must admit. I was becoming callous.

That was more than a month ago. The police obtained an excellent description of me from the fellow behind the counter, a scruffy old man who hardly seemed capable of such a feat of memory. Luckily the description could fit a multitude of people. A policeman made a sketch from it, but thank goodness, the poor lad was no draughtsman. My fame has increased. There have been several articles in national magazines on "The Boston Borgia" or "The Strychnine Maniac"—none very complimentary, though. One such actually showed a picture of Belisle in convulsions, which I thought in rather poor taste. I have collected the pictures and the stories of all the murders and keep them in a little folder. I feel very close to these people and often look at these scraps of paper. I'm getting as bad as Faber with his trunks of memorabilia.

But I am still one victim short and I am anxious to finish up and meet God. I carry the strychnine with me always, hoping for an opportunity to put it to use, but I have been to Framingham, Worcester, Lawrence and Lowell without finding a bowl of sugar. It will be very difficult, I imagine.

And now all the treasures of my studio have been embezzled.

STILL NO news. Leo's lawyer says we should go to the police, but I won't allow it. They attribute my attitude to a lingering affection for Veronica.

As I left the house today, that mad harpy, Mrs. Dandelion, was lurking about the front door. Those pigeons on my window ledge—does she direct them? I raised my hand as if to strike her and then scratched my head. She flinched, glared, scowled and then hurried across the street.

Sleep has become a problem for me. I think those pills have thrown me off completely. All sorts of mad visions have broken loose in my head. They're not dreams and they're certainly not reveries. Each time I close my eyes to sleep, some horrid scene develops, and though it may last no more than a second, it is nonetheless terrifying. Last night I kept falling from a high building, down, down, down—with all the actual boundless fright that would attend such a plunge. Later in the morning I was plagued by a vision of being guillotined. I was lying face up and could see the descent of the blade and hear its shriek. The night before a huge truck was about to run over me. I was able to make out the herringbone pattern of the giant tires and feel the wheel start across my body. Needless to say, I open my eyes quickly. The mirage goes away, but how am I to sleep with open eyes?

I have stopped taking the pills. They add to my nervousness. My nerves are really very bad. I've got dangling, jangling ganglion. I am going to drink less coffee and try not to think of my paintings.

I saw Randolph in the Garden a little while ago. He is quite sad. He has lost Sebastian, the frog.

"He was made in Germany," he told me. "There was a label on his hand that said so, but I took it off. I wonder where he is right now."

I made an effort to console him. I told him that I was Lindsey Eiderdown, an undercover agent on the trail of the beautiful Eurasian spy, Samantha Cobblebanger, alias Samantha the Panther, alias the Boa of Goa, who had stolen a formula for invisible ink, written in invisible ink. But neither of us felt very much like fantasy. He thinks Johann and Mr. Beels stole Sebastian, because he left him on the bench yesterday and no one else was around. He was deeply attached to that little piece of cloth and papier-mâché. After a while he went home. I tried to reverie but my mood made it a fiasco. There was a bunch of gallants in galligaskins in some kind of public house but I couldn't hear what was going on. I tried a couple of times more, with no result at all. I am beginning to be apprehensive. What if I lost my reveries forever?

I sat for a time gazing at a mauve balloon that was caught in the topmost branches of one of the elms. It drifted back and forth, at the end of its tether. It, too, represents a little (or big) misery for someone, I thought. What is the sense of separating Sebastian from Randolph or a mauve balloon from some other child? I hoped that all that could be changed.

As I walked out of the Garden, I passed Beels and Johann. As hot as it's been, that deformed little man continues to huddle beneath his woolens. His face seemed redder and more pinched than usual. I nodded to them. Johann, as is his way, looked straight before him like a man in a trance, but Mr. Beels waved his cigar in greeting.

"Have you decided on anything yet, Mr. Barber?" he asked in his adolescent voice.

"Decided? I have nothing under consideration," I said.

"Time has a way of evaporating on us, Mr. Barber. Even tomorrow may be too late."

"I might have more time than you, Mr. Beels. The fact of the matter is that I've stored some away in a closet at home. I put aside an hour or so, each day, and now I've several years," I said, pausing for a few seconds before going on my way.

His dry, crackling laughter followed me.

80 ଛ

TODAY I saw Darius in a taxicab. I'm sure of it. The cab was turning into Berkeley Street as I came down Beacon and I saw him in the back quite clearly. Leo thinks I might have imagined it, but I couldn't be mistaken. I doubt if he saw me. I began to run after the cab, but the lights were green and it was gone before I could draw near.

I have been trying to put the whole thing out of my mind for a while, in order to regain some of my composure, but the sight of him has set me off again. I spent the rest of the day calling hotels, but none had a Victor Darius registered. He must be staying with someone—but who? Or maybe he's here under an assumed name, considering the iniquitous nature of his business. Tomorrow I will patrol Newbury Street and keep an eye on the galleries. He's sure to appear there sometime.

I long for a good night's sleep. Those horrible little visions are maddening. They're like momentary motion pictures, projected on the inside of my skull—but oh so real!

I am thinking of hiring a private detective to look for Darius. I made another unsuccessful reverie attempt. I am too upset, too discouraged. How I would like to get off to another life, even for only an hour or two.

81 &

SUDDENLY ALL is clear. The filthy wretches! I understand now. It is unbelievable. The magnitude of their villainy leaves me aghast. I discovered the truth today. Victor Darius is nothing but a swindler, a confidence trickster. There was his name, right in the article. They called him "the London expert, renowned for his skill in detecting the spurious." Renowned for his infamy would be more exact. What a spider the man is! He has woven a web of such intricacy that I cannot see the beginning or even imagine the end, but I am truly snared in its glittering filaments. What fantastic knavery.

It was all in this magazine. I have gotten into the habit of looking at the magazines on the newsstands because of the poisoning stories they have lately carried. Today, when I glanced at the display, I was staggered by what met my eyes. I have gone completely insane, I thought. There, on the cover of the most successful weekly in the country, was my painting of Lisabeta! I nearly fell to the sidewalk. It can't be, I thought. But it was.

This English gangster, this British brigand, has passed off my picture as an original Leonardo! Yes, it's what he's done. My Lisabeta of Maine is now the grand Lucrezia Crivelli of fifteenth-century Milan. There is no shortage of fools in this world, that is certain.

I must calm myself. It will do no good to lose my mind. I am so filled with rage that I could explode into a million pieces. But I must hold myself in. Restraint, will power, discipline and, above all, lucid thinking—that is what is needed. But oh, those thieves—the two of them, in it together. I'll get them both. I will crush them; I will granulate them. But no. I must be calm. Calm and canny.

Here is the article with a dozen photographs. The lovely Lisabeta is here before me, just as I did her—the hand before her breast, the inclination of her glance, that transcendent jaw. A Leonardo, they have proclaimed it. Why, the portrait is scarcely five years old. Are they all mad?

Faber isn't home. He's giving a lecture in Albany but he'll be back tomorrow. I must contain myself. I haven't eaten anything and my hands tremble like those of a palsied old man. I must compose myself. I will take two of those pills tonight, otherwise I'll get no sleep.

What scorpions! Is it possible? I must regain my self-possession.

82 &

WELL, I have slept the night through but I cannot say that I feel particularly refreshed. My mind feels sluggish and I have an ache behind my eyes. But I do have more control over myself. I am less agitated.

After breakfast I went down to Charles Street and bought copies of all the magazines that mentioned this "Leonardo" and returned to my room with them. The *New York Journal of World Art* contained the most complete account. It is an involuted, revoluted, convoluted tale of sepentine wile.

In Pavia, Italy, there is a *palazzo* belonging to a Count Ugo Feranti, it seems. This property has been in the possession of the Count's family since the time of the Napoleonic Wars, coming to them through a marriage with a daughter of a family named Roccia. According to the town's records and a history kept in the local church, the Roccias built the palace in 1450. They were connected with the powerful Viscontis of Milan.

This present-day Count owns a number of paintings, many of which are three or four hundred years old. Little value, however, was placed on his collection because the artists were second or third rate. Recently he decided to have some of these pictures cleaned and restored and, accordingly, called in a man named Dalpozzo to do the work. All the articles agreed that Dalpozzo was a restorer of unassailable reputation. He had worked at the Vatican and at the finest museums and churches in Italy. He was skilled, experienced and absolutely honest, they said.

Dalpozzo removed four of the Feranti paintings to his shop and set to work. He quickly noticed that one of them—a young boy in a blue doublet, done on wood—concealed an older work beneath. The panel was cracked, and where a flake of the outer layer of paint had broken away, the restorer espied the tip of a finger, complete with fingernail, executed—he observed later—"with the unmistakable flair of a master artist." He then asked the Count if he might remove a little more of the pigment—from the background, which was dark and without detail—so that they might have a better idea of the underlying picture. The owner was at first reluctant but eventually gave his permission.

With great care Dalpozzo cleared a small area. Underneath he found a portion of the breakwater at the Potter place in Camden, Maine, but, of course, he took it for something quite different. To him, it brought to mind the setting of the "Virgin of the Rocks." He grew excited and called in another restorer and a man from the Brera. On the strength of their remarks, Feranti allowed them to lift off more paint. The sea and some more rocks appeared, and three additional wise men were called in to make a judgment. After a long discussion it was decided that the painting should be x-rayed.

There was Lisabeta. The panel was taken out of the hands of Dalpozzo, to his chagrin, and given to two of the best restorers in the world—a Roman and a Florentine—who undertook, for the now eager nobleman, the delicate task of removing all the overpainting. The work was done slowly and with maximum care. Rumors circulated, and a graduating stream of art historians, museum officials and other experts began to flow into Milan, where the work was being done.

Under such supervision, the portrait was slowly unveiled. What was the verdict of these supervisionaries? All but a few pronounced it a major painting of Leonardo da Vinci. Of those who refused to accept it as such, one called it the work of Solario, a couple attributed it to Leonardo's pupil, Giovani Boltraffio, and one sage—from Venice—said it was clearly Venetian in spirit and might have been done by Lorenzo Lotto. The shrewdest appraisal was made by a Frenchman, who denied that it was a Leonardo and remarked that "the whole affair is very curious."

But these words of dissent were drowned in a tidal wave of critical affirmation. Exhaustive tests, said the article, proved the antiquity of the picture, and the manner in which the paint was applied was that of the master. There followed a little dissertation on how each painter does noses a certain way and treats hands a certain way, or drapery or hair in a distinctive way, so that it was impossible to duplicate these idiosyncrasies. It was, however, the pre-eminence of the entire painting that convinced the authorities. Some of the foremost acknowledged it a Leonardo after comparatively brief examinations. A distinguished German scholar—a Leonardo specialist—was quoted as saying: "At no point does it deviate from the master's method. I could not be mistaken about this one. It is the easiest attribution I have ever had to make."

As there was no question about the identity of the artist, there remained only the identity of the subject to consider. This, too, was established in dazzling style. Pavia having been a dependency of Milan in Leonardo's day, the picture had to be one of his Milanese works. Strengthening this hypothesis was the interesting discovery that the reverse side of the panel, when photographed at a raking angle, revealed the scratched outline of a mulberry tree—one of the devices of Lodovico Sforza, the then Duke of Milan. This "doodle," as the *Journal* called it, was also thought to be from the hand of the great artist, though it was only an outline and barely visible even to the camera. The subject, they reasoned, had to be Lodovico's mistress, Lucrezia Crivelli, for it was known that such a portrait had been painted by Leonardo though it had long been missing. The estimated value of the picture was two million dollars. It was called the most important discovery since the disinterment of the Venus de Milo.

That is the rigmarole they have presented to the world. It's like something from the pen of Molière. Those puffed-up oracles! Those simple-minded savants! How could they possibly mistake a five-year-old painting for a five-hundred-year-old painting? But I am becoming excited again.

To begin with, the support for my picture was a piece of pine no more than fifty years old at most. It wouldn't have the patina, the texture or even the smell of wood five centuries old. As for the paint, it is true that I employed only the old colors but they couldn't dry out in so short a time. Old paint— paint that is a hundred or more years in place—is almost as hard as glass, but a recently painted surface can be penetrated by the point of a pin. All of it surpasses belief. I am not really familiar with this seamy side of art, still I have read that x-rays, ultraviolet lighting, photographic enlargements, chemical analyses and all the rest have made fakes and forgeries a thing of the past. The *Journal,* however, said that all these tests were used and nothing suspicious was detected. How can this be?

And what of documentation? It is certainly not enough to know that Leonardo painted this girl; there must be a reasonably clear trail, leading from that time to this, to support such an authentication. Where are the inventory records, the bills of sale, the letters or diaries that make mention of its survival?

But here is the strange history that is put forth in the article. The "Boy in the Blue Doublet," which concealed Lisabeta, was the work of Salvatore Paglia, and Paglia died in 1514! He was a somewhat rudimentary portraitist, but according to his contemporaries, an extremely handsome and witty fellow and much in demand by the matrons of Milan. No one questions the authenticity of this overpainting, but if it is genuine, how does my painting come to be beneath it? The Paglia painting, they claim, is mentioned in a letter from a mother to a daughter, and this letter, though undated, is believed to have been written in the latter part of the sixteenth century. Another letter, dated 1721, makes a reference to the "Paglia painting of the boy with the dog" and in the "Boy in the Blue Doublet" there is a pottery dog on a table. Both these documents were found among some trash at the palace. As for more recent proof of its existence, there are dozens of witnesses who will attest the presence of the picture on the Count's dining-room wall for the last twenty or thirty years! The art historians have suggested that Paglia superimposed his own painting over the Leonardo in order to smuggle it out of Milan after the city fell to Louis XII of France in 1500.

My mind is in a turmoil, trying to understand this tortuous plot. Faber should be home by this afternoon. He may be able to make some sense of it. How can Darius expect to get away with it? Everyone in Boston knows he represented me. Of course, only the people in Maine saw the Lisabeta portrait, but my style is certainly distinctive even when I am imitating another. Yet I went to great pains to simulate the style of that strange old Florentine.

Ah, I have only now remembered that all my sketches for the painting were stolen from the car that day. It is not hard to imagine who the thief was. If he was scheming that far back, what a Machiavelli he must be.

Ach! Those pigeons are all over the ledge again.

And I can't reverie.

83 ɤ

FABER IS still not home. He is always off somewhere. I have been calling his house at fifteen-minute intervals.

I have been thinking about this Salvatore Paglia and the impossibility of his painting over the Lisabeta. Could it be that Leonardo and I have, by an astounding coincidence, painted identical portraits? Maybe the Milan picture really is genuine. Time is the most slippery of the dimensions. Could I have conceived the same composition that he created first, five centuries earlier? I have read of stranger things. It could well be that I am a reincarnation of the man and that my memory of this previous existence was not entirely effaced in the course of my metempsychosis.

But this is nonsense. It is all foolish speculation. Some of those books that I've been reading . . .

A reverie might explain it, though. If I saw him at work on the picture, I might have unconsciously duplicated . . . No, that's not possible. I wasn't having reveries five years ago. There is no explanation. It is all impossible—except that it's happened.

Darius is the mover behind this miracle. He had me work in Maine so that none would see the picture. He and Veronica are manipulating everything. Yes, and that is the explanation of my empty studio. That is why they took all my work. I will have nothing for comparison, nothing to back my claim. What slyness!

I cannot understand the Italian end of it, try as I may.

Ah, if the Maestro were still alive, he would know how to fox these wolves!

84 ßœ

I HAVE been looking into my crystal ball, hoping to find a clue. There was nothing there but it was very soothing. While I scried, my tic ceased. Almost all the tension left me and my thinking became more orderly.

To have one's work mistaken for that of Leonardo da Vinci is no small thing, I've decided. I have never been a modest man—it would not have been honest to pretend to be less than what I was—but I would never have considered myself quite the equal of such a master. Now I am not so sure.

When I ponder the inhospitable atmosphere in which I have been obliged to work, my achievement seems all the greater. Leonardo lived in a milieu that loved art; my age abhors it. Artists usually draw their strength from their environment, but I have had to free myself from mine in order to do creditable work. I have had to fly in a vacuum.

Will I paint again? Can I? I do not know. I may have to if I'm to prove my allegations. It's been more than a year since I touched a brush.

EACH DAY brings new detonations! My life is becoming an endless series of surprises. Today I saw Darius and spoke to him. Yes, Victor Darius—here in the apartment. It was a great stroke of luck, really. What a consummate rascal he is. And what a monstrous labyrinth of deceit he has constructed. Yes, a labyrinth—for he is a devious Daedalus, that Darius. But I think I handled it all very well, though it will be no simple matter to expose the scoundrel.

I came home for lunch, thinking that Leo might telephone. My morning had been spent in roaming about the city, trying to make sense of what I knew. When I reached my door, I heard a faint noise from within. I inserted the key very quietly and opened the door. There before me, his coat off and one of Veronica's suitcases in his hand, was Darius. It would be hard to say which of us was more startled, but my surprise—unlike his—was a very pleasant one. I felt like a child on Christmas morn when he first sees the tree.

"How nice to see you, Victor," I said, and I have never been more sincere.

He was quite disconcerted. He set the bag down and watched me warily. "Hello," he said finally.

I closed the door behind me. "Is Veronica in her room?"

He coughed. "Veronica is in New York. She asked me to stop by for these things." He took a very white handkerchief from his hip pocket and patted the perspiration on his brow. It was very warm in the apartment.

"Take what you like," I said amiably. But I was disappointed in not having caught her as well.

"Very decent of you," he said, reviving a little. "Rather awkward, this. Frankly, I had hoped we wouldn't meet. I'll only be a minute or two. There's another valise."

I made no answer but continued to look at him, just as that Christmas child might gaze at one of his new toys before testing its durability.

"I'll be out of your way in a trice." He offered me a small smile and walked off to my wife's bedroom.

For a moment I stood there marveling at the circuitous ways of chance—then I went into the kitchen to get a bread knife. Before I reached the cutlery drawer, however, my eyes alighted on a long package that stood in the corner near the refrigerator. This, I remembered, was the ornate scimitar that I had bought at the new antique shop. Thinking how right the stars were for me this day, I snatched it up and hurried back to the living room. I could hear him moving about in the bedroom as I undid the brown paper wrapper. When he emerged with the second suitcase, a while later, I was admiring the weapon's edge.

"Have a seat," I offered.

"Sorry, no time." He had donned his suit coat and looked his usual spruce self. "Have to be on a two-thirty plane. What in the world is that?" He eyed the scimitar speculatively.

"A scimitar, of course—from Damascus."

"Oh. Well, I'll be on my way." He lifted both bags. "Not much we can say to one another, I'm afraid."

I walked toward him. There must have been an odd expression on my face because he suddenly looked uneasy.

"No foolishness now," he said.

I placed the tip of the blade where his thorax joined his abdomen, just below where his jacket buttoned. His delicate features, always pallid, rapidly became more so.

"You're wrong," I said. "We have a lot to say to one another." Then, with a sudden, swift upward slash, I snipped off the button. It flew through the air like a tiny black bird. The point of the sword swept to within an inch of Darius' nose. He dropped the suitcases and leaped back, his coat swinging open.

I scowled. "Sit right there," I commanded, indicating a Victorian settee that had been a favorite of Veronica's. "Do it at once, before I unbutton your flesh the way I've unbuttoned your coat."

"You're unbalanced!" he said, his eyes starting from his head.

"Hurry. My supply of patience is low." I added a malign leer to my scowl.

He circled around me and sat down.

"Good," I said. "Sit back and put yourself at ease, Victor. There's whiskey in that cabinet at your elbow. Lovely marquetry, isn't it? Open it up. Go ahead. Don't be shy." I waved my Syrian cutlass like an admonitory finger. "Pull out the stopper. That's it. Now pour yourself a little drink."

Reluctantly he put an inch of whiskey in a gilt-edged tumbler, then held it in both hands. His expression was anxious. I dragged a straight-backed chair closer to the settee and sat down.

"Now," I said reasonably, "you must tell me about the recovery of the lost Leonardo, the one—in the event that you've forgotten—that I painted for you five years ago in Camden, Maine."

He stared at me for a moment, sighed, looked morosely into the brown fluid in the glass and then took a drink of it. "That's it then," he said. "You know. I had hoped you wouldn't learn of it for a year or two. Veronica said you never read papers or magazines. All this damned publicity." He crossed and uncrossed his legs nervously. "There's really no need for any unpleasantness, you know. There will be a great deal of money and you're certainly entitled to your share."

"How was it done?" I asked casually.

He bit his lip. "I can hardly tell you that, can I? It would be self-incriminating. If you threw in with us, of course, that would . . ."

I bounded from my chair, suddenly furious. "I'll kill you," I shouted, brandishing the scimitar. "I'll lop off your head, you brazen, double-dealing reptile! You're a liar, a cheat, a thief, a charlatan, a hypocrite and a philanderer. You have caused the suicide of my friend Littleboy, run off with my wife, ransacked my studio and damned me as a faker and forger. I will slit open your belly and festoon the room with your entrails. Do not trifle with me. See how I am trembling!" I was holding the blade edge just beneath his chin and it was shaking dangerously. "Be careful that I do not twitch you into oblivion. I want to know about the fraud. I want to know it all. I want to know it at once."

Darius pressed back against the sofa, his eyes glued on the quivering scimitar. "Very well," he said, the words nearly strangled. "Very well. I'll tell you. Whatever you like. But do sit down, won't you? You've quite convinced me."

I lowered my weapon. My heart was pounding. I went back to my chair as Darius finished his drink in two quick swallows and poured himself another.

Pressing his handkerchief to his forehead, he looked longingly in the direction of the door. "It was the 'Mona Lisa' copy, you see, that gave me the idea," he began. "The fact is, I've been in the fakery end of the business since I was hardly more than a boy. It kept me in pocket money at first. Now it's a bit more than that. Genuine things are almost impossible to come by these days. Everything's been bought up by the museums or the collectors. I found that if I wanted to have something to sell, I had to make it myself—or have someone else do it for me. You might find an occasional good old piece, but you'd never find enough of them to stay alive in the profession. I suppose it sounds awful to you, but you'd never dream of what goes on in the art world. You have to be a cynic to survive. It's a world of lions and jackals. They may speak of aesthetics and beauty but they do not believe in them. American museums are stiff with counterfeits—and how do you think they got there?" He pulled his coat about him but it wouldn't stay closed. A thread hung where the button had been.

"I kept my reputation clean, however. When I came upon your work, it was like finding a goose that laid golden eggs— if you'll pardon the uninspired comparison. One of the great difficulties in making forgeries is the near-impossibility of producing free, unlabored work. As soon as a painter tries to imitate another, he is forced to apply his paint in a strained, unnatural manner. This stiffness is what betrays most forgeries. But in your case, none of this applied. You painted like a Renaissance artist and you did it naturally, because it was your style and not someone else's. And you did it incredibly well." He laughed but it seemed forced. "They sold very well. I had to treat them, give them vague identities and be careful whom I sold them to, but it was relatively easy and they fetched good prices.

"If I could have approached you openly on the matter of making fakes, it would have greatly simplified things, but I feared that you would refuse—and I would've given myself away. Instead, I sent an associate of mine to test you. You may recall him—a burly fellow who wears garish clothing. I believe he bought an ivory carving."

"The man from Detroit," I said, remembering.

"Detroit? Is that what he told you? No matter. In any case, he returned with the answer I expected. You were a moral type. It was annoying but not fatal. I continued to buy all I could. I tried to keep other dealers away from you and I was anxious to keep you from traveling to Europe. You might learn that the buyers I mentioned were nonexistent or, worse still, see one of your statues in an antique shop window."

"Ah, Victor!" I exclaimed, shaking my head. "What a waste of everything."

He looked at me in silence for a moment. "Perhaps—but I've always had an inclination toward intrigue and skulduggery. A weakness, no doubt, but it was Leonardo, appropriately enough, who said, 'A straight line offers the most resistance.' I've always found it that way." He sipped the whiskey. "Be that as it may, the 'Mona Lisa' replica came to me and set my mind on fire. I knew an authenticated Leonardo would bring an astronomical price. Indeed, nothing in the entire art world would command more. But money alone was not the goad; the possibility of setting the scholars on their ears, of foisting on the world at large a bogus Leonardo da Vinci was an even greater spur. I began to dream about it.

"Do you see my dilemma? With your cooperation it would have been, not easy, to be sure, but much less impossible. I had an artist who could paint like Leonardo but who wouldn't. It required a stratagem. We wove a tale. Then we found a girl with a quattrocento face and brought her to America."

"She was not the daughter of a marquis, my Lisabeta?" I asked, surprised in spite of myself.

Darius smiled wryly. "She was a prostitute from Bergamo. Her name wasn't Lisabeta; it was Caramella. The arrangements were costly but the expectations were awesome. You accepted the challenge. I was sure you would. We are all of us the victims of our pride. You agreed to use only pristine paints and you asked no embarrassing questions. In short, you played your role perfectly." He smiled again and took another swallow of whiskey. "Only when you lost your touch and returned to Boston, did you give us cause to worry. Once you finished the picture, however, we soon forgot our anxieties. All of us were astounded. It really is a masterpiece, you know, regardless of who painted it.

"We smuggled it into Italy—the first time the traffic's gone in that direction, I imagine—and we processed it there. It was two whole years in a special gas oven, drying out. There was a danger of the pine shrinking more than the portrait and the paint layer buckling, but our luck held and it didn't happen. When the colors were quite hard, we covered it with layers of starch paste and cotton fabric. The entire paint surface was firmly fixed on this new reverse support. Then we removed the pine panel from the painting itself."

"Transference?" I asked incredulously.

"Yes. Transference—that most clever invention of Monsieur Picault. How else? Of course, it's more difficult with wood than canvas."

"I didn't know it was possible with wood."

"Oh yes," he said. "They can even take frescoes off walls these days. With a panel, you must saw the back off as closely as you dare, plane it down further, sandpaper what's left and pick off the remaining fibers with tweezers. But the reverse support of paste and cloth has to be firm. I gave you pine to use originally because its softness would make the task easier —though it was tedious enough, all the same."

There was no denying the cleverness of the rogue. He had planned well. As he related these details, his confidence began to return.

"At that stage your masterpiece was a sheet of hard, dry paint only a millimeter in thickness—about a twenty-fifth of an inch. We had to give it a new home—or rather, an old one— and we had to provide it with a credible provenance. The 'Boy in the Blue Doublet' was on a piece of poplar, as were most things of that period. We removed this panel, too, and placed the paint layer of the boy next to that of the girl. They were, I need hardly mention, the same size. We then fixed your work onto a second aged poplar panel, cleaned the muck from Lucrezia's pretty face, varnished it anew and placed the Paglia painting over it. The lost Leonardo was now the meat in a cunningly contrived sandwich. It remained to be seen whether the professors would nibble at it. We hoped they'd swallow it whole." Darius giggled at his conceit. The drink, evidently, was getting to him.

"Ingenious," I said, wondering if it would be possible to kill him once I had all the information.

"It was more than that," he replied, his eyes shining. "It was masterful. But let me go on. The stage was set. We put the picture back where it had hung for years and the restorer came and carted it away."

"The Count was in on it, then."

"Oh yes, but not the restorer. It was best to have the discovery made by an honest outsider. It lent verisimilitude. Naturally, we made it easy for him to detect the hidden portrait."

"How many of the experts were privy to the plot?"

"None. Good heavens! There isn't a one of them I could trust."

"You're an authority on trust," I said, but without bitterness. "But come now, Victor. You must have done more than that. No matter how much you dried the colors, they'd still look bright and new. What else did you do to it?"

"Not a thing, my dear fellow. It wasn't necessary. For one thing, your dark ground came through to some extent during the baking. For another, the portrait was supposed to have been covered over by Paglia only a short time after it left Leonardo's hands. Light is what fades color. The experts in Milan could see that the thing was bright, but they put it down to its having been protected all these years by the 'Boy in the Blue Doublet'—and quite reasonably so. How could it fade when it was so well protected? The richness of the color is one of the aspects that delights them most. They feel that they are looking at the only Renaissance masterpiece that still retains all its original freshness."

Everything worked in their favor, it seemed. I said, "Let me have a drop of the whiskey."

"Certainly," he replied. He poured some into a second glass and added to his own. The paleness had left his cheeks and he was no longer jittery. He appeared, in fact, to be enjoying his confession.

"The article said that the panel was cracked," I said, taking the glass from him.

"Simplicity itself. It was cracked before we put the paintings on it. One of the cardinal rules of the trade is never to produce a too-perfect article. Damage influences even the wisest of the wise. If it's knocked about some, it must be old, and if it's old, it must be legitimate, they reason. So the poplar support was cracked and warped as well. But we cradled and braced it and fixed the pictures to it. Then, little by little we released the clamps, and since the crack wasn't glued, it reopened and tore the paintings as realistically as Dame Nature herself. The warp returned, too. Did they mention the mulberry bush? 'All around the mulberry bush,'" he sang.

"Yes, they did." I watched him narrowly.

"That was my idea. A little hint for the connoisseurs. Clever, too, if I do say so. It was invisible to the naked eye, you know. Only the camera could make it out. I had a chap from Florence do it with a stylus. Leonardo liked to fool with intricate foliage —not that this was all that intricate. The Benci portrait in Liechtenstein has quite a tangle of it on the back. We couldn't use ink or those tin-lead pencils they had in those days, because the drawing would have been on top of the patina, and that would have given the whole show away. So we hit upon the stylus. A lot of genius besides yours went into that picture, believe me."

If I killed him, I thought, he would be my seventh victim. The idea was a charming one. What could I do with his body, however?

"But this is all nonsense," I told him, standing up. "What about all the scientific apparatus that they have now—the ultraviolet light, the infrared photography, the high-powered microscopes . . ."

"Yes, and the radiography, the spectroscopy, the spectro-photometry—I know them all. After all, it's my specialty. The best thief is a policeman. We subjected the picture to every known test before we let it out of our hands. Had you used a single dab of anachronistic paint, we'd have found it. As for the varnish, that was my own secret concoction. I'm a fair chemist, as perhaps you've heard. New varnish has a nasty habit of fluorescing under ultraviolet. Mine doesn't give a glimmer. We considered everything. We even checked for tobacco in the paint. You don't smoke but it could have gotten there a number of other ways; it would never do to have tobacco dust mixed in pigments that were made before Raleigh brought the stuff to Europe.

"At one point we considered aging the pine panel so as to eliminate one of the transferences, but in Italy no wood that old could escape the depredations of termites and you really can't simulate worm holes. Not only do the tunnels twist and turn, but the insect lives and dies in them." He giggled again. "We'd have had to fake termite cadavers, which was a bit much. Besides, there was always the chance that they'd carbon-fourteen the thing." He came to a halt and drank some of his whiskey. A flush had crept into his poet's face. Suppose I put strychnine in his drink? To see him in a paroxysm on the floor would cure all my illnesses.

"I still can't believe that the foremost Leonardo scholars in the world could be deluded by such machinations," I said. "How could they certify such a pastiche?"

"Well, they did, didn't they?" he asked triumphantly. "It was like selling the Eiffel Tower to the head of the Sûreté. The ultimate in deception, dear boy. Actually, the audacity of the enterprise was its strongest point. The old graybeards never dreamed that anyone would attempt a Leonardo fake. What, Leonardo? He was inimitable. Utterly unique. So they were caught in the toils of their own self-confidence. But, you know, the picture really is a wonder. It certainly looks more like the genuine article than that portrait the Poles insist is Lodovico's other mistress, Cecilia Gallerani. Remember, too, that every expert wants to be in on the discovery of a treasure. Think what it means to them. Their dreams are filled with such things. We have given them a chance to realize their fantasies, eh?"

I began to pace back and forth, my mind grappling with the details he had given me. What an edifice of artifice! There had to be a chink in so complex a structure.

"That's how it was done," he said, smirking. "And now, if you don't mind, I'll be on my way. None of this information will do you any good, I assure you. It's too late to alter anything."

"What about the brush stroke?" I cried, the idea suddenly entering my head. "Haven't you forgotten that? It's my brush stroke and not the good Leonardo's that's impressed in the paint of that portrait."

"The brush stroke! The brush stroke!" he exclaimed loudly, slapping his thigh. "That was the beginning of it all. When my man in London saw the 'Mona Lisa' caricature, he noticed it at once. He ran with it to the window and looked at it edge-on. 'It looks like the same stroke,' he said to me. The same stroke, don't you see? It was uncanny. We checked it against enlarged photographs of all the Louvre Leonardos and we couldn't believe what we saw. There was a difference, but one so fine that even we, who knew it existed, were unable to define it clearly. It was like finding two people with the same fingerprints. Is it any wonder that we attempted the hoax? The stroke made it possible. Without it, we'd never have dared cross swords with all those brainy coves."

I was stunned. Could it be true? Or was he lying? I returned to my chair and sat down. "It isn't possible," I muttered.

He laughed happily. "But it happened, nevertheless."

Identical brush strokes? Brush strokes are the most distinctive characteristic of painting. I took a gulp of whiskey and revived my reincarnation theory.

"That's why you should join us," he continued. "Think what we could do to them. We'd drive them up the wall. Do you know what the 'Lucrezia Crivelli' will fetch?"

"Two million dollars, they said."

"Double that! Maybe more. There isn't a decent Leonardo in all Italy. The 'Last Supper' is a ruin. The 'St. Jerome' and the 'Adoration of the Magi' are unfinished and the 'Annunciation' is only ascribed to the master. Many think it's a Ghirlandaio. It's too precise, you see. And what else is there? The picture can't leave Italy but the competition between Milan, Florence and Rome will cause the price to soar. We'll make them pay—otherwise it will go back on the *palazzo* wall. As a tourist attraction alone, it's worth the four million. Why, already throughout Italy they are saying it is better than the 'Mona Lisa.' The cast of Lucrezia's eyes, they say, is a miracle in paint—one that surpasses the Gioconda smile."

"Who are all these mysterious associates you mention, Victor?" I asked, hoping to get hold of something substantial.

He looked at me slyly. "No names, old boy. You've been trying to get me drunk, haven't you? A waste of time."

"You might still die," I reminded him.

He shook his head. "You'd be killing your hopes if you did away with me—not that I think you're serious," he said, slurring his s's. "I'm your only link with the picture, you know. You'd be cutting yourself adrift."

He was right, as far as he went. I studied him. His eyes radiated craftiness. "Darius the nefarious," I said. "Don't be so cocky. You're not all that clever. What about Buster in Maine and Caramella in Bergamo? What about Veronica? And suppose I paint another Leonardo with my uncanny brush stroke? What about that?" I emphasized my words with a flourish of the scimitar. "What about the people here who know my work and know you represented me?"

"Too late, much too late. And you needn't wave that thing about like some beggar in the Arabian Nights. Buster's dead

—coronary thrombosis, I'm told. Caramella? How would you find her? Girls like that are forever on the move. And if you did, how would you recognize her? Whores can change a bit in five years. And why would she admit to being a party to a fraud? The Italians do not treat art fraud as lightly as they do here. She'd draw a couple of years in quod if she talked. As for Veronica—you now know more about it than she does." He finished his drink. "I have to run."

"But suppose I paint another Lucrezia?"

"The answer to that is easy. They'd say that it was as different from the other as night is from day. And they'd believe it, too. You just don't know what you are up against. These people are experts. They can't change their minds. When they make an ascription, it's forever. How can you be an authority if you vacillate? Having once committed themselves, they'd die on the rack rather than admit they were mistaken. No, you haven't a chance. It would be what we called in public school a scalene contest—unequal sides, you see." He chuckled at his joke. "You on the one side, and all the world authorities on the other."

If I poisoned him just before he left, they'd still trace him back here, in all likelihood. His delicate face with its smug, sly expression was an invitation to murder. I felt the corner of my mouth begin to twitch. I can't kill him, I decided, much as I'd love to. It was too risky.

"You may go, Victor," I said, standing. "You've been closer to death, this past hour, than you imagine. Circumstances have preserved you. But you'll be hearing from me. Perhaps someday in the distant future, we'll have another long talk. By then you'll be able to tell me what life is like in an Italian jail." I walked toward my bedroom.

"Not likely! She said you were crazy, and you are," he called after me. "I was the only one to recognize your genius. To whom are you being loyal, eh? You could be a millionaire, with that brush of yours. You could have your revenge on the boors. Instead, you'll live and die in this apartment—like those silly termites in their worm holes."

I shut my bedroom door, cutting off his voice.

When I returned to the living room an hour later, he was gone. Only a depression in the Victorian settee and a black button on the rug revealed that he'd been there at all. But it proved that I hadn't imagined it all.

86 ౿

IT SEEMED to me that I would have to call in the police, like it or not, and get them to arrest Darius. Olsen, the janitor at my studio, could identify him. If I could get my work back, it would substantiate my claim. Moreover, the mere fact that they had stolen the things would surely have some bearing on the Leonardo business. But Faber would have to handle it for me. My nerves just weren't up to police interviews.

I ate two eggs and some salami and went down to the Garden. It was a pleasant day. I sat quite still. After a while I became calmer. I hoped for a reverie, but none came. I stayed mired in Boston amidst my problems. If I have lost the ability to reverie, I do not know what I shall do. The future would become impossible. Today I thought I was tranquil enough for a simple excursion but I couldn't produce a flicker. It's almost as if someone has thrown a switch and disconnected me. I don't like it at all.

Beels came along. Johann parked him right beside me, and, of course, he commenced his prattle immediately.

"Well, well, well. I've come upon you at last," he said in his weird voice while looking sideways into my face. "I never see you, it seems. You used to be quite regular in your appearances here, but lately it's difficult to know when you'll arrive. Have you been ill? You look a bit wan, if I may say so. No? You must take care of yourself, my good sir, in any case. Life is perilous and unpredictable. Have you given any more thought to a policy? Perhaps a trust would be more to your inclination. I have many fiduciary arrangements. You can't possibly imagine the multitude of benefits to be derived from some of my contracts. Benefits, I mean, that you can take advantage of while you are alive. Then, when life comes to an end—as sadly it must—you will have made the most of your sojourn here on this planet, eh, Mr. Barber? But I was forgetting. You intend to take a short cut to contentment, by killing God, isn't that so?" He was holding a German magazine in one hand and he now waved it playfully before my nose.

"Yes," I said, wondering how the old fool could keep from suffocating under such a mass of clothing—and in such heat.

He sucked on his cigar and sent a volcanic cloud up toward the sheltering treetops. "And then," he said, wiggling the periodical, "you intend to usurp His throne on high. Is that it?"

"I hadn't planned a general election," I admitted.

He discharged his inimitable cackling laugh. "You really are most humorous, sir. A dazzling wit. But where are you going? You must leave so soon?"

I had risen. "Business," I said. "I must call a man about a four-million-dollar fraud."

"Really? What an inventive mind you have! But I really do think that you are deliberately avoiding me," he said mildly, "and I did want to discuss a policy with you."

"I have no need of any kind of policy."

"You are certain?"

"Yes."

"And that decision is final and irrevocable?"

"Nothing could be more so," I said, walking away from the two of them.

His voice followed me. It contained a chilly, almost macabre, quality. "Very well, then. Time will determine which of us was right," he said.

87 ❧

"I'VE JUST come in the door," Faber said, sounding out of breath over the phone. It was one o'clock the next afternoon. "They talked me into staying for a *vernissage*—some awful mannerist. How are you?"

I wasted no time in telling him of the wild and amazing discoveries I had made in his absence, from the picture on the magazine to the final words of Darius in my apartment. I suppose I rambled in my narrative, for he was, at first, unable to grasp the story, but when he did, he was thunderstruck. After a rapid series of astute questions, and many cries of astonishment at my answers, he fell silent. I waited impatiently.

"Do you remember your visit here," he said finally, "shortly after I returned from Vermont? I was going to ask you about this lost Leonardo then. I had seen it in a New York paper and it struck me as familiar."

"How could it be?" I asked. "You'd never seen the original."

"No, but you sent me a sketch of it in Europe and the black and white newspaper photograph brought it immediately to mind. I wanted to show it to you, but it seemed too fantastic. It's unbelievable even knowing the tale behind it. How could they hope to fool all those scholars? And they did it. Later I assumed that you must have seen the picture. The story was printed everywhere. It's been the biggest sensation the art world has known for years and years." Suddenly he whistled shrilly in my ear. "I believe I still have that letter with the sketch. It's in a box in storage in Cambridge or possibly Dorchester. I'm sure of it. All my European correspondence is there—along with the water colors I did at Capri and Sorrento."

"That would prove my authorship!" I exclaimed, nearly dropping the phone in my excitement. "It would prove it. How could they refute it?"

"I don't know if it would be enough, in itself, but it will certainly be a help. As I recall, you described the painting at length. I think, too, that the original envelope is probably with the letter and that would be postmarked with the date and place of origin. If we can get experts to establish the authenticity of the sketch and the letter, we ought to be able to cast serious doubt on the whole question of the attribution, and one serious doubt will compel them to investigate further, I should think. It's a question of setting the ball rolling. If we can present a strong enough case, we'll begin to get rival connoisseurs to support us. The Louvre, of course, has that painting that they've put forth for years as the 'Lucrezia Crivelli' and they would probably be eager enough to listen to us. And those people who specialize in uncovering frauds—the letter should attract a few of them. The man who exposes this one will make his reputation. But come up. Take a cab."

I ate a quick sandwich, downed a cup of coffee and rushed from the house. My spirits were soaring. The letter could change everything.

"You look ready to burst," Leo said when I arrived. "Sit down. Would you like a drop of Courvoisier? I'm completely out of coffee. I should have told you to bring some along. The cleaning woman drinks it all. Tell me again about those transferences. What a job it must have been. Yet, if they'd had you paint it on canvas, the experts would have realized from the surface that it had been transferred from cloth. And Leonardo wasn't a canvas painter. A fiendish plot."

We spent the afternoon going over every facet of the swindle. The similarity of the brush stroke stunned him as much as it had me, but he agreed that it might yet work in our favor. He regretted not having spoken to me about the portrait when he first saw it. The tardiness of my speaking out could weaken my claim. It was essential, therefore, to get the letter in the morning and to bring it to a Boston newspaper. Its publication would begin things swiftly. Leo knew a very clever restorer in New York who had great experience with transferring, and we would consult him. The studio theft would have to be turned over to the police and Leo's lawyer brought into the affairs. Faber made a listing of the influential people he knew and whose aid he thought he could enlist. Things looked brighter.

"Do you remember the Flora case?" he asked at one point. "It happened in the nineteenth century but you might have read of it somewhere. It was a wax bust of a woman that some dealer sold to a museum."

I had never heard of it and told him so.

"I don't remember the details. It was authenticated as the work of Leonardo by most of the top people in Europe. Then an Englishman announced that his father had made it some thirty years before. He had a little evidence to substantiate his claim but nothing conclusive. The experts fought fiercely. Reputations hung in the balance. In the end the figure was repudiated, taken from its place of prominence and put in the basement. I believe the museum was in Berlin."

This anecdote further buoyed my optimism. He related other stories of exposed impostures, and by the time I left I was sure that we could topple Darius and his confederates. Leo's knowledge and his distinction, not just as an artist, but as a writer and lecturer as well, were bound to add great weight to my assertions. They would listen to him. I promised to call for him at nine the next morning.

88 ❧

WHEN I reached the street, the heavy hot atmosphere, added to the excitement and the three or four brandies that I had drunk, made me drowsy and I stopped in Ringle's for a cup of coffee. In the days when Faber had a furnished room on Brookline Avenue, Ringle's had served as our headquarters. Many an hour was spent there in lively debate. Benjamin's booming laughter had often resounded off the walls in those far-away days. Our customary table was vacant, and I sat at it and tried, as I drank my coffee, to recall those happy conversations of my youth.

But the problems of the present soon pushed aside the pleasant musings of the past. I took a pencil and a scrap of paper from my pocket and began to write down all the arguments in our favor. There were far more than I expected, though some, admittedly, were not too convincing. I had mentioned their checking the paint for tobacco, and Leo had raised the possibility of further checks—automobile exhaust chemicals, maybe, or traces of coffee powder, since that, too, was a new-world product. He said that pollen was sometimes used in identifying archeological finds, and that if the picture contained the spores of any plants from the Western Hemisphere, that could raise doubts.

I must have sat there for some time, for when I looked out the window, the sun was setting behind the bulk of the Hotel Westminster. I did not want to be caught by darkness. I finished my cold coffee.

Suddenly I noticed that there was a sugar bowl on the table. The turmoil of the past few days had so distracted me that I had failed to perceive, directly in front of my nose, the very object that I had hunted for in so many cafeterias in so many suburban towns. I looked about me. The woman at the counter was a total stranger. It had been a couple of years since I had been here last and three times that since it had been our meeting place. The nearest customer was an old man with his face an inch away from his evening paper. The bowl was open, the cover replicated. I dug into my pocket and got the fold of wax paper. Two or three seconds passed, then the woman at the counter turned her back to me and I emptied the packet into the bowl. A moment later I was out in Kenmore Square, on my way home. I congratulated myself.

If I fail in my struggle with Darius, I reasoned, I will have my consultation with God to fall back upon.

89 ⮞

I DIDN'T take any pills that night but I slept very soundly—more soundly than I had at any time in the past month. The street noises, when I awakened, told me that it was past my usual rising time and I washed, dressed and ate hurriedly. There was much to be done that day and I didn't want to be late getting to Leo's. While eating, I remembered all the reworking I had done on Lisabeta's hand, and it struck me that this should be visible to the x-ray camera and that my awareness of it would do a lot to advance my suit. With this happy thought to start the day, I skipped down the stairs confident that things would be successfully arranged. I even waved to Mr. Barletty.

It was not until I came out on Beacon Street that I remembered the poisoning of the sugar the evening before. The clock in the florist's showed it to be a quarter to nine. I might well have my seventh and last victim, I thought. With bouncing step I walked to Charles Street to get a newspaper and a taxi. While I was still several yards from the newsstand, I discerned a tabloid headline that made my heart leap. *Seventh Borgia Murder* it proclaimed. I had them all. I was finished.

"The *Chronicle*," I said to the newsdealer, glancing at the rows of papers. One edition carried a picture labeled at the top: *Latest Target of Killer,* but only the crown of a man's head was visible because of the fold in the page. I lifted it and turned it back to have a look at him.

The next instant I felt myself falling forward, and almost simultaneously, someone grabbed me by the arm. My eyes filled with blackness, as though a sable pall had dropped before my face. But it lasted for only a second.

"You all right, Mac?" a voice asked in my ear. I turned and saw the paper seller's anxious face.

"Yes, yes," I responded, in little more than a whisper. "I've been ill. I'm still weak—but I'll manage. Thank you."

"Ought to get home to bed," the man advised gruffly, as I tottered away with the *Chronicle* under my arm and the change still in my hand.

The face in the picture had been that of Leo Faber.

I SPENT all of yesterday trying to escape into a reverie of some kind—any kind would have been welcome. It was a hopeless endeavor. Whether I lay trembling beneath my bed or sitting catatonically in the Garden or in the courtyard of the library, I could not flee this odious setting, this hateful time. By nightfall I was so racked with melancholy that my heart actually hurt—as if it were breaking, the way hearts are said to shatter in romantic poetry. Dejection closed over me like a shroud. My head became a bedlam of mad and dreadful notions. Nightfall found me under my bed, the tears warm upon my cheeks, my limbs shivering.

When I closed my eyes, he was there. Through the door of Ringle's he comes, walking with that graceless shuffle of his. I see him with perfect clarity. He is tired, but he hasn't had a cup of coffee all afternoon. Perhaps he came out to buy a tin but the grocer had closed and he was too weary to trudge to the market on Massachusetts Avenue. He goes to the counter and the woman serves him; he turns and looks for a table. Down the aisle he comes. But where will he sit? At the old table, of course. In his usual place. He will sit there, just as I sat there—guided by nostalgia and habit.

"Away, Leo, away!" I cry out. "Do not sit there! Not at that table, please. Get away from it at once." But these words are pronounced here in my apartment. They reach only the mattress above me. In Ringle's there are only the small sounds of people eating. I watch him in horror as he sets the cup down, pulls out the chair and sits. His spoon dips into the bowl, then reappears filled with sparkling crystals, which he carries to the coffee. Down into the steaming brown fluid the lethal grains tumble. The perspiration trickles down my face and stings my eyes. "But don't drink it, Leo," I implore. He stirs it, puts it to his lips. "No!" I scream into the palms of my hands. Hoping to stop the action, I beat my head against the floor. My fingernails dig into my cheeks. But the mouth opens, the cup tilts.

I am suddenly aware that it is all over—but I continue to look at him as he puts the cup down and watches the traffic in Kenmore Square. What are his thoughts? No doubt he is pondering ways to help his friend. No doubt he is considering the incredible tale he heard that day. He drinks slowly. There is no need for him to hurry. He might even have a second cup in mind. But he begins to feel strange, uneasy. He puts his hand to the nape of his neck. The sinews are curiously tense.

After that his agony begins. It is all there. The hideous grin and the twitching muscles, the bending of the body and the look of impending doom in the protuberant eyes. Then the deceptive relaxation of the muscles and the seeming recovery of the sufferer that is, all too soon, followed by new and even more severe spasms. The pattern is repeated until death, at last, arrives.

I open my eyes and look blankly at the coiled steel springs of the bed. In the gloom my gaze wanders distractedly among these twisted strands of wire, and my brain cringes. I close my eyes and there is Leo walking into Ringle's. He marches to the counter, and I whisper, "Away! Away! Don't stay there, Faber. Go away."

At one point, well into the night, I heard three chimes of a church bell and found myself sitting at the window, staring at the street lamps in the Garden. Two in particular, because of their seeming proximity, resembled giant orange eyes—and not just any eyes, but a familiar pair. One appeared slightly larger than the other. I suddenly realized that they were Mitya's crooked oculi and I leaped from my chair and ran from the window.

When the sun rose, I awakened in the kitchen with my head on the table. I managed to eat a hard-boiled egg and then left. The newspapers announced the formation of a special committee to consider new ways of trapping the Borgia. The Governor offered every assistance; the Mayor declared this, the Attorney General warned that and the Police Commissioner hinted at fresh leads.

I took a long walk. It was past noon when I returned to the apartment, and I boiled another egg and drank some tomato juice. After that I lay across my bed and fell fast asleep, thinking—just before losing consciousness—that Leo would still be alive if I had killed Victor Darius the day he was here.

91 ঌ

I MUST have slept two or three hours. The pigeons awakened me with their disgusting gurgling. I got up and chased them. The nap had cleared my mind of guilt and wretchedness and I felt much better. Indeed, I was able to view things with an almost paranormal tranquillity. My nerves were gone. I was as calm as on the day I had killed the Mahoney girl.

I went into the kitchen and made coffee, and as I sat drinking it, I noticed Casimir's *Life and Precepts* on the window sill. For a while I stared idly at it. The window was open about an inch and a slight breeze stirred one of the yellowed pages, moving it up and down in gentle undulation. All at once I understood what I must do. It was perfectly clear. I must summon God and have Him return Faber to life. That was the solution to everything. I did not know how God could do this —whether He could reverse time or, perhaps, erase the memory of Leo's death from the consciousness of the world—but I was confident that He would have a means. It was all so simple that I was amazed at my not having thought of it yesterday. I had the victims and the ritual; now was the time to put them to use. I picked up the book and went back to my room.

The pigeons stared in at me. Out in the Garden I could see the swan boats gliding serenely upon the lagoon. Some sailors in white uniforms and girls in pastel dresses strolled across the little bridge, while near the main Charles Street gate a vendor hawked celluloid pinwheels. As I looked down, I wondered. Could I really bring God here? Could I fetch Him from wherever He might be in the universe and cause Him to materialize in this city, in this room? Would He respond to the incantation? Or was it all folly? Was I merely a homicidal maniac, as the newspapers insisted? A cloud passed before the sun and I turned and looked at the Bourg Angel on the mantel. Beside it stood the vial of *nux vomica*. The two had shaped my destiny. The Angel stared back at me in concentration. She had called Him "the Lord God."

I spread the newspaper clippings on my table and counted the people I had murdered, to be certain there was no error. There were seven, beyond a doubt, though I had no clipping for Leo. I thumbed through Casimir and found the section dealing with conjuration.

"Having done to death these seven fellow creatures," I read, slowly and carefully, "you must secure a piece of fine white cloth or parchment or paper and lay it evenly before you. Upon this surface describe in black a spiral, with pommels on the terminal points—the whole slightly larger than your left hand. This is the sign of God, being the one figure that begins at the beginning, which is the inner pommel, ends at the end, which is the outer pommel, and encompasses all and everything within its helix. When you have done this, you must

take up in your right hand a stick or wand of wood, and recite
the names of those you have sacrificed. Wait, then, for the
space of seven breaths, raise the wand and say these words:

> God, God of all gods, Spinner of space and substance,
> Master of men, All of everything—I would speak to Thee.

As the word 'Thee' leaves your lips, place the tip of the rod
on the inner knob of the spiral. God will then appear."

It was simple enough. I read it through a second time and
then began to look about the apartment for a stick. There
wasn't one and I was obliged to wrench a rung from one of
the less sturdy Windsor chairs in the kitchen. Returning to my
room, I pushed the newspaper accounts to one side, put a
clean piece of paper on the table and placed the rung beside it.
Then I read the passage a third time and looked out the window. I could see a bundle of clothing that was Mr. Beels, and
Johann—angular and motionless as a menhir—standing behind
him. The mauve balloon was still the captive of the elm, and
near the drinking fountain the mad Mrs. Dandelion—pallid even
at such a distance—scattered birdseed and wagged her head.
The sky was filling with black clouds.

From the drawer I took a charcoal pencil. Then I sat down,
drew a small circle in the center of the sheet and filled it in so
completely that it looked like a hole in the paper. Beginning
there and working outward, I traced a neat, perfectly propor-
tional spiral. The room suddenly grew still. I worked deliberately and with a steady hand, and when after the fourth loop
I ended the coil, I did so with a second black ball exactly the
size of the first. Putting the pencil aside, I surveyed the design. The concentric lines formed a whirlpool that pulled the
eye into the spot at the center, while the spot itself appeared
to expand and gape. I compared it with my left hand and was
satisfied that it was a little larger.

The sky without was growing darker. Only two pigeons remained on the ledge, but they watched me closely with glassy

amber eyes, though they had ceased their warbling gabble.
Below, the automobiles raced down Beacon Street, but no
audible evidence of their career penetrated into the room.

I rubbed my hands together—the fingertips felt cold—and I
picked up the chair rung.

"Janice Mahoney," I said in measured tones. "William Hunt.
Peter Skibinskoi. Aldo Muja. Isabel Bailey. Gary Belisle. Leo
Faber."

I inhaled and exhaled seven times, a great excitement growing in my breast. Then, clearly and rhythmically, I recited the
prayer:

> "God, God of all gods, Spinner of space and substance,
> Master of men, All of everything—I would speak to
> Thee."

I hesitated for a fraction of an instant before pronouncing the
final word, but when it did leave my lips, simultaneously I
placed the tip of the rung on the spot in the center of the
spiral.

I do not know how long I waited—hardly more than three
or four seconds, I would guess. The pigeons were now not only
silent but completely motionless as well. Utter quiet pervaded the room. I knew that I was breathing heavily but
I made no sound. A fear of moving gripped me, as though
the nod of a head or the gesture of a finger might bring on a
calamity. It was as if everything was arrested and frozen in
place. Three or four seconds thus—and then there came a sharp
and imperious knock upon the apartment door.

A cold jagged sensation traversed my body. The silence of
the room, shattered by the knock, now disappeared completely
as the accelerated pounding of my heart filled my ears. The
hair on my arms and on the back of my neck bristled in horri-
pilation. Slowly I got up from the chair, like an invalid standing for the first time in many months. Through the bedroom
doorway, through the arch of the dining room and the foyer,

I could see the cream-colored panel of the front door. My eyes strained to look through it. I took one step in its direction, but then the muscles in my legs ceased to function and I could go no further. I became as still as a piece of furniture. A strange, unintelligible murmuring seeped into the apartment from the hall and was quickly followed by a series of blows on the door of such potency that the pictures quivered on the walls.

I thought of Casimir's tall stranger, of the burning inn and the screams of the old man and his wife and of the consternation of the Bourg Angel at the mention of God. My nerves, so lacerated by the appalling incidents of the past few months, snapped. Under the bed I went, my teeth clenched to prevent them from chattering, my hands tightened into fists of fright. And then the door opened. I took a deep breath and held it. I held it for a long time. In all my life I have never contained a single lungful of air for such a lengthy period. Were I suspended from a gallows, I doubt if I could hoard my breath with greater avidity. In spite of the pulsing in my ears, I heard footsteps. I closed my eyes.

"Hello, hello!" said a voice, rich with Irish brogue, from the living room. "Anybody home? Hello. Who's there? Anybody at home?"

I opened my eyes, releasing the breath silently. More footfalls sounded.

"I guess not," the voice said. "Not a soul. Nothing to fear, Mr. Barletty. The fellow's out. Is that the window? Oh yes, there's the bread all right. Don't worry about a thing. We'll be out of here in a minute."

The meddling Barletty spoke. "He'd make a fuss, I'm sure. He's a queer one, believe me. But he's always out at this time. Regular as clockwork, he is. He sits in the park a lot but I never saw him feeding the pigeons. I'd never do this in the ordinary way of things, but a police matter is something else."

A window went up. "Well," said the brogue, "it saves trouble—and who's to know? I'll just take a bit of it and be on my way. Look at it. There is some kind of white stuff on it. Probably sugar but I'll let the boys at the lab have a peek. Me science is a bit rusty and I don't think I'll take a taste of it."

"Do you think it could really be him?" Barletty said.

"Who knows? It could be anybody. What's that?"

"Why, it's a broken chair."

"Is it, now?"

Their footsteps shuffled off to the kitchen. I could still hear their voices but I couldn't make out the words. After a while they returned.

"His wife left him," Barletty was saying. "They used to pass one another in the lobby without even speaking. Made me feel creepy just to see them. Can't say I blame her any. She was a real lady, but him! Very peculiar. He walked around with dust on his clothes, as if he'd been rolling about on the floor."

I shuddered beneath the bed.

"Well, maybe the crazy old biddy is on to something. By Jasus, it was a treat to see the way she collared the Captain. Of course, anyone who says the word 'poison' to him gets the full use of both his ears. And waving that dead pigeon in front of his nose sort of held his attention, too. What is that room there?" They drew nearer.

"One of the bedrooms," Barletty said.

I shut my eyes again and tried to contract my body within its skin. I had gone from terror to mere fear and was now on my way back to terror.

"Ah-h-h-h!" the policeman said, lengthening the aspirate until it sounded like a moan.

"What's that?" the janitor asked.

I opened my eyes very slowly, in case the lids should make a noise. Before me, not a yard from my nose, was an enormous black shoe with a thick sole and a worn-down heel. Above the shoe a white sock gleamed, and above that rose the blue serge trouser leg of the policeman. I watched the foot with as much interest as the rabbit is said to bestow on the weaving head of the hungry cobra.

"Now that's interesting," said the voice at the other end of the foot. "Clippings about the murders is what they are, you see. Right from the beginning. I'd say that was more than natural interest. What do you make of this thing, here?"

"A design of some kind. He's supposed to be an artist. But all of those newspaper stories—that's very suspicious."

"I'd say so. A morbid curiosity, eh?" The shoe and the leg moved from my field of vision. A silence followed, and then the cop spoke once more but his voice had changed. It was suddenly strong with emotion. It seemed to shimmer.

"Now, now. I see something—yes, I do," he said. "It's a sight to make me want to sing a song. Oh, do I see something, by Gawd. Touch nothing. Don't put a finger on a thing in this room. I think our names are going to be in the morning papers, and I think I'll find meself in the Detective Division soon after that."

"What do you see? Why do you say that?"

"That bottle there on the mantel—that's what I see. He'll be back around six, you think?"

"That's when he usually gets back, yes. That's a medicine bottle, that is. Do you mean it's the poison?"

"*Nux vomica,* me boyo, and that's not *Dominus vobiscum.* We'll have to get out of here. There's a lot to be done." The Irish voice was gay and lyrical. "We'll need a warrant now, you understand. As the Sergeant says, 'Always do things legally —whenever possible.' We'll grab him downstairs when he comes in the door, and then escort him up here with the warrant."

"That's the strychnine? You mean it's really him?" Barletty was saying incredulously as their footsteps retreated from the room.

"Mum's the word. Don't go flapping your lip, now. You can talk all you want once we've got him in the Charles Street Jail. I have to get me partner to move the bucket of bolts away from the front door. Wouldn't want to scare me promotion away."

"My God!" Barletty exclaimed theatrically.

The front door opened and closed.

92 ﹖

I REQUIRED only three minutes to pack my things. When I was certain that they were gone, I slid out from under the bed and dusted myself off. Tiptoeing, I made my way to the kitchen and got a large paper shopping bag. Into this inconspicuous portmanteau I tossed the Bourg Angel, all my papers, the Casimir book and the vial of strychnine, covering the lot with socks and underwear. I was forced to abandon the crystal ball, the scimitar and my phonograph and records. To alter my appearance, I put on a gray straw hat and an olive linen jacket that I hadn't worn in years. After a moment with my ear to the door, I slipped into the hall and made for the stairs.

Down I went, into the basement, out into the backyard and through the door in the wall to Byron Street. A drop of rain touched my cheek as I strode with casual speed out to Charles Street. Another tapped my hat as I bounded across Beacon Street. A cautious peek in the direction of the apartment showed neither police cars nor constables. I ducked into the Garden. Randolph, resplendent in new white sneakers, shot out from behind the gatepost and caused the blood to congeal in my veins.

"Where'd you get the hat?" he asked bluntly.

"A gift," I replied, my heart flopping about in my throat, "from my sister's brother."

"My cousin Claude has one like it. He's seven."

"Really?"

"Yes. Want some Turkish taffy? It's good. Don't you like candy? If lemons are sour all the time, how can they tell when they're ripe?"

"Because," I said, "when they're not ripe, they're green."

"Oh." He looked thoughtful. "How can they tell with limes?"

"I'm in a great hurry today," I said evasively. "Who is that?" He had produced a crococile puppet from inside his shirt, fitted it over his hand and was now snapping its jaws in my face.

"My name is Anthony," the thing announced, "what's yours?"

A folded newspaper on a bench caught my eye. *Total Liquidation* was inscribed in large block letters over an advertisement.

"My name is Totality," I said, "Mr. Totality."

"What's your first name?" Anthony asked, champing the air.

"I don't have one—not any more, young man—or crocodile, I mean to say. Did once, but it wore out. People were always using it, you see. They all wanted to be friendly, I guess. Had it repaired once or twice, but in the end it just fell all to pieces. Happened one day when my wife was calling me in to help move the piano. She never got past the first syllable and even that just crumbled into dust. I swept it up into a dustpan and that was the end of that." Out of the corner of my eye I discerned Johann wheeling Mr. Beels in our direction. "Mind if I walk a little faster?" I asked, stepping up the pace.

"Yes, I do," Anthony said. "Crocodiles have very short legs, you know. What's the rush, anyway?"

"Well, being Mr. Totality carries certain responsibilities. You have to be everybody—and when you're everybody, you have to be everywhere, right? And to be everywhere means you have to dash about a bit."

"Where are you scampering to?" Mr. Beels asked, pulling alongside me and pointing his gnarled black cigar at me like a pistol.

"It's going to rain," I said, casting a glance at the threatening sky.

"What of it? You've been wet before." He laughed evilly. "I'd say you were running away from more than the rain. I'd say you're in some kind of difficulty. But you wouldn't take out a policy, would you? Thought you'd go it alone, eh? Now you have no protection, you fool, none at all. He's a fool, isn't he, Johann?" He turned his pinched red face around to look over his shoulder at the giant. But Johann made no reply. Impassive as stone, he looked straight before him.

The daylight was rapidly succumbing to the assault of the clouds.

"What's that in the bag?" Beels asked raucously.

"A dead body. God's, as a matter of fact. You didn't think I could do it, did you? Turns out He wasn't such a big Chap, after all. He's there at the bottom, beneath my T-shirts. Pity He didn't have some of your excellent coverage. But no matter. I'm going to give him a decent Christian burial over in the fens."

"Don't be clever with me," he barked. A lobster claw of a hand darted from the folds of the blanket and tried to grab the shopping bag.

I yanked it out of his reach. By now I was walking very fast, but the wheelchair stayed with me on the one side, while Randolph, with Anthony bobbing on his hand, skipped along on the other. More raindrops fell.

"Do you think all your nonsense deceived me?" Mr. Beels asked. "I've been on to you from the very beginning, you damned ninny. You've had your dance, and a merry one it's been, but it's time to pay the fiddler."

At his words I thought it was prudent to break into a trot. "Seize him, Johann," he cried shrilly. "Seize the ruffian!"

I ran. Behind me there was a scuffling noise and some sharp words in German. I chanced a backward look. Johann was sprawled on the ground, while Randolph, white sneakers flickering in the gloom, was racing nimbly away in the opposite direction.

"You damned idiot! Get up and get him—fast!" Beels screamed, rising in the wheelchair. But evidently, in addition to his other errors, Johann had neglected to engage the brake. Thus, as the cripple stood, the vehicle rolled out from under him and he pitched forward, woolens and all, on top of his servant. The cigar fell from his hand and sent up a great shower of sparks as it struck the ground. The tweed hat, an instant later, rolled on its brim like a cartwheel, gaily pursuing the stogie. Mr. Beels, it appeared, had dark hair, though two short plumes of white ran up from his forehead in striking fashion. His face was now so congested with blood that it was almost black and his green eyes flickered up at me in helpless, seething rage. I wasted no further time in idle observation but lengthened my stride and improved its frequency. The rain was now falling in fat blobs that splattered noisily on the pavement. With the shopping bag pounding against my leg, I made for Arlington Street.

Who is that man? I wondered. What's his game? Is he a detective? Some kind of an agent provocateur? I ran lightly but swiftly. Then a new and far more curious thought came to me. Those streaks of gray in his hair—were they really that or something else? I got only a fleeting view of them. Might they not have been—horns? Yes, horns! Was the fellow Old Nick himself? And those tiny, tiny shoes—did they hide hooves? Yes, yes. It could be. It could be and it would explain a great deal. His talk of contracts and of it being too late. He was after a hellish compact. Wait! Before he fell, did he shout, "Get him—fast," or was he saying in his outlandish accent, "Get him—Faust"? What about that? Was the silent Johann the ambitious Dr. Faust? Is it possible? Could it really be? The world is coming apart. This rickety universe has at last begun to crumble.

I had no time to continue these strange and terrible speculations, for I now saw before me a flock of pigeons milling jerkily about on the path. Setting my jaw, I lowered my head and charged. Neither the lancers at Quatre Bras nor the Numideans at Cannae could have advanced more fearlessly. The beastly birds swarmed upward, creating an almost solid gray wall of thrashing wings. Feathers brushed my face and a foul poultry smell assailed my laboring nostrils, but I persevered stoutly and suddenly the way was clear.

At that moment a cold bony hand grasped my wrist.

"Poisoner," a shrill voice screeched in my ear. "Killer! Murderer!"

There beside me, running along as best she could, her gaunt face contorted by fury and her yellow hat flopping about precariously on her head, was April Dandelion. With a cry of anger and loathing I shook her off and ran still faster. A man under an umbrella glanced at me suspiciously, but as the rain was now coming down quite heavily and others were running nearly as vigorously as I, I did not hold his interest long.

On I sped, past all the handsome elms, the carefree magnolias, the delicate tea crabapples and the dolorous willows. At last, clutching my bag to my chest, I reached the Garden exit and dashed out. At that very moment the blackened sky was torn asunder by a flash of lightning brighter than the midday sun. A second later the ground beneath me was rocked by an ear-shattering clap of thunder. I nearly stumbled and fell. My heart skipped several beats.

But across the street I galloped, and into the alley behind

Marlborough Street. There I slowed my stride long enough to raise my fist aloft, direct my eyes to the heavens and bellow defiantly, "You missed me, You great, silly Ass!"

Then away I went.

93 ❧

NOT UNTIL Exeter Street did I emerge from the alley. A cautious few minutes spent in a doorway assured me that I had not been followed. The rain had slackened but my clothes were damp and my shoes filled with water. To supplement my discomfort, I had a flaming pain in my left side from my cross-country gallop. An umbrella is what I need, I decided. It was then that I realized that I had no money. A rapid and frantic exploration of my pockets produced eighty cents and a bus token. Eighty cents. Hardly enough for lunch! And to return to Charles Street and my savings bank was to walk into the arms of the police. My career as a fugitive was off to an inauspicious start.

"This, too, is His work," I mumbled to myself bitterly. "He thinks that because He is God, He can do anything."

But without money, I was lost. The corner of my mouth commenced to twitch busily.

I began to look in the gutter, trying to recall Benjamin's remarks about money-looking. What had he said? Bus stops, parking meters, something about windy days, coins glistening in the rain—snatches of his ramblings rose to the surface of my memory as I trudged along Commonwealth, studying the rivulet of murky water at the curb. Dead leaves, match sticks, rusty nails, cigarette packets, pebbles, grease spots, bottle caps, cigar butts, bobby pins, candy wrappers—everything in the world but money. At Hereford Street, I at last came upon a shiny new penny, but this success was overshadowed a few moments later when I collided with a mailbox and nearly lost an ear. Benjamin had made no mention of mailboxes.

On the other side of Massachusetts Avenue, I caught a glimpse of myself in a store window and shuddered. The straw hat (which transmitted the rain with one hundred percent efficiency), the sodden jacket and pants, the lumpy shopping bag and the hangdog expression on my wet face, all combined to drag down the few hopes I still harbored. I was a picture of desolation. I, who had always cherished order, was now as disarrayed as everything else in this discordant world.

What am I doing? Where am I going? Why? I laughed mirthlessly. It's impossible. Hopeless. Crazy. Ridiculous. The whole city of Boston is looking for me. In an hour the Commonwealth of Massachusetts will be on my trail, and shortly thereafter the United States of America—with its illimitable resources—will be joining in the chase. Nor is that all, for God and (I have good reason to believe) the Devil are pursuing me as well. And to confront this formidable alliance, what force can I muster? A shattered nervous system, a battered intellect and eighty-one cents! What foolishness this is. There is no chance at all. Not a single one. Everything is finished. All that remains to be done is for me to hop off the Cottage Farm Bridge—to tidy up my life by concluding it. That's it, of course. The way of Themistocles, Hannibal, Brutus, Cato the Younger and Littleboy.

> To cease to be,
> Is best for thee.
> Felo-de-se,
> Will set you free.

The greatest truths are the simplest. And at this time of year the Charles is not even cold. I will pull it up over my head like a goosefeather quilt and nestle down in its soft folds for a sweet, dreamless, wakeless, endless slumber.

"Yes, on to the bridge," I said aloud as I neared Kenmore Square. "It will, after all, be only a semi-suicide, since I am half-drowned already."

I felt pleased with this logical solution. Why hadn't it occurred to me sooner? Who ever had greater cause to take his own life? Consider what I have had to endure. All I sought was to live in peace and create beauty. A crust of bread, a little appreciation, a few congenial comrades and a modicum of immortality—I desired nothing more.

But what was I given? A faithless, empty-headed, burglarious woman for a wife and a conscienceless, philandering English phlebotomist for a business agent. This precious pair of vipers began it all. These two adders divided my life, subtracted my happiness and multiplied my misfortunes. It was they who tipped me into that maelstrom of false marcheses, mercenary Bergamese whores, slippery Italian counts, witless German art experts, villainous Peruvian generals, paranoiac harpies, spiteful Russian cats, specious Polish wizards, spying pigeons, nosy janitors and ambitious Irish cops. My closest friend was driven to hang himself by my closest enemy. Somehow, through cunning insinuation and obscure machinations, I was inveigled into murdering six poor strangers and the kind and generous Leo Faber—in the name of humanity! I have been slandered, lied to, cuckolded, robbed and persecuted. My lovely reveries have been snatched from my head and replaced by nightmares. The fruit of my years of labor—enough beauty to stock a museum—has been carried off to a foreign land, while one of my masterpieces has been plagiarized by a man dead five hundred years. I've been thwarted by an angel, duped by God and stalked by the Devil. Who would believe such things could happen in Boston?

Tonight I will sleep in the river bed. It's time for me to depart, to go west, to head for the wings, join the majority and call it a day. Into the Charles—and no nonsense.

Across the square I marched, savoring this sensible resolution. The rain had stopped at last but the sidewalks were black with puddles. All at once a great fear came over me. Suppose my guileful adversaries are luring me to suicide? Isn't it entirely possible that every move in this intricate chess match, from the subtle opening to the dreadful endgame, was designed solely to entice me into the trap of self-destruction? And if that is so—what awaits me afterward? I shuddered violently. My heart felt like a clenched fist, my stomach like a flattened palm. The rest of my organs commenced to palpitate.

"Ah. Even death has become a luxury that I can ill afford," I muttered in despair. "I am enveloped, encompassed, enmeshed. Every door is nailed, every window barred."

But even as I dwelt upon this dismal possibility, another idea leaped into my feverish brain. What if it is all groundless nonsense? What if I have only imagined these things? Casimir, the Bourg Angel and all the rest may be nothings—mere fancy. The arrival of the policeman at that moment might have been a mere fortuity and not a divine prank at all. And as for Beels being the Devil and Johann, Faust—looked at with circumspection, it is patently improbable. There is nothing unusual about an invalid being forever cold. Then, too, when he fell to the ground, I saw no evidence of a tail. He must've been some kind of detective. Either that or the importunate insurance agent he professed to be. His sales approach was odd but hardly unique in this day and age.

At Brookline Avenue, I came wearily to a halt and set my bundle down. My brain was a Gordian knot of doubt and perplexity. Should I flee? Should I surrender? Should I live or die? Was I right or wrong? Wise or stupid? Mad or sane? I leaned against the stop-light stanchion and my eyes filled with tears. I wanted to shrink—to grow smaller and smaller, to shrivel and contract until I was no more than a mote and then, absolutely nothing at all.

A motorcycle pulled up directly in front of me and went *buroom!* It was purple with pink trim and flaunted tawny foxtails from its handlebars. The head of a snarling leopard and the designation *Tiny's Torpedo* were stenciled on the fuselage. *Buroom, buroom!* it snorted, and then, *Butter, butter, butter, butter, butter, butter, buroom!*

The conductor of this obstreperous vehicle was a fellow no bigger than a Japanese jockey. He had a goatee, long thin mustachios and curved sideburns—all as blond as gold. The longest cigarette that I have ever seen dangled languidly from his mouth, while wound about his little head was a tall silk turban—orange-vermilion in color. Above a hooked nose, two coffee-bean eyes surveyed the world with a total disdain.

Buroom, buroom! roared the machine impatiently. *Buroom, butter, butter, butter, butter, butter.*

Riding tandem behind this remarkable person was a figure nothing less extraordinary. This one was a woman—and no mistake. Three times the size of her companion, she was constructed along the lines of a neolithic fertility idol. No matter how you looked at her, you saw breast, hip or buttock. She had red hair (restrained by a bice-green ribbon), emerald eyes, a broad sun-tanned face and a wide coral mouth. With one fleshy hand she held to her expansive bosom a dainty greyhound puppy, while with the other she tried earnestly to feed him a chocolate ice-cream cone.

The motorbike, *burooming and buttering,* inched forward aggressively, and as it did, I noticed a sign on its rear fender. It was the size of a cake plate, yellow with blue lettering. *Give us a smile, ya slob!* it said. I blinked away my tears and read it a second time. The light changed and the motorcycle *buroomed-buroomed* and *buttered* off. I watched it weave its serpentine way amongst the automobiles until it disappeared. I took a sock out of my shopping bag and wiped my wet face.

Stuck to the sock was a triangular-shaped piece of white candy.

"Turkish taffy," I murmured, putting it in my mouth. "What a good boy you are, Randolph." Then I picked up my bundle and crossed the street, chewing pensively. I felt better. I smiled, and as I did the toe of my shoe struck something. I looked down. There on the pavement was a thick, dark green, crumpled mass of banknotes, gripped in the jaws of an outsized clothespin. I stared—but only for a fraction of a second. Like a chameleon tongue flicking out to take a fly, my hand darted down and seized the treasure. One glance showed me bills of the highest denominations. I thrust the precious wad into my shopping bag, looked about to make sure I was unobserved and then hurried on with steps light and brisk.

"Benjamin, it is you who have sent me this," I whispered. "Your recurring dream, the orange hat, the clothespin—I remember it all. Thank you, thank you, Benjamin, my old friend."

All at once I was happy—more than happy—transported. My damp cold body began to surge with warmth and my tortured brain assumed an airy quiescence it hadn't known since childhood. My cares had all vanished. I was as free as a puff of summer wind.

"You've given me a sign, Benjamin. I'm not to surrender. I'm to continue, to go forward," I declared joyously.

A huge bus rushed by me, the words *New York* emblazoned above its windshield.

That is where I shall go, I thought. To New York. I can lose myself easily there. The bus, too, is a sign. I'm to go to New York. Yes, down the old Boston Post Road. Why, it begins only a few blocks from here, I believe, if I am not on it already. I'll walk to New York while the police guard the airports, the train stations, the bus terminals and the docks. How simple! In this era, who would suspect such a getaway?

And once there, I will work it all out, after I've rested a little. Perhaps I will grow a goatee and mustachios and don a silk turban and even buy a violet and pink motorcycle that goes *buroom, buroom, butter, butter, butter.* That was a sign also.

All my powers will return to me. I'll go out at night and on Sundays and holidays. I'll reverie. I'll paint and carve and read and study again. I might even send a few more Leonardos to Milan, since they are so fond of them there. And I'll make a whole new set of plans—and no blunders this time.

A broad beam of sunlight fell through a hole in the black clouds and landed at my feet. I eyed it suspiciously. Another sign? It looked like a spotlight. Is He trying to make friends with me? Does He seek a reconciliation, an end to the war? He must be frightened. I must have put a scare in Him. And You have good reason to be afraid, God! Oh yes. I will find You one day, and when I do, I'll straighten out Your spiral for You and tie a knot in it as well. Yes, even if it is as vast as the one in Andromeda—and with my bare hands. Then it will no longer be You and me, God, but Me and you. I will have it all. I will capture infinity for eternity.

And Benjamin—I will make you an archangel. And you one, too, Leo. Yes, that is what I will do. Why not? And all my victims—Janice and Aldo and the rest—you will all be seraphim. I give you my word. That is how it will be. I will bring everyone who has ever lived back to life. Never again will anyone die. I will kill death!

"Hey, mac!" The voice came from an automobile that had pulled alongside the curb and was now moving apace with me. I pretended not to hear. "Hey, buddy!" the voice called, more insistently. "Come over here a minute." I looked at the car and saw that it contained two men; the nearest had his arm out of the window and was beckoning. I kept walking. The sound of metal doors opening forced me to look once more. Both men had emerged from the automobile and with purposeful step were coming toward me. I looked wildly about. On my right were some of the buildings of Boston University. There were scattered groups of summer students standing around but not enough of them to provide me with protective cover. My heart began to dance in my breast—a quick, joyless caper. I must flee, I realized, and with the greatest speed.

The nearest building had three arched entrances set at the top of a flight of broad granite steps. I made my move. Up the steps I dashed. It was then the silly shopping bag, weakened by the rain, burst. Out came the Bourg Angel, my underwear, all my papers, the bottle of strychnine and the roll of money.

"Damnation!" I shouted, casting the empty sack from me and lunging for the heavy brass handle of the center door. Frantically pressing the latch, I pulled with every morsel of strength that was left in me. It would not open. I wrenched the handle a second time and then a third. It wouldn't budge. Frenzied, I threw my body against the oaken panel. It was as solid as the face of a mountain.

I spun around and saw the two men advancing up the steps. Their faces were all jaw and chin, their eyes dispassionate. "You're the one, now, aren't you?" the closest declared casually.

It was too late to try the other doors and impossible to evade them if I fled back down the stairs. Suddenly I realized that it was over. Suddenly I knew that the end had come at last. Suddenly I saw that I was in the final trap; that I was, once and for all, terminated. The men came unhurriedly. I looked out over their heads at the speeding traffic. Raising my arms, hands in fists, I screamed.

At the end of the road was a city on a hill, surrounded by a topaz wall of striking symmetry. Parallelopiped houses of colored crystal rose imperiously above this marvelous parapet. A great dipyramid balanced in perfect equilibrium upon its apex. An egg-shaped structure lay on its side on an oval platform near a ring, seven or eight stories high and made of octagonal bricks. Two flawless spheres of equal size sat one above the other. A massive honeycomb edifice, its cells utterly precise, appeared to float above the ground like a kite. There was a dodecahedron resting easily on the knife-edged juncture of two of its planes and a lovely scroll-like building whose curves were a joy to see.

Astonishing as were these forms, the colors that they radiated were more amazing still. Garnet and amethyst mingled with black and brown onyx. Emerald and gold were there alongside transparent terra-cottas and steel-blues. Nacre and sapphire and jade vied with the hues of the diamond, of silver, of rose quartz, ruby and chrysoprase.

Above this magical place, the sky was a bronze bowl encrusted with a pair of blood-red suns whose rich beams flashed through the countless prisms of the houses and reflected from the millions and millions of minute surfaces, so that everything was sprayed with rainbow and opalescence. The scintillation of this light was such that it bestowed a palpitation on the scene. Some of the structures appeared to be actually growing.

And how delightfully proportioned it all was. Each form—incredibly exact, intrinsically—harmonized completely with the whole. Each shade of color blended beautifully with all the others. Nowhere were there clashes, rough edges or cacophony. The city was perfect.

My eyes, drunk from these wonders, now saw a group of twenty or twenty-five berobed people issue from a gate in the topaz wall and proceed down the road in my direction. They moved in sedate procession, an elderly man with a wispy beard at their head. How beautiful they were! Their faces were like flowers. A dozen feet from where I stood, they came to a halt. The old man stepped forward and I saw that he held a white velvet cushion upon which rested a truncated crystal cone of luminescent azure. With great dignity he set the cushion on the ground, lifted the crystal and advanced toward me.

I saw, then, that it was a crown. He placed it on my head.

About the Author

RUSSELL H. GREENAN was born and educated in New York, where he worked briefly at banking before enlisting in the Navy. After war service, he received his B.A. from Long Island University, sold industrial gas and diesel engines, then opened a curio shop in Cambridge, Massachusetts. In the next four years he opened and closed four such shops, discovering that he was singularly ill-equipped for the retail trade. He went back to the machinery business, and continued to read voraciously about art and the art world, always his major interest. Twice he saved enough money to quit his job and go to Europe, the last time with his family. It was in Nice, France, where they settled for a fifteen-month period, that his first novel was written. His favorite modern authors include Céline, Nathanael West and J. P. Donleavy, but his talent is uniquely his own.